Die, damn you! Hubbard thought and marveled at the fury that possessed him, facing down these cowards who had come to murder him, his wife, his friends. The thought of Josey weakened him, but only for a heartbeat, sending up a silent prayer that she'd be safe with Emma's trusted men.

He dropped behind a hedge of shrubbery. No decent cover there, but it was better than the porch. He fired the second barrel of his twelve-gauge blindly at the lynchers, trusting buckshot to find someone as they scattered, then he drew his Colt and cocked it, seeking targets on the street. As in their first engagement, most of the assembled "Knights" had dropped their torches, fearful of attracting gunfire with their light. Some ran toward nearby houses, then discovered that the neighborhood was turning out against them in a rage.

Encouraged, Hubbard rose to join the charge against the mob. He'd taken two long strides when something struck his chest with a sledgehammer's force and drove the breath out of his lungs.

You never hear the shot that kills you, Hubbard thought as he collapsed.

Titles by Lyle Brandt

The Gideon Ryder Series

SMUGGLERS' GOLD
ROUGH JUSTICE

The John Slade Lawman Series

THE LAWMAN
SLADE'S LAW
HELLTOWN
MASSACRE TRAIL
HANGING JUDGE
MANHUNT
AVENGING ANGELS
BLOOD TRAILS
RECKONING
WHITE LIGHTNING

The Matt Price Gun Series

THE GUN
JUSTICE GUN
VENGEANCE GUN
REBEL GUN
BOUNTY GUN

ROUGH JUSTICE

A GIDEON RYDER NOVEL

LYLE BRANDT

BERKLEY BOOKS, NEW YORK

THE BERKLEY PUBLISHING GROUP
Published by the Penguin Group
Penguin Group (USA) LLC
375 Hudson Street, New York, New York 10014

USA • Canada • UK • Ireland • Australia • New Zealand • India • South Africa • China

penguin.com

A Penguin Random House Company

ROUGH JUSTICE

A Berkley Book / published by arrangement with the author

For information, address: The Berkley Publishing Group,
a division of Penguin Group (USA) LLC,
375 Hudson Street, New York, New York 10014.

ISBN: 978-0-425-26798-1

PUBLISHING HISTORY
Berkley mass-market edition / November 2014

PRINTED IN THE UNITED STATES OF AMERICA

10 9 8 7 6 5 4 3 2 1

Cover art by Bruce Emmett.
Interior text design by Kelly Lipovich.

For Agent Joseph A. Walker

End of watch: November 3, 1907

★ It was a good night for a lynching. No moon to speak of, and a dark ceiling of clouds concealed whatever starlight might have helped illuminate the streets of Corpus Christi. Streetlamps, few and far between, guttered and did more to accentuate the lurking shadows than relieve them. Anything could happen on a night like this, and something was about to.

Gideon Ryder lay prone on the flat roof of a cotton warehouse, peering north along the dark street below him, waiting for the lynchers to arrive. They were late already, likely drinking courage to prepare for their adventure, getting fired up for the task they'd set themselves. Hanging a man was thirsty work. Toss in his wife, and it could be downright nerve-racking.

Ryder was as ready for them as he'd ever be. His lever-action Henry rifle was loaded with sixteen .44-caliber rounds in its tube magazine, plus one in the chamber. His

Colt Army Model 1860 revolver, holstered on his left side for a cross-hand draw, was likewise fully loaded, and he carried three spare cylinders to save on time, if it became a standoff. Finally, a Bowie knife was sheathed inside the high top of his right boot, but it wouldn't come to that.

Or, if it did, Ryder supposed he would be out of luck.

One blade against a mob armed to the teeth wasn't the kind of odds he favored. Not for getting out alive, at any rate.

The house across the way, intended target of the raid, was dark and still. He almost envied those inside, likely asleep, or maybe making love. Ryder would happily have taken either option, if he'd had a choice, but duty placed him where he was, another shadow in the night, waiting to see if someone had to die.

At least, he thought, *I'm on dry land.*

His last job had involved considerable sailing on the ocean, not a circumstance that he was anxious to repeat. He was a landlubber, no doubt about it, and would take a desert over rolling wave crests any day. Not that the choice would necessarily be his. He went where he was told to go and dealt with what he found awaiting him, upon arrival.

Last time, it was pirates smuggling gold. This time . . . he wasn't absolutely sure yet, but planned on finding out.

His first job was to keep the mob from stringing up a man who might be able to supply the information Ryder needed to complete his task. He'd snooped around the town sufficiently to get a feel for what was happening, but details had been sparse to nonexistent. Rumors wouldn't get him far, distorted as they were from traveling by word of mouth, and maybe by design.

He knew a group of terrorists was operating in the neighborhood of Corpus Christi, making life a hell on Earth for former slaves and anyone who offered them a helping hand, but that was it, so far. No names, no addresses, and dropping hints in various saloons had gotten him more dirty looks than answers.

But he *did* know whom the night riders despised. That much was common knowledge, more or less, and when a plan was hatched to throw that fellow a nocturnal necktie party, word of it had filtered to the streets. Ryder supposed it must have reached the local law, as well, but they were steering clear, probably shaking down some of the city's countless pimps and prostitutes to supplement their meager city wages.

So, he'd do the job alone, or try to. Preferably without anybody getting killed.

But if he had to make that choice, Ryder intended to go home alive tonight.

Home in this case being a small room in a boardinghouse that cost him two dollars per week, no extra for the privy out back. His real home was in Washington, D.C.—or had been, until recently. He had been happy with the U.S. Marshals Service, till they'd sacked him for shooting a senator's son. It had been self-defense, and not even a mortal wound, but rich men got their way in Washington, like anywhere else.

Now he was lying on a roof in Texas, six blocks from the waterfront, waiting to see if he would live to see another sunrise.

Now, as if in answer to his thought, he saw light breaking to the north—which made no sense, time-wise, or in relation to geography. A second look told Ryder he was staring at the lights of torches, thirty-five or forty of them, held by ragged ranks of marching men. The torchbearers wore hoods resembling flour sacks, a few with hats planted on top of them at awkward angles, and the firelight showed that all of them were armed. Two of the men in front had long ropes coiled over their shoulders, nooses dangling at their hips.

No false alarm, then.

Ryder watched the mob approaching, peering over rifle sights, wondering how many of those faceless strangers he might have to kill.

What is it, Tom?"

The sound of Josey's sleepy voice distracted Thomas Hubbard, kneeling in the darkness, fumbling for the Sharps breech-loading shotgun he kept underneath their bed. When he'd retrieved the long gun, Hubbard pulled a heavy Colt Dragoon revolver from its hiding place inside the top drawer of his night table.

"Thomas?" Her tone had grown more urgent now, frightened.

"We're having visitors," he said, half whispering, although they were alone inside the small frame house.

"Oh, God!"

"Be calm now," he commanded. "We've rehearsed this."

"But I never thought—"

"Where do you go?" he interrupted her.

She stopped, moved close enough to touch his shoulder in the dark. "The bathtub," she replied.

Cast iron, it was, and capable of stopping bullets once they'd spent force punching through the walls. She would be safest there, unless—

"What if there's fire?" he pressed her.

"Run out through the back, to Mammy Waller's."

"And if someone gets past me?"

"I fight, if I can't run. Thomas—"

"Go fetch your implements. Quick, now."

She ducked into the kitchen, not a long walk in the little house, and came back bearing steel, a cleaver in her right hand, and foot-long butcher's knife in the left. Settling beside him on the floor, she said, "Thomas, I don't know whether I can—"

"You'll do what you have to do," he said, trying to reassure her. "Kiss me, now, and then go hide."

She made it last a moment longer than he'd planned, enough to stir him at this least appropriate of times, then Josey bolted for the bathroom. As they'd planned, she did not shut the door behind her. With it open, she could keep track of the action in the house and on the street outside, and it would be more difficult for anyone to corner her. Hubbard could hear her as she crawled into the tub, her nightgown rustling, weapons clanking as their blades struck iron.

Hubbard still didn't know exactly what had woken him. He barely slept, these nights, and hadn't had a full night's sleep since he arrived in Corpus Christi, but tonight was different. He'd bolted upright in the bed he shared with Josey, knowing there was danger on the way and that they did not have much time for preparation.

Just as well, then, that he'd been prepared for trouble from day one. He wished that Josey had stayed in St. Louis, but she wouldn't hear of it, insisted on living their vows to the utmost, for better or worse.

Till death do us part, he thought, trying to swallow the lump in his throat.

Hubbard saw torchlight in the street outside and shifted his position at the window for a better field of fire. He hoped it wouldn't come to killing, but in Corpus Christi, when a mob showed up outside your home at night, it was a safe bet they had murder on their minds. Hubbard had half a dozen buckshot cartridges preloaded, half a dozen pellets each, which ought to do some damage in a crowd. After he fired the first round, they'd be shooting back, and it would quickly go to hell from there, no matter how he tried to hold the line. The mob would have mobility and numbers on its side, and he could only hope that Josey would be able to escape before they stormed the house or burned it down around him.

Was it worth it? Hubbard asked himself. And once again, he had to answer, *Yes.*

For him, at least. But Josey . . .

Now the mob was coming into view, their torches giving him a halfway decent look at them. They all wore hoods, of course, embarrassed to be seen doing their "patriotic" work. Most of the group wore workmen's clothes, although a couple out in front were dressed in suits and had their shoes polished, reflecting torchlight, so the flour sacks pulled down over their heads looked all the more ridiculous. All of the men that he could see were armed, most of them packing guns, although a few carried axes and long-bladed cane knives. The two well-dressed leaders had ropes, their hangman's nooses dangling. *Two* nooses, he noted, which meant they planned on killing Josey, too.

A brutal rage welled up inside of Hubbard, blotting out most of his fear. Attacking him was one thing; he'd invited it, even expected it. But setting out to lynch a woman in the middle of the night was something else. A new low for the sneaky bastards who pretended everything they did was in the interest of defending "southern womanhood."

Tonight, he swore, at least a few of them would pay for their effrontery. They'd pay in blood, by God, and if they took him down—which he supposed, based on their numbers, they were bound to do—at least the sons of bitches would remember they'd been in a fight.

He eased the window open, shy of smashing it himself, and called out to the street, "What do you want?"

"You need to ask?" one of the rope bearers yelled back to him, making the others laugh.

"I reckon not," Hubbard replied, hoping they didn't hear the tremor in his voice. "But you'd be wise to turn around and go back home."

"Soon as we're done here," said the other rope man, while the others laughed some more.

"You've got no right to do this," Hubbard answered back.

"We're doin' this for God and for the State of Texas," said the man who'd spoken first. "We aim to set a clear example for the other carpetbaggers."

"And my wife?"

"Be pleased to entertain 'er for a spell, before we string her up," said someone in the hooded ranks.

Hubbard cocked the Sharps and shouted back, "Come on, then. It'll cost you."

He was ready—thought he was, at least—but when the first shot echoed in the street, he flinched away and wondered where in hell it had come from.

Ryder didn't plan on killing anybody when he fired into the crowd. He sighted on a torch one of the hooded men was holding overhead, off to the far edge of the mob from where he lay atop the warehouse, held his breath, and squeezed the Henry's trigger just as gently as you please. The .44 slug found its mark, the torch head detonating, raining sparks onto the man who held it. When his hood caught

fire, the would-be lyncher started whooping, running aim-
lessly in circles while he batted at the flaming flour sack.

The others froze, then panicked, trying to determine
where the shot had come from. Several turned their weapons
on the house they had been planning to attack, blasting away,
and someone at the nearest window fired a shotgun blast
into the crowd.

Damn it!

He couldn't blame the mob's target for fighting back, but
Ryder hoped to scare the lynchers off, not start a battle in
the middle of the street. If the police showed up, he knew
there was a fair chance they would take the lynchers' side
and rush the house, claiming its occupants had started
everything.

And Ryder hadn't planned on shooting any coppers.

Not yet, anyway.

He pumped the Henry's lever action, hoped no one would
spot his muzzle flash, and fired a second shot above the
shrouded heads below him. This one didn't have the same
impact, with the other weapons going off down there. In
fact, it almost seemed as if no one had noticed. Ryder cursed
and took a chance, picked one of the mob's leaders, standing
with a large revolver pointed at the house, and sighted on
his gun hand.

This time, there was no mistaking the reaction. Impact
sent his target's pistol flying, and a couple of the shooter's
fingers with it, spinning through a puff of crimson mist. The
man on the receiving end let out a howl of pain and dropped
his torch, clutching the wrist below his mangled paw with
his free hand. He wouldn't bleed out if he got some help
before too long, but at the moment he was miles away from
thinking straight.

One of his cohorts tried to help; he rushed forward with

his torch and grabbed the leader's wounded hand and brought it to the flames. That raised another cry of agony, more shrill and high-pitched than the last, before the leader snatched his helper's torch away and smashed it down atop the other's hooded skull. That set the pair of them to brawling, and it quickly spread among the others, fists and gun butts swinging, leaving bloody stains on cotton sacks.

So much for brotherhood.

Another shotgun blast came from the house and struck one of the brawlers in his hind parts. He went down, then struggled to his feet again and limped off toward the melee's sideline, hands cupping his wounded buttocks. Others, maybe stung by stray shot, bolted from the fight and started running back the way they'd come, dropping their torches in the street.

Ryder was leery about firing any more shots toward the mob, chaotic as it was. The chance of seriously wounding somebody was too high, in his estimation, so he sent a parting shot over their heads and heard it smash a window, two or three blocks farther down. That kept them moving, and the man they'd come to hang was smart enough to let them go without another blast to motivate them.

In the street, where hooded men had gathered moments earlier with murderous intent, there lay close to a dozen torches, sputtering. Their light showed Ryder that the mob had dropped some of its flour sacks, two six-guns, one cane knife, and two bloody fingers blasted from their spokesman's fist. It wasn't much to show for a heroic outing, no bodies suspended from a tree and shot to shreds, or set afire.

Ryder supposed that he could log that as a victory of sorts, but he still had more work to do. He rose and crossed the rooftop, hurried now, and scrambled down a ladder fastened to the outer southeast wall with rusty bolts. Checking the street once more for enemies, he ran across and made his way around the backside of the little, bullet-punctured house.

Thomas?"

Josey's voice surprised him, made him whip around and nearly point the shotgun at her, but he caught himself in time. "You weren't supposed to come until I called you," Hubbard said.

"I had to see if you were hurt, with all that shooting," she replied.

"I'm fine. Can't say much for the house, though."

"I don't care about the house."

"You may, next time it rains."

"Thomas, what's happening?"

He glanced back toward the empty street outside and said, "They ran away. I think someone was shooting at them."

"That was *you*. I know that much."

"Not me," he told her, frowning at the night. "Somebody else."

"Make sense," she chided him.

"I'm telling you, somebody opened up on them before I did."

"But who?"

"I couldn't answer that. It sounded like a rifle. Shot one of the torches"—Hubbard had to smile as he explained—"and set one bastard's hood on fire."

"Language!"

"Be serious," he said, losing the smile.

"Who'd help us out against that mob, in Corpus Christi?" she demanded.

"They don't speak for everyone. You know that, well as I—"

"What's that?" she interrupted him.

A rapping at their back door, soft but clearly audible.

"Back in the tub!" he ordered.

"Tom—"

"Do like I tell you!"

Josey ducked into the bathroom. Hubbard checked the street again, saw no one lurking there, and started moving toward the back door, shotgun ready in his hands. It struck him as peculiar, that the mob or members of it would come creeping back and knock politely on his door after the skirmish sent them fleeing. Still, he knew they weren't all idiots. Some of them might try stealth, where a direct attack had failed.

Halfway between the bedroom and the back door, Hubbard paused. What if the knocking was a trick to draw him from the street-side window, while the mob or part of it came back? They wouldn't have to rush the house, just sneak back long enough to pitch a torch or a kerosene lamp through one of the windows. Hubbard couldn't fight fire with a shotgun, and once he fled the house with Josey, they would be exposed to gunmen waiting in the dark.

He almost doubled back to watch the street, then realized that someone with a mind to burn the house could set a fire as easily behind it as in front. He mouthed a silent curse, then detoured to the tiny bathroom and spoke into its shadows.

"Be ready to run if I tell you," he said, then retreated, not waiting for Josey to answer.

It was imagination, he supposed, that made him hear her whisper back, "I love you, Thomas."

Only half as much as I love you, he thought.

Hubbard would die defending her, and gladly, but he

knew it wouldn't help if she was trapped inside the house by flames or gunfire, with him dead.

Moving toward the back door, Hubbard placed each step precisely on floorboards, cringing when they groaned beneath his weight. The little noises he'd grown used to in the weeks they'd occupied the rented house all worked against him now, marking his every movement for whoever waited in the night, outside.

Go slow and take it easy.

Hubbard knew it wasn't the police. Most of them thought no better of him than the men who'd come to lynch him, and if they'd arrived belatedly, they would be kicking in his front door, probably arresting him and Josey for the crime of self-defense. He thought about the man he'd wounded in the butt and knew that if he died, Hubbard might well be charged with murder.

Hang me one way or another, will you? Then I may as well die fighting.

He was almost at the back door when the knocking was repeated. Slightly louder now, or was that just because he'd moved in closer? Hubbard stayed as far to one side of the doorway as the narrow hall permitted, knowing that a fusillade of gunfire blasting through the door could cut him down before he had a chance to use the Sharps.

What now?

The knock came for a third time, urgently, and someone whispered through the door panel, calling his name. A man's voice, but he couldn't place it.

Should he answer, or just blast the prowler straight to hell?

"Who is it?" Hubbard asked, throat dry and croaking.

"I'm a friend," the disembodied voice replied.

And what else would it say? *I'm here to kill you?*

"State your name," Hubbard demanded, knowing that the answer might well be a lie.

"Gideon Ryder."

"Never heard of you."

"Be disappointed if you had," the stranger said.

The Sharps was trembling in his hands like a divining rod with water underfoot. "What do you want?"

"You're in a spot of trouble here."

Hubbard choked back a sudden bleat of hysterical laughter. "You think so?" he answered. "Thanks for the tip."

"I want to help you, if you'll open up."

"Mister, I've had all the surprises I can stand for one night," Hubbard warned him. "If you're laying for me, I can promise you we'll die together."

"Trust me," said the voice. "A minute's all I need."

"It's all you've got," Hubbard replied.

Half crouching, apelike, sweating through his nightshirt even with the chill breeze from the broken windows trailing him, Hubbard inched forward, cautiously unlatched the door, then flung it open, leveling his shotgun at a solitary stranger's face.

The tall man had a rifle in his left hand, while his right was holding up some kind of badge shaped like a shield, with a five-pointed star in its center.

"Gideon Ryder," the man said again. "United States Secret Service."

2

★ I don't know what that is," Hubbard said.

"That's because it's a secret," said Ryder. "You mind?"

Hubbard checked the back alley for lurkers, then let him come in, latched the door at his back, and stood watching, the long shotgun ready. A woman emerged from a room to the left, alluring in a nightgown, less so when he saw the cleaver in her right hand and the long knife in her left.

"Are you all right, ma'am?" Ryder asked her.

"So far. Who are you?"

He introduced himself again and let her see his badge.

"The Secret Service? What's that?"

"We can talk about it while we're moving. If you have a safe place you can go—"

"And leave our home?" Hubbard managed to seem dismayed by that idea. "I won't be driven off by ruffians."

"Right now, I'd worry more about the cops," Ryder

replied. "They're bound to show up here, sooner or later, and with two men wounded that I'm sure of, there's a good chance they'll arrest you."

"What? For defending our lives and our home?" Hubbard's wife sounded outraged.

"You're Yankees, they're Texans," Ryder reminded her. "Some of them—most of them, maybe—are friends of the men who attacked you. The police see you disrupting their established way of life and don't appreciate it. They'll use every means at hand to stop you."

"But—"

"We don't have time to argue," Ryder cut her off. "There's nothing I can do to help you, if they show up while we're standing here."

"What can you do to help us, anyway?" asked Hubbard.

"Stash you somewhere," Ryder said. "Then see what I can do about the KRS."

"You know about them?"

"Save the questions," Ryder said, "and pack now. Anything you can't collect within five minutes, leave it here."

He watched them scrambling through the darkened rooms, collecting their possessions, while he stood guard at the street-side window with his Henry, counting off the seconds in his head. They whispered as they worked, the woman tearful, Thomas Hubbard trying to be strong on her account.

And Ryder knew about the KRS, all right. Knights of the Rising Sun, they called themselves, an outfit that had sprung up in Texas soon after Robert E. Lee surrendered to General Grant at Appomattox Court House, in Virginia. They were regulators of a sort, sharing some traits in common with the vigilance committees that had operated in California, Kansas, and Montana before the war broke out in '61. The major difference was that they didn't target gamblers, whores, and rustlers, but were focused on the northern carpetbaggers and home-grown "scalawags" who thought black people, liberated from their bondage at war's end, should have a say in government and how they led their lives.

In Dixie, talk like that could get you ostracized, boycotted if you ran a business, murdered if you didn't see the light and knuckle under on command. The Hubbards had come down to Texas from St. Louis, with a plan in mind to help the freedmen gain equality, and they'd been butting heads with local whites since they arrived.

That wasn't Ryder's problem. He was not a do-gooder in any normal sense, although he tried to do the *right* thing when he could. His mission, delegated to him by Secret Service chief William Patrick Wood in Washington, was to find out whether members of the KRS were bent on stirring up a new rebellion from the ashes of the old one, or if they were just another gang of crackers persecuting people they regarded as a servant class ordained by God.

If they *were* Rebels, Ryder had been told to use his own best judgment in discouraging their treason. That sounded familiar to him, after being left to deal with Galveston's smugglers and pirates alone, on his first assignment. Plenty of excitement, working that way, but the tough part could be getting out alive.

The Hubbards beat his deadline by the best part of a minute. They had given up on salvaging whatever dreams inhabited their rented home, dressed warmly for the night, and packed sufficient clothes to get them by, with ammunition for the husband's guns. Josey Hubbard, he observed, had also packed the cleaver and the knife, wanting to do her part if there was trouble.

"Ready, then?" he asked them, when they stood before

him, bags in hand, Tom Hubbard with his big Sharps shotgun.

"As we'll ever be," Hubbard replied.

"So, where's your safe house?"

"I can guide you there," said Hubbard. "Emma Johnson's place, a half mile west of here, or so."

"Among the Negroes," Josey added, as if she expected Ryder to object.

"You think she'll take you in?" he asked.

"I'm sure of it," Thomas replied. "She's offered more than once, but I was leery of directing trouble toward her family."

"That still applies," said Ryder.

"But we seem to have no choice. And the police aren't likely to go looking for us there."

"How dumb are they?" Ryder inquired.

"Not dumb, so much, as raised to think a certain way. The thought of whites and Negroes sharing quarters likely won't occur to them."

"Okay, let's go," said Ryder. Thinking to himself, *I hope you're right*.

If the police or vigilantes did go looking for the Hubbards among black folk, it could spark a massacre, and Ryder didn't want to have that on his conscience. The alternative, however, was abandoning them to their fate, and he wasn't prepared to live with that, either.

"Shall I lock up?" Tom Hubbard asked.

"Your choice," Ryder replied.

They both knew that if the police arrived, or members of the scattered mob returned, they'd simply force the doors, ransack the house, and burn it if they had a mind to. Still, the simple act of locking doors felt civilized and might dissuade some random thief from entering.

"I'll lock it," Hubbard said and plied his key, while Ryder and the lady stood by, waiting. When he'd finished, he directed Ryder westward, following an alley littered with rubbish. Rats ran squeaking from their path, together with a couple of the cats that preyed on them. They did not speak until they'd crossed a line that Ryder couldn't see, and Hubbard said, "We're in the Negro quarter now."

It didn't look much different in the dark, the homes seen from behind, but Ryder saw that some of them were smaller and in need of more repair than those they'd walked past earlier. The former slaves of Texas and the other Rebel states had been emancipated to a state of abject poverty, in most cases, the vast majority illiterate because the governments that held them captive also punished anyone who taught them how to read and write. Some had been promised forty acres and a mule to call their own, but hasty offers made in wartime were forgotten easily with peace restored. Ryder thought simple fairness might require a helping hand, rather than simply striking off their chains, but it was not his place to meddle in official policy.

They reached a side street, Hubbard pausing there with Josey at his side. "We turn here," he told Ryder. "If we meet someone, let me do all the talking."

Ryder nodded, thinking, *That depends on who it is and what they want.*

They turned the corner, walked about ten yards, and then were suddenly surrounded by a dozen men with guns, pitchforks, and clubs. The men were black and emanated raw hostility.

"The hell you want round here?" one of them asked.

"Is that you, Lazarus?" Tom Hubbard asked the man who'd spoken.

"Mr. Hubbard? We wasn't expectin' y'all. And who's that with you?"

Ryder went through his introduction one more time, flashing his badge and waiting while a number of the freedmen scrutinized it by the little light available.

"First time I heard of any Secret Service," said the one called Lazarus.

"I'm getting that a lot," Ryder acknowledged.

"Maybe oughta put the word around some, in the newspapers and such."

"I'll pass that on."

Hubbard broke in to say, "We've had some trouble, Lazarus. The KRS—"

"Already heard about it, Mr. Hubbard. Wasn't sure you made it out alive, but we're right glad to see the two of you." Lazarus peered at Ryder, asking Hubbard, "Can you trust this one?"

"He helped us out tonight," said Hubbard. "I will trust him till he gives us reason not to."

"Be too late by then," another member of the group declared.

"If Mr. Hubbard trusts him," Lazarus announced, "that's good enough for me." He cut another look toward Ryder, adding, "If he prove me wrong, we'll deal with it accordingly." Then, back to Hubbard, "Where you headed?"

"Emma Johnson has offered several times to let us stay with her, if there were . . . difficulties. It's an awful imposition, but we'll try to keep it brief."

"Let's get you there," said Lazarus, "before the wrong eyes see us lingerin'."

Surrounded by the freedmen, Ryder and the Hubbards walked another three blocks north, then stopped outside a little house that had a knee-high picket fence around its scrap of yard, more dirt than grass, and bricks laid down to form a walkway from the street, up to the porch. Gate hinges squealed as they passed through, and Ryder saw a giant rise up from a rocker on the porch to bar their way.

"Teeny," said Lazarus, "we brought some visitors to see Miss Emma."

"Do she know you's comin'?" asked the giant.

"It's the Hubbards. She invited 'em."

"I know my numbers," Teeny answered. "I count three white peoples."

"That's a fact," admitted Lazarus. "Third one's some kinda secret fella."

"Hunh. Wait here a second."

Teeny went inside, stooping to clear the lintel with his head, and shut the door behind him. When he came back, half a minute later, he seemed more relaxed.

"Miss Emma say c'mon inside, them that'll fit."

"Rest of y'all stay out here and keep a watch," Lazarus told his armed companions. "Jonas, you and Ezekiel go scout around. Make sure they ain't no crackers comin'."

Tom and Josey Hubbard followed Lazarus into the tiny house, with Ryder bringing up the rear. Teeny regarded him with thinly veiled suspicion, maybe wondering if he should ask for Ryder's weapons—or, perhaps, just twist his head off like a jar lid. Either way, he let them pass, then moved to block the door. Ryder imagined that he might not leave the house alive if this Miss Emma looked at him and disliked what she saw.

She was a tiny woman, as befit her miniature home, in stark contrast to the behemoth standing watch outside. Ryder could not have guessed her age, although he reckoned she was somewhere on the downhill side of fifty, gray hair pulled back in a bun that drew most of the wrinkles from her sharp, angular face. He would have been surprised if she weighed ninety pounds.

"Miss Emma," Hubbard said, "I must apologize for this intrusion on—"

"Invited ain't intrudin', Mr. Hubbard."

"Thomas, please."

"Ain't gonna call you by your Christian name. I told you that before."

"Yes, ma'am, you did."

"They run you off, I guess."

"They're trying to," Hubbard replied. "We're not done, yet."

"This fella helpin' you?"

"I'm trying to," said Ryder, speaking for himself. He offered one more introduction, hoping it would be the last tonight.

"I heard somethin' about your Secret Service."

"Ma'am, I'm pleased somebody has."

Her sly smile twinkled. "Wouldn't be much of a secret if they all knew, would it?"

"I suppose not," Ryder granted, smiling back at her.

"You gonna make these lousy crackers stop what they been doin' to my people?"

"That's my plan," he said. "I'm working out the details."

"Somethin' tells me you are a determined man. That right?"

He nodded. Said, "I like to look, before I leap."

"But mostly, you leap anyway."

"Sometimes."

"There's somethin' to be said for pure audacity."

Surprised by her turn of phrase, Ryder smiled and said, "Yes, ma'am, there is."

"You know about these fellas, call themselves a bunch of Knights?"

"We've had reports in Washington."

"Before the war, they woulda been the paddyrollers hereabouts. What you'd have called the slave patrol. It kept some of 'em out of battle, after the secession, ever'body and his donkey scared to death about some kind of uprisin' amongst my people. Hear 'em talk today, o' course, it sounds like they won every scrap from Bull Run down to Chickamauga by theirselves. Windbags, but that don't mean you get enough of 'em together, they won't kill you."

"I saw some of that tonight," said Ryder.

"Did they wear their pillowcases?"

"Something similar."

"I haven't seen 'em, personally," said Miss Emma. "Mebbe they'll come by to check on me one of these nights."

"I'll try to see that doesn't happen," Ryder said.

"How you gonna do that?" she inquired.

"I'm not sure, yet. Maybe get close to them, see what they're up to."

"Better lose that Yankee accent, first," Miss Emma said.

"Is it that obvious?"

"Except to deaf folk, I imagine." She was laughing at him now.

"I'll do my best."

"Them Knights ain't very smart, but they's suspicious. Best remember that."

"I will."

"Miss Emma," Hubbard interrupted, "we don't mean to rob you of your sleep."

"Don't need much, when you get to be my age," she told him. "Long sleep's comin' soon enough. Your missus, on the other hand, looks like she needs some ole shut-eye."

"We can sleep out here," said Hubbard.

"That you will," Miss Emma said. "Ain't room for two

in my bed, anyhow, but I can spare a couple blankets. Get them pillows off the chairs." She paused and asked, "You stayin', Mr. Ryder?"

"No, ma'am. I'll be on my way, if everything's secure for now."

"Teeny won't let nobody in, 'less I instruct him to," she said.

"Good night, then. Thomas, Mrs. Hubbard, you'd be wise to stay out of the public eye, the next few days."

"They'll be right here," Miss Emma said. "Gwan, now, Secret Service man."

Teeny stood far enough aside for Ryder to edge past him, on the porch. The other freedmen watched him go, a nod from Lazarus to see him on his way. Ryder imagined a policeman passing by would be alarmed, seeing the group of them outside with weapons, but he guessed that warning them about white law would be superfluous. They'd all been born and raised under the gun and lash. Nothing in Ryder's personal experience could match what they'd lived through.

He had kept track of streets, while he was escorting the Hubbards to Miss Emma's, and he knew the way back to his rooming house. It had a private entrance, at the rear, and no curfew on boarders. The walk let Ryder clear his head and gave him time to think about his plan, such as it was.

Miss Emma had a point about his infiltration of the KRS. He had done something similar in Galveston, on his first job, but posing as a smuggler obviously differed from pretending to be Texas born and bred. He'd need another angle of attack to make it work—but what?

It hit him when he'd covered roughly half the distance to his rooming house. With only minor effort, Ryder thought that he could turn himself into a copperhead, one of those northerners who'd given aid and comfort to the Rebels while the war was on, and who were clamoring for readmission of the states that had seceded on their own terms, meaning that the freedmen would not vote, hold public office, or by any other means disturb the "southern way of life." He knew the arguments by heart, believed that he could sell himself as a Confederate devotee, but a slip could get him killed.

What else was new?

He detoured past the Hubbards' place on his way back and smelled the smoke three blocks before he got there. Closer in, he saw the house engulfed in flames and sagging at the roofline, almost ready to collapse. The street was lined with sullen-looking men and members of the Corpus Christi fire brigade, their horse-drawn ladder wagon standing idly by, its Deming four-man end-stroke hand pump unattended. Someone had decided just to let the house burn down, and no one was prepared to buck that plan.

He moved on, keeping to the shadows, unobserved. All eyes were on the fire, some of the watchers doubtless disappointed that the house would be unoccupied when it collapsed. Police were just arriving on the scene—some kind of record for a slow response, Ryder supposed—and huddled with the fire brigade's commander on the sidewalk opposite the blaze. They didn't notice Ryder passing, Henry rifle down against his leg and mostly out of sight.

Another block, and he was clear, the fire and crowd behind him. Ryder knew he should feel something, maybe outrage, but he'd seen too much during the war and since to make believe that much of anything surprised him now. Brutality was commonplace, and he was not above employing it himself, as need arose.

There were no guidelines, in particular, for how he did

his job. The Bill of Rights applied, of course, but Ryder's chief in Washington seemed less concerned with legal niceties than with results. His first case hadn't gone to trial, but Ryder had achieved what he set out to do, albeit at a bloody cost. This time, he hoped it wouldn't turn into a massacre.

But if it did, he planned to be the one who walked away.

Two blocks west of the boardinghouse, he passed the Stars and Bars saloon, a favorite watering hole for Knights of the Rising Sun. The tavern's name was borrowed from the Rebel battle flag, commonly mistaken among Yankees with the national flag of the late Confederacy. In fact, the real flag of the severed southern states had changed three times during the four-year Civil War, and while the last two versions had incorporated versions of the stars and bars, most Yanks—and many southern partisans, besides—still mistook the national banner for that of General Lee's Army of Northern Virginia.

Ryder stood across from the saloon a while, watching the celebration that was going on inside. He doubted that the man whose hand he'd shot away was boozing with the others, or the one whose backside Tom Hubbard had ventilated with his Sharps. Both of them likely would survive, unless a clumsy sawbones made things worse, but Ryder wasn't overly concerned with them. It was the rest of their fraternity that worried him, a gang of thugs and louts bent on undoing what had cost four years of blood and sweat, more than one hundred thousand Union lives, and untold millions from the U.S. Treasury in order to achieve.

The slaves were free. They needed help beyond lip service out of Washington. And any die-hard Johnny Rebs who thought they could refight the war, and maybe win it this time, had a rude surprise in store for them. The lesson that they should have learned at Appomattox needed to be driven home, by any means available.

Was Ryder the man for that job?

Maybe not. He just happened to be the man sent to perform it, however. And one thing he'd never been able to master was quitting.

Ryder knew the leaders of the KRS, had shadowed them around town for the past four days and nights, getting a feel for their routines and methods of communication with their underlings. The man in charge for Corpus Christi, Chance Truscott, sold dry goods when he wasn't putting on a flour sack and terrorizing former slaves. He was a portly fellow, with an extra set of chins and a peculiar sense of personal superiority that wasn't borne out by his tubby frame or waddling gait. Ryder had also learned that Truscott didn't run the whole shebang but took his marching orders from a "grand commander" named Coker in Jefferson, Texas, some four hundred miles northeast of Corpus Christi, near the border of Louisiana.

One step at a time.

The local chapter had been raising hell to beat the band, and had attracted Chief Wood's interest in the process. Bad mistake—and one they didn't even realize they'd made, as yet.

Those were the kind that brought men down.

One thing that Ryder would not do was let himself grow overconfident.

Which was the quickest way he knew of getting killed.

3

★ "It doesn't look so bad," Chance Truscott said.

"Don't look so bad?" Rex Fannon raised his bandaged hand, wincing. "I only got two fingers left, Cap'n!"

"Two fingers and a thumb," Truscott reminded him. "I've seen men do with less."

"Easy for you to say, still sportin' ten."

"Your wounds are badges of honor," said Truscott.

Same speech he'd made to mutilated members of the Texas Invincibles—Company K of the Ragged Old First Infantry—during wartime. It turned out that they weren't invincible at all, with most of the ones who managed to survive scattering bits and pieces of themselves on battlefields so far from home they didn't understand what they were doing there. Truscott himself had managed to come through unscathed, at least in body, and had soon discovered that the long war wasn't over yet.

Fannon was simmering with pain and anger, needed

someplace to unleash it, but he wasn't fit for battle at the moment. And, if Truscott was being honest with him, they were short one major target now, because of him. Fannon had cut and run when he was wounded, which encouraged his companions to desert the battlefield.

"How's Stacy?" asked Fannon.

"He lost some hair. Has burns around his face and neck, but not too bad. He got the hood off pretty quick, all things considered."

"Not too bad. Like me, huh?"

"That's the way I look at it."

"And Abe?"

"Shot in the ass. He won't be sitting easy for a while."

"I guess we missed the carpetbagger."

"That's a fact," Truscott agreed. "His house is gone, though, so that's something. If he's still in town, we need to find out where he's hiding."

"Ask the darkies," Fannon snarled.

"It's something to consider, but I doubt they'd be forthcoming."

"Make 'em talk. I know some ways."

"I'm sure you do, Rex. But we have to keep from overreaching, after last night's failure."

"Wadn't my fault," Fannon told him, sullenly. "Nobody told me he was gonna have a sniper lookin' out for him."

"In combat, we expect the unexpected," Truscott said. "And speaking of the sniper, did you catch a glimpse of him, by any chance?"

"Nossir." The sullen tone shifted toward bitter. "Shot come outta nowhere, hit ol' Stacy's torch 'n' set his mask on fire. Next thing I know, there's shootin' back 'n' forth between us and the carpetbagger, then some bastard shot my hand off."

"Not your hand. Two fingers."

"Feels the same to me."

"I'm sure it does, but try to focus now. The sniper."

"Told you that I never seen him. He was off behind us somewhere, mebbe on a roof."

"And to your right," said Truscott.

"What the doc says, way the bullet hit me."

"I don't suppose it could have been the woman?"

Fannon snorted. "Shot like that? You joshin' me?"

Somebody else, then, handy with a rifle. And he didn't have a clue who that might be.

"All right, Rex. If you think of something else—"

"I'm gonna practice shootin' with my left hand," Fannon told him. "Hope you'll save the carpetbagger for me, since I owe him one." He raised the bandaged paw again and glowered at it. "Make that *two*."

"We can't do anything until we find him," Truscott said. "You just fix your mind on healing up."

"Ain't much else I can do," said Fannon. "Last I heard, there's no call for one-handed farriers."

"You won't go wanting. Brothers take care of their own."

"I'm comin' back, Cap'n. Won't let this hold me down."

"Good man. Now, try to get some rest."

Outside, the early morning sun already warming Corpus Christi's streets, Truscott turned toward the waterfront, where he helped run a hiring hall for stevedores. He had to earn his keep, like anybody else, no matter what the cause demanded of him after hours. Dealing with the freedmen made his skin crawl, an infuriating imposition that he had to pay them for the same work they'd have done for free last year, but cursing circumstances would not change them.

Only force would put things right.

He had to take it one step at a time, remembering that

Texas and the other Rebel states were occupied with blue-coats now, and some of them were black. The bottom rail on top, for God's sake, and he wouldn't have believed it when he first marched off to war. Truscott had never owned a slave, himself, or ever wanted to, but the society he had been born and raised in was dependent on its human chattels for a multitude of dirty jobs that kept the system ticking like a fine ten-dollar watch. That watch was broken now—or, rather, its components had been forced out of their rightful slots, ordained by God Almighty at the moment of creation—and it wouldn't work again until true order was restored.

That might require another war, one fought by different rules, guerrilla-style, but Truscott figured he was up to it. He'd come through four years hale and hardy. If it took another four, or more, to put the South back on its feet, what pure, red-blooded son of Dixie would refuse?

Rex Fannon, maybe, now that he was wounded, though he'd seemed to have a measure of the old fire welling up in him again, when Truscott left his company. As for the others, he would have to wait and see.

Their first task, he decided, was to find the sniper who had interrupted them.

And after him, the carpetbagger.

Ryder had breakfast at the rooming house that morning: hash, fried eggs, and biscuits, washed down with strong black coffee. His fellow boarders were an elderly woman who wore her hair pinned at the top of her head, and a sallow ex-soldier who walked with a limp, as if one of his legs had been shortened a couple of inches. The landlady helped out with small talk, but got little back for her effort.

No one at the breakfast table talked about the shooting overnight. The only newspaper in town, the *Crier,* came out in the afternoon, but Ryder guessed that word of mouth would spread distorted versions of the incident to every corner of the city by midmorning. Whether it had reached his landlady or not was anybody's guess. The other tenants, if they knew, were keeping mum.

From breakfast, he went out to find Chance Truscott. It was time for him to be at work, although the prior night's bloody business might have altered the routine. Ryder went by the dockside hiring office first and was relieved to spot his target through one of the windows facing out to sea. Selecting stevedores to load and unload waiting ships would keep Truscott tied up for two, three hours minimum, and Ryder could return to check on him before the one-time Rebel captain went to have his lunch.

That left the Hubbards, but there wasn't much more he could do for them, until his business with the KRS was settled. In the meantime—

He was heading back uptown, considering how he could try to get some information from the local cops, when something caught his eye. A poster on a lamppost, red letters on white, trimmed all around in black. It read:

Knights of the Rising Sun!!!

Our State requires assistance in her hour of need! All able-bodied men are summoned by the call for selfless heroes! Rally to the cause this evening, 7 P.M., at La Retama Park. Bring friends and comrades! Come to hear the word of reason and to consecrate yourselves anew! Remember glory days and make them come again!! Hail victory!!!

Ryder read it twice, wondering how the third sentence had managed to escape without an exclamation point. It was an invitation to rebellion, and he wondered how the local garrison of Union troops would take it, but he didn't plan on asking them. The last thing Ryder needed was to be seen consorting with the bluebellies. He was a foreigner, by Corpus Christi standards, but he hadn't drawn any undue attention yet and hoped to keep it that way for another little while, at least.

On the other hand, an open invitation to a rally of the KRS was something Ryder couldn't very well pass up. Truscott would probably be there, speaking as their commander, and it should help Ryder pick out other members of the brotherhood. He'd watch for wounded suspects—one short-handed, one scorched, and another limping—but he couldn't count on those three turning up in public for a while.

If they were taking applications, he'd consider it, but cautiously. The Knights were likely watching out for infiltrators, and a Yankee suddenly appearing in their ranks would be a prime suspect. They might decide to ease the pain of last night's loss with an impromptu necktie party, if he pushed too far, too fast.

That was the rub. His mission was to pin the local outfit down and trace its roots back to the men in charge. Ideally, he would manage that before the KRS found Thomas Hubbard's hiding place and other chapters started raising hell all over Texas. The attack on Hubbard's home had been the first raid staged against a white opponent—and, from what he understood, had mustered up the largest mob of Knights fielded so far. Each raid encouraged more and drew more backers to the group.

The war, as Ryder knew too well, had left thousands of men soul-seared by the atrocities they'd witnessed and

committed. Some would never be the same again, trans-
formed from modest patriots or hapless draftees into killers
who'd forgotten what remorse felt like. Given the least
excuse—or none at all—they'd run amok, and if they had
a cause to fight for, sanctified by loss and suffering, so much
the better.

Ryder did not aim to fight another civil war, or let some
gang of yahoos start one, if he had the means to stop it.
Heading off one lynch mob was a start, but more would be
required to nip a new uprising in the bud.

More work, more risk. .

And, he supposed, more blood.

One way of gauging local sentiment was through the
Crier. While its afternoon edition wasn't ready yet, the editor was fond of posting bulletins outside his office—"extras,"
as he called them—with selected snippets from the day's
top stories. Ryder could discover what officials had to say
about the shooting and destruction of the Hubbards' home,
then he'd check back on Truscott and begin preparing for
the KRS hoedown.

He planned to show up early and prepared for anything.

A smart man made his own luck, when he could.

The *Crier*'s office had a crowd of middling size outside
it, reading the day's posted extra and jabbering about its
contents. Through the broad front window, Ryder saw the
presses rolling, turning out that afternoon's edition of the
paper. Two men operated the machinery, while one—
presumably the editor, based on the visor and the oversleeves
he wore—was supervising. Ryder eased in through the
crowd, trying to keep from jostling anyone, and read the
extra from the second row.

Its headline announced: "Mysterious Blaze; Couple Missing." The rest of the short piece declared that Thomas Hubbard's home had been razed by a "conflagration of unknown origin." Hubbard was missing, along with his wife, and police professed to be baffled as to both the couple's whereabouts and what had caused the fire. The story quoted a police lieutenant's statement that no witnesses had seen "any unusual activity" around the house before it burned. A captain of the fire brigade declared the house was "too far gone" and "beyond saving" when his men arrived. Investigation was "ongoing," with a plea for information that would help authorities locate the Hubbards.

It was more or less what Ryder had expected. The authorities in question, he surmised, were sympathetic to the thugs who'd torched the house and would make no serious attempt to solve the crime. If Hubbard and his wife had been strung up, as planned, Ryder supposed the extra's headline would have blamed their deaths on "persons unknown," perhaps adding a blast at "carpetbaggers" who intruded where they were not wanted in the South. As for police seeking the Hubbards, Ryder would have bet his next month's pay that they were not concerned about the couple's welfare.

Better off right where they are, he thought and banished any lasting thought of visiting them at Miss Emma's house by daylight, when he might be followed.

Not that he'd detected anybody trailing him since he had arrived in Corpus Christi. His cover, as a cattle buyer down from Kansas, checking out the local livestock, had been holding up as far as he could tell. Yankees were welcome, more or less, if they arrived with promises of cash and showed no interest in upsetting southern customs, where the races were concerned. Ryder had spent enough time prowling local stockyards to establish his identity, then left the sellers hanging while he checked on current prices with his people up in Wichita.

Which people? No one asked. And since they were ephemeral, they couldn't be contacted with demands to verify his story. Meanwhile, any other questions that he asked—about the war, the Knights, or local politics—were simply those of one more stranger being nosy. Two ranchers had asked him what he thought about the "darky situation," but he'd shrugged it off, pled ignorance, and said it wasn't his concern.

From what he'd gathered, roughly half the slaves in pre-war Texas had been held on farms along the Nueces River, which rose northwest of San Antonio, meandered through Texas hill country, and finally spilled into the Gulf of Mexico at Corpus Christi Bay. As elsewhere in the South, most bondsmen were employed to plant and harvest crops, though some worked sheep and cattle ranches, and a few were skilled at breaking horses. Ryder had heard stories of black cowboys—Charles Goodnight was sometimes mentioned—but he hadn't seen one in the flesh, so far.

He wondered why they stayed in Texas, or in any part of Dixie, after they had been enslaved and brutalized for generations. Now that they were free, why not move on to someplace where their color didn't draw a stark dividing line between them and the rest of humankind? Did Texas feel like home, somehow, in spite of all they'd suffered there? Did poverty alone prevent them from escaping?

Or was it ridiculous to think that anyplace on Earth existed where the population drew no color lines?

Ryder had seen too much to think the best of people anymore, at least until they'd proved themselves deserving of respect and trust. He knew that race relations in the nation's capital, in New York City, and in Baltimore were

tense, at best. The New York draft riots of 1863 had claimed
at least a hundred lives and injured some two thousand,
mostly black, when Irish laborers rebelled against conscrip-
tion in the name of ending slavery. They didn't want to die
on distant battlefields for someone else, of course—who
does?—but it had turned into a race war that had threatened
to destroy the largest city in the Union.

Cheered along, no doubt, by scheming copperheads.

His job, if he could handle it, was to prevent a similar
eruption in the Lone Star State. Ryder believed an army
regiment might be more suited to the task, but since no one
had asked for his opinion, he would keep it to himself and
forge ahead the best he could.

Trying to stay alive.

It crossed his mind to check up on the Knights who had
been wounded in the past night's skirmish, see if any of
them felt like talking, maybe giving up a lost cause while
they had a chance. Ryder dismissed the notion instantly,
knowing it would involve too many questions, likely bring
him into contact with physicians sympathetic to the Rebel
cause or others who'd betray him without giving it a second
thought.

No, he would save it for the meeting and discover what
the night might hold in store.

For supper, Ryder found a restaurant two hundred yards
from La Retama Park that specialized in barbecuing
beef and pork. He ordered ribs, baked beans, and coleslaw,
with a mug of beer to cool his palate from the spicy sauce.
The restaurant featured long, rough-hewn tables, forcing
strangers into close proximity with one another, which
encouraged eavesdropping.

The main subject of conversation, as he'd hoped, was the impending KRS rally. The men surrounding Ryder—and the diners were *all* men, perhaps because the seating was unsuitable for ladies—seemed to favor any reasonable action that would keep the freedmen "in their place." There might be arguments over what constituted reasonable action, but he came away with an impression that if violence was necessary, most of those he heard would be neither surprised nor saddened. They were rough men, many of them probably illiterate, and had been raised in an environment where each man looked out for himself, without expecting any aid from government officials.

Ryder knew, from personal experience and briefings he'd received, that parts of Texas had been slipping into anarchy since Appomattox. Whether it had always been this way, he couldn't guess, but between losing one war and bracing to fight another with hostile Indian tribes, while trying to replace the vast slave labor force that had supported their economy, most Texans were in no mood to be bound by rules dictated out of Washington.

Secession hadn't worked, but some of those he listened to that evening weren't entirely clear on who had lost the war. Instead of bowing in defeat, they seemed to think that they were resting up before they fought another round.

General Philip Sheridan, assigned to command the military district of the Southwest in May 1865, was on record as saying that if he owned both Hell and Texas, he would rent out Texas and live in Hell. Ryder thought that might be stretching it a little, but he couldn't speak for former slaves or any local whites who thought the war had been a fool's errand.

When he had cleaned his plate and had a second beer in lieu of pie, Ryder paid up and left the restaurant. Outside, dusk had begun to settle over Corpus Christi, and the lamp-lighters were out, beginning to illuminate the streets favored with lighting. Ryder checked his watch, saw that he still had half an hour left to go, and started ambling down toward La Retama Park.

By day, the park served as a combination marketplace and haven for a class of men who either couldn't find a job or didn't want one. After sunset, when the market stalls shut down, the park played host to public meetings, sports events, and the occasional near-riot fueled by alcohol. Ryder guessed he would have to wait and see which category fit Chance Truscott's gathering of Knights.

Something about the outfit's terminology struck Ryder as absurd. As far as he knew, from his readings into history, there were no Knights in the United States, and never had been. Royal titles were forbidden by the Constitution, but he guessed the label had been chosen to suggest a link with ancient days of chivalry, when bold men dressed in shining armor, jousted for a smile from a princess, or crossed swords in a king's defense. That didn't square in Ryder's mind with putting on a floppy hood and going out at night to terrorize women and children. Something had been lost in the transla-tion, he supposed.

A crowd had gathered by the time he reached the park, and it was growing by the moment. Most of those who had turned out so far were men, but Ryder spotted several women of the crib-and-tavern type moving among the fel-lows, likely seeking customers. Ten minutes after Ryder arrived, Chance Truscott showed up with a clutch of body-guards around him, moving toward a low stage someone had erected on the west side of the park. Ryder moved closer, reached the dais just as Truscott mounted it, watching from the third row back as Truscott launched into his speech.

"My friends and neighbors," he began, "I want to thank you all for turning out this evening. We stand at a momentous crossroads, with the fate of our fair city hanging in the balance. Will we fight for all that we hold dear, or see it swept away and turned into a charnel house?"

The crowd was silent, nearly breathless, as he paced across the stage, commanding full attention. "Citizens! The radicals in Washington tell us we must accept the nigra as our brother, lift him up from the subservience ordained by God Almighty, and endow him with the full rights of a free white man!"

Some muttering had started now, angry, but not at Truscott.

"White men! Will you take it lying down, or will you stand and fight?"

A voice cried out from somewhere in the crowd's rear ranks, but not in answer to the question. "Soldiers!" it proclaimed.

Another raised the shout, "Bluebellies!"

Ryder turned and saw a squad of Union troops approaching, some of them black men, armed with Springfield rifles sporting bayonets.

4

★ The crowd convulsed, hundreds of throats raising a sound of mingled fear and anger as the troops advanced. Some individuals among the audience were shouting racial epithets and curses, others scouring the ground for stones to hurl against the marching men in blue. Ryder could see no happy outcome for the situation and had no desire to be there, but his focus was on Truscott and his corps of bodyguards.

Atop the dais, Truscott pointed at the soldiers, shouting out above the growling of the mob. "Brothers! Behold the enemy! They've laid waste to our homes, and now send *niggers* to oppress us! Where's their sacred Constitution and its freedoms when *we* try to use them?"

More excited, angry babbling from the crowd, where several of the men Ryder could see were drawing knives and pistols. Most of Truscott's bodyguards jumped down and joined the mob, forcing their way up toward the front ranks where the troops would make first contact. Two men remained on stage, flanking their boss with six-guns drawn, ready for trouble.

Ryder eased in their direction, still not certain what he planned to do. His first instinct was to get out of there before the bullets started flying, knowing he could just as easily be killed by Union bullets as by Rebel fire. His mission, as he understood it, didn't call for him to fight an army in the open, at a time and place of someone else's choosing, but he needed something that would get him close to Truscott, and he might not get another chance like this.

He reached the close end of the stage, ignored by Truscott's two remaining bodyguards. That was a lapse in judgment on their part, apparently unable to conceive there might be enemies among the snarling crowd. If he'd been an assassin, Ryder could have dropped his man from fifteen feet away, an easy shot, and vanished in the mob before the guards could take him down.

Something to think about, but since he *wasn't* an assassin, it was useless.

Rocks were flying now, along with curses, and the troops were taking hits. Their bayonets were lowered, aimed directly at the crowd, while their commanding officer bawled orders, brandishing a saber. If a shot was fired from either side, the scene could turn into a massacre. Ryder was measuring the space beneath the dais, wondering if he could fit in there and use the stage for cover, when it happened.

At the far edge of the crowd, a pistol cracked. He thought it might be one of Truscott's men but couldn't tell for sure, with all the ducking, heaving bodies in his line of sight. He saw one of the bluecoats stumble, going down, and then the officer in charge of them was shouting, "Halt! Aim! Fire!"

The first blue-suited rank dropped to one knee, clearly a

movement they had practiced, so the second rank could aim over their heads. At the shout of "Fire!" a dozen rifles spoke as one, their .58-caliber Minié balls ripping into the crowd through a mist of black powder smoke. Men fell, some of them screaming, others deathly silent, as the third and fourth ranks slipped around their comrades and assumed firing position.

"Ready!" their commander ordered. "Aim!"

Truscott was leaving, leaping off the stage, trailed by his last two bodyguards. Ryder ran after them, was almost close enough to touch them when they met a second file of soldiers jogging toward the park along Mesquite Street, from the north. Truscott stopped short, pushing his men in front of him, as others from the fleeing crowd caught up and found their angle of retreat cut off.

The bodyguards stepped forward without hesitation, obviously seasoned fighters from the war years, with their pistols raised. Before they had a chance to fire, though, someone in the blue ranks shouted, "Charge!" The troops came racing toward them, polished blades adding a good foot to the forty-inch barrels of their Springfield rifles. Ryder saw his opening, moved forward, Colt Army in hand, and clutched Chance Truscott's arm.

The startled rabble-rouser jerked around to face him, saw the pistol and recoiled, but Ryder's grip restrained him. "Follow me," Ryder demanded, "if you want to live the night."

After a heartbeat's hesitation, Truscott did as he was told. Behind them, as they fled, the charging troops skewered a wall of frightened flesh, more gunshots ringing out, men shouting, cursing, wailing as they fell.

Ryder led Truscott on a tangent from the park, leaving its battleground behind. He wished the soldiers well but had no sympathy for any of the Rebels or the painted doxies who had come to take advantage of their gathering. They must have known trouble was likely when they came together, and they'd gotten what they asked for.

Ryder ran all-out for three blocks, then slowed down and turned to look back at the park. Gun smoke hung in a haze over the scene, but active fire had nearly petered out, resistance broken. Members of the crowd were running hell-bent from the troops in all directions, and that seemed to satisfy the soldiers as they finished mopping up, arresting those they could identify as having fired on them during the clash.

"Who are you?" Truscott asked him, breathless.

"Gary Rodgers," said Ryder, plucking the name from thin air.

"You're a Yank!" Truscott pegged the accent.

"Born and raised. Doesn't mean I agree with the government."

"Oh?" Glancing at the Colt Ryder still held in his right hand.

He put the gun away. Told Truscott, "Look, you needed help back there, to keep from being gutted. Now we're clear, you go your way and I'll go mine."

He turned from Truscott, took two steps before the voice behind him said, "Hold up a minute."

"Why?"

"I'm grateful for your help," Truscott replied. "Least I can do is stand you to a drink."

The saloon was called the Southern Cross. It wasn't old, per se, but had seen better days before the war. The bartender was nearly bald and compensating for it with a thick black beard. He put two whiskies on the bar at Truscott's order, backed by mugs of beer.

Trustcott thanked Ryder one more time for helping him, then downed his whiskey in a single gulp. Ryder did likewise, liquid fire searing his throat, and wheezed, "No problem."

"But it would be," Truscott said, "if I'd been killed back there, or taken into custody."

"Because you head up the resistance?" Truscott eyed him, didn't answer. Ryder forged ahead, saying, "It stands to reason. You're the spokesman. 'Less you've got a boss somewhere, afraid to show his mug."

"No, you were right the first time," Truscott granted. "What brings you to Corpus Christi?"

"Cattle. I'm a buyer out of Wichita."

"I know some people. Get ahold of me tomorrow or the next day, and I'll make the introductions."

"Thanks."

"Least I can do, considering."

As Truscott spoke, a group of men entered the Southern Cross, disheveled, dusty, some of them with fresh scrapes on their faces, bruises darkening. For having been defeated, though, they seemed in rare good spirits as they crowded up against the bar and ordered drinks. Some spoke to Truscott, one clapping him on the back, while others cut suspicious eyes toward Ryder.

"Wish you coulda stayed and seen the windup, Mr. Truscott," said a man easily six or seven inches taller than the rest.

"Were they defeated?" Truscott asked. "The bluebellies?"

"Well . . . no," the big man said. "They took some losses, though. I seen two a their nigras bite the dust."

"That's progress," Truscott said, raising a twenty-dollar bill to get the bartender's attention. "One round for the house, on me."

Ryder saw the twenty was a U.S. gold certificate issued in 1862, showing an eagle vignette on the front. It disappeared into the barkeep's hairy paw before he started setting glasses on the bar and filling them with whiskey. The talk was all of fighting, some raising comparisons to battles from the recent war that told him they had never witnessed any of the action they described.

Funny, he thought, *how liars always tell the best war stories.*

Ryder finished off his whiskey, sipped his beer, and watched Truscott working the room. He had the quality of leadership, there could be no disputing that, but he was using it to keep a wounded land divided, sowing hate and rage in place of healing. That was not a crime, as far as Ryder knew, unless he carried it too far and blood was shed—as it had been that night.

There were two sides to every story, Ryder knew, as there had been during the dark years of the war. Truscott's adherents would proclaim that Yanks had sparked the violence at La Retama Park, conveniently forgetting that the first shot came from their side. Why split hairs, when they were the aggrieved side, with their homeland occupied by hated enemies? Aggression could be cast as self-defense, if you kept one eye shut and squinted through the other.

It was easy. People did it all the time.

Ryder was wondering if he should slip away and meet Truscott tomorrow when a new arrival pushed up to the bar and leaned in close, half whispering in Truscott's ear. Ryder was close enough to catch the words "Hubbard" and "nigger town," but lost the rest.

It was enough. Somehow, he realized, the KRS had found the Hubbards.

"How many are going?" Truscott asked the man who'd spoken to him.

"Twenty, twenty-five. Enough to get it done."

"That's what you said last night," Hubbard replied. "Make sure it gets done properly this time."

"Yes, sir."

The new arrival left, and Ryder was about to follow him, when Truscott turned and caught his arm. "Leaving so soon?"

"I've got some early rounds to make," Ryder replied.

Truscott produced a business card and slipped it into Ryder's hand. "My office address. Come to see me around noon, if you can make it."

"Do my best," Ryder agreed and drained his beer for show before he left the Southern Star. It was a challenge, walking normally until he'd cleared the bat-wing doors and passed the windows facing on the street, before he broke into a run.

The Hubbards and Miss Emma were just sitting down to supper when a tall man burst into the house and blurted out, "Dey's comin!"

Thomas didn't have to ask who "they" were. He could hear the guards outside Miss Emma's house preparing for a fight and, with the windows open to a cool night, heard the tramp of many feet approaching from the north, along the unpaved street. A rising grumble-growl from voices of the mob reminded Hubbard of the recent battle and the home that he had lost.

Josey reached out to clutch her husband's hand. "Thomas, we have to get away from here, before—"

"Too late for that," Miss Emma interrupted. She had risen from the table and was moving toward the porch with stately grace. "Crackers'll go ahead with what they come to do, whether they find you here or not."

"I'm sorry," Hubbard said. "We never should have come here in the first place."

"Where else would you go?" Miss Emma asked. "You risk your life to help my people. How could we refuse you?"

"But—"

"These people need to learn they lost the war," Miss Emma said. "And things is different now."

Hubbard left Josey at the supper table and retrieved his weapons from the small room they had shared the night before. He checked the shotgun and the pistol, making sure that both were fully loaded as the mob drew closer, torchlight visible by now, coming along the street that had no lamps.

"Thomas, where are you going?" Josey asked.

"To meet them," he responded. "I'm done running."

"Then, I'll have that pistol," Josey told him, rising to approach him.

"No," Miss Emma answered, sternly. "When the shooting starts, you skin on out the back. A couple of my boys will see you someplace safe."

"I can't leave Thomas!"

"Fightin' is a man's job, more or less." As Miss Emma spoke, she smiled and drew a Colt Model 1855 Sidehammer pocket revolver from somewhere beneath her long shawl. "O' course, it's my home, too."

"Thomas, I—"

"Josey, go!" he ordered.

Two young freedmen suddenly appeared beside them, having come in through the back door, and they listened to Miss Emma's orders, spoken in a kind of patois Thomas barely understood. They nodded and stood waiting, muskets cradled in their arms, but Josey made no move to exit. Thomas finally dismissed her with a kiss and gentle shove in their direction, then turned back to join Miss Emma and the others on her porch.

The mob had nearly reached the house by then. He guessed that there were seventy or eighty men in all, half of them bearing torches, faces hooded, all well armed. Their leaders hesitated for a moment, maybe startled by the sight of freedmen bearing weapons of their own, but then they spotted Hubbard on the porch, beside Miss Emma, and a howl went up among them.

"There's the nigger-lover!" someone shouted, followed by a storm of cursing.

In the front rank, one of the mob's leaders raised his free hand—no torch in the other, but he carried a revolver—and called out to Hubbard, "Come with us, and no one else needs suffer for the crimes that you've committed!"

"Crimes?" Hubbard could barely keep from laughing at him, even in the face of mortal danger. "What crimes?"

"Comin' here, where you ain't wanted, rilin' up our nigras," said the spokesman. "And woundin' three of our brave Knights."

"Did you say *brave*?" Hubbard replied. "Coming around to lynch a woman in the middle of the night? And when did Knights start wearing flour sacks to hide their faces?"

That provoked more snarls and curses from the mob. Their leader hollered back, "Your time is over, carpetbagger! If you want to spare these darkies, lay your weapons down and come along with us."

Miss Emma spoke before Hubbard could answer. "Darkies gonna send you straight to hell, if you don't mind your manners!"

Hubbard saw the muzzle flash and heard the bullet whisper past him, almost felt the slap of lead on flesh before Miss Emma gasped. Then she was falling, two strong freedmen rushing up to catch her, and her Colt spoke once, sending a shot into the crowd. A masked man fell, and then all hell broke loose.

Gunfire rattled along the skirmish lines, black facing hooded white, unleashing clouds of gun smoke in the street. Hubbard squeezed off one barrel of his shotgun, aiming for the masked man who had called him out, and saw the faceless stranger lurch back, free hand clutching at his side, the first shot from his pistol going high and wide.

Die, damn you! Hubbard thought and marveled at the fury that possessed him, facing down these cowards who had come to murder him, his wife, his friends. The thought of Josey weakened him, but only for a heartbeat, sending up a silent prayer that she'd be safe with Emma's trusted men.

He dropped behind a hedge of shrubbery, no decent cover there, but it was better than the porch. He fired the second barrel of his twelve-gauge blindly at the lynchers, trusting buckshot to find someone as they scattered, then he drew his Colt and cocked it, seeking targets on the street. As in their first engagement, most of the assembled "Knights" had dropped their torches, fearful of attracting gunfire with their light. Some ran toward nearby houses, then discovered that the neighborhood was turning out against them in a rage.

Encouraged, Hubbard rose to join the charge against the mob. He'd taken two long strides when something struck his chest with a sledgehammer's force and drove the breath out of his lungs.

You never hear the shot that kills you, Hubbard thought as he collapsed.

R yder heard distant gunfire as he ran through Corpus Christi's streets, but it had stopped before he reached his destination, following the smell of gun smoke in the air.

Dozens of torches scattered in the street were burning out, but still gave light enough for him to see by, coupled with the glow of lanterns held by neighbors as they moved among the bodies sprawled around Miss Emma's place.

White men and black together, dead or dying where they'd been cut down.

Three freedmen intercepted Ryder half a block from Emma's home. One aimed a six-gun at his chest; the others held a pitchfork and an ax, respectively. Ryder saw a dark trace of something on the ax blade, hoping it was rust.

"Where you think you's goin', buckra?" the man with the pistol demanded.

Ryder tried to keep his tone respectful, anything but agitated. "I was here last night, to see Miss Emma, with the Hubbards," he replied. "I heard there was some trouble here, and—"

"Come along to pitch in, didja?" asked the ax man.

"Hoping I could help," said Ryder.

"White trash he'ped enough for one night," said the short man with the pitchfork.

"If you'd only ask Miss Emma—"

"Cain't ask her," the gunman spat back, nearly sobbing. "She be daid."

Ryder was groping for a comment, when another voice rang out behind the trio that had stopped him. "Matthew! Cyrus! Jethro! Let 'im pass!"

Reluctantly, the three obeyed. Ryder eased by them, saw one of the men he recognized from last night moving toward him, grim-faced, with a musket cradled in his arms.

"You come too late, lawman."

Ryder nodded. Said, "I see that. Is it true about Miss Emma?"

"She's crossed over," said the freedman. "Ain't about to be forgotten."

Hesitant to trespass on his grief, Ryder still had to ask the question. "What about the Hubbards?"

"He gone with her, or wherever white folks go. His missus got away in time, I think. Still need to check on that."

"If you could tell me where she went—"

"Don't know, right off. An' you'll appreciate a certain lack o' trust right now, for white men that I only met last night."

Ryder could sense where that was going, and he moved to head it off. "You don't think I had anything to do with this?" he asked, and nodded toward the nearest of the corpses sprawled around them.

"If I did, you'd be amongst 'em, Mister. One more dead'un, more or less, don't make no difference now."

"I mean to see the men responsible for this are punished," Ryder told him.

"And I wish you luck. You gonna need it."

From behind him, Ryder heard more angry voices. Turning, he saw freedmen moving out from both sides of the street, to meet a line of uniformed policemen trooping toward the scene. Late as they were, he saw the cops were armed with rifles, shotguns, all with sidearms strapped around their waists. The leading officer wore captain's bars and signaled his authority by scowling, barking orders like an army drill sergeant.

"Squad, halt! Form into firing lines! Three ranks!"

"This don't look good," Ryder's companion said.

"I'll talk to them," said Ryder, reaching for his badge.

"Think that'll help?" the freedman asked. "More likely get you shot down for a nigger-lover. They see white men dead, we bound to have a scuffle."

"There's been too much killing, as it is," said Ryder.

"Maybe not enough. You best clear out, now, 'less you dumber than I think you is."

Ryder considered saying more, or staying on to face whatever happened, then thought better of it. Showing his credentials to the coppers likely wouldn't help—in fact, it might have just the opposite effect, making him a marked man in his own right. His advantages, so far, were anonymity and a connection, frail as it might be, to Chance Truscott. There might be nothing he could do for Josey Hubbard, but he could press on to see her husband's killers and the men behind them brought to book.

He *could* do that.

And if a few of them were damaged in the process, well, that was the price you paid for dressing up at night and going out to terrorize your neighbors.

Ryder did not feel like waiting till tomorrow for his chat with Truscott, or the time it would require to worm his way into the Rebel's confidence. He guessed that the survivors of the raid against Miss Emma would be celebrating, likely at the Southern Cross, to make it feel like a resounding victory. Why not drop in and visit them, while they were swilling booze and patting one another on the back?

Why not, indeed?

But he would stop off at the boardinghouse, first thing, to fetch the Henry rifle from his room.

It was a lesson he had learned the hard way: always be prepared.

5

★ **R**yder heard the celebration when he was a block out from the Southern Cross. Men laughing louder than they had to, fueled by alcohol, congratulating one another on a job well done. It didn't sound like any wake he'd ever been to, making Ryder think they'd managed to forget about the comrades left behind them, lying in the street outside Miss Emma's house.

At half a block, he slowed his pace, keeping to shadows in the long stretch between streetlamps. There was no sign of the police, so far, and Ryder had an inkling that they wouldn't bother dropping by to question Truscott or his men about the shooting across town. Why bother, when the so-called lawmen were in sympathy with Truscott's aims? More likely, they'd arrest some freedmen on a charge of killing helpless white men who had been out for a stroll.

There was no point debating with himself about the local

"justice" system. Ryder saw the writing on the wall and knew that any justice carried out this night would have to be a one-man job.

A shout went up from the saloon, as if in answer to a toast. It was a big night for the KRS, between their riot with the bluecoat soldiers and eliminating Thomas Hubbard. Losses on their own side would be irritating, maybe sadden some of them to a degree, but they were getting over it in record time. Between the combat veterans and those who'd stayed at home during the war, guarding their human live-stock, these were men inured to death and cruelty. For some, he guessed, it was precisely what they lived for.

He'd checked his Henry at the rooming house and knew that it was fully loaded, with a cartridge in the chamber. Likewise with the Colt, six chambers loaded and three extra cylinders weighting his pockets, just in case he had to reload in a hurry. Some men kept an empty chamber underneath their pistol's hammer, to prevent a nasty accident, but Ryder wasn't careless with his sidearm, didn't go for all that fool-ishness of twirling it and whatnot. It was a destructive tool, and always treated with respect.

As he approached the saloon, the revelers inside began to sing. It was a song he'd heard before, though never sung with quite as much enthusiasm as tonight.

Oh, I'm a good ol' Rebel, and that's just what I am.
For this fair land of freedom, I do not give a damn.
I'm glad we fought against it, I only wish we'd won.
And I don't ask no pardon for anything I done.

By the time he reached an alley west of the saloon and slipped into its deeper darkness, they were on the second verse.

I hates the Yankee nation and ever'thing they do.
I hates the Declaration of Independence too.
I hates the glorious union, 'tis drippin' with our
    blood.
I hates the striped banner, and fit it all I could.

"Keep singing," Ryder muttered. "You'll have more to hate in just a minute."

At the rear of the saloon, no lights at all back there, he heard a scuffling sound of boots on sand and gravel. Slowing down, he edged up to the northwest corner of the building, risked a peek around, and saw a drunken man, unsteady on his feet, preparing to relieve himself against the wall. Distracted as he was, trying to sing along with friends he'd left inside the Southern Cross, mind blurred by whiskey fumes, the pisser didn't notice Ryder creeping up behind him in the dark.

"Three hunerd thousand Yankees lie still in southern dust," he crooned, then lost the words. "Dah, dah-dah, dah dah *dah* dah—"

Ryder stepped in and slammed the Henry's butt into the drunkard's skull, just where it met the spine. The impact drove his target's head against the wall, a second solid *thunk,* then he rebounded and collapsed, his privates on display.

Unconscious? Dead? Ryder considered it, then heard the traitor's lyrics in his head. *I do not give a damn.*

The back door wasn't locked. In fact, it stood ajar, left open by the man he'd just knocked out. Inside the Southern Cross, the noise was louder than it had been in the alley, but at least the song was winding down.

I can't take up my musket and fight 'em down no more.
But I ain't gonna love 'em, and that is sartin sho'.

And I don't want no pardon for what I was and am.
I won't be reconstructed, and I do not give a damn.

Ryder had almost reached the barroom entrance when
the singing died, replaced by Rebel yells. He cocked his
rifle, set his teeth, and stepped into the crowded room.

The first whiskey too many had a sour taste. Chance Truscott grimaced, knew if he kept drinking he would have
a rotten, sickly head tomorrow morning, but his men were
in a mood to celebrate and clearly didn't want him letting
down the side.

The bartender noted his empty glass and grabbed a bottle
from the shelf behind him, moving in to top it off. Truscott
blocked him, placing a hand over the glass and saying,
"Think I'll switch to beer."

"Okay, then."

When it came, the beer was warm, but that was normal.
Few saloons in Texas—none in Corpus Christi that he knew
of—bothered keeping ice on hand. A cold drink would have
helped to cut the smoky, sweaty atmosphere inside the Southern
Cross, but Truscott knew he'd have to do without that luxury.

It was a night to celebrate, regardless. Sure, they'd lost
some men taking the carpetbagger down, but it was worth
the cost and had his men fired up, pretending that they'd
fought a battle on the scale of Gettysburg. The ones who'd
been in combat knew better but wouldn't spoil it for the
stay-at-homes. Tonight, they felt like winners, and he meant
to keep them feeling that way, since they had a long fight
still ahead of them.

Since Lincoln's death in April, the Republicans in

Congress had been clamoring for stiff reprisals. Booth was dead, and his accomplices had stretched rope in July, but killing off five southern patriots had failed to satisfy the Yankee craving for revenge. President Johnson seemed to think that he could hold the radicals in check, but Truscott didn't think so. There were hard times coming for the late Confederacy, and she would need hard men to preserve the treasured southern way of life, even in part.

One of his men nudged Truscott's elbow, nearly spilled his lukewarm beer, but Truscott bit his tongue in lieu of cursing. "Cap'n, we done good tonight," his soldier slurred, already three sheets to the wind.

"You did, indeed," Truscott replied—although, in truth, he wasn't happy to have lost the men who'd fallen, and to have the coppers picking over their remains. It was unlikely that there'd be any investigation worthy of the name, but clumsy tactics made for sloppy outcomes.

They would have to do much better in the future.

Someone at the far end of the bar was calling for another song. "Dixie" this time, and the piano player started hammering his keyboard without hesitation, singing in a loud, slightly discordant voice, as others joined in with him.

"Ooohhh, I wish I was in the land of cotton, old times there are not forgotten—"

"Look away!" the rowdy chorus echoed. "Look away!"

"Look away, Dixie Land!"

Somebody tugged on Truscott's sleeve, the left. He turned in that direction, lowering his eyes to meet those of a shorter man whose whiskey breath was nearly overpowering. Truscott wondered if he had grabbed the nearest solid object to support himself, but then the short man gave another tug and asked, "Cap'n, who's that?"

"Who's *who?*" Truscott replied, raising his voice to make it audible over the singing.

"There," the shorty answered, pointing toward a doorway that gave access to the Southern Cross's storeroom, owner's office, and a back door exit from the place. Squinting against tobacco smoke, Truscott picked out a figure that he recognized and came up with the name of Gary Rodgers.

Pushing past the man who had alerted him to Gary's presence, Truscott moved in that direction, smiling. "You came back," he said. "I'm glad to see you. Let me—" Glancing down, he froze, then asked the man who'd saved him earlier that evening, "What's the rifle for?"

Unsmiling, Rodgers kept the Henry's muzzle pointed at the floor, as he replied, "Truscott, it's time for you to come with me."

Ryder hadn't considered what charge he could file against Truscott. Nothing came instantly to mind, except a vague count of conspiracy he knew was likely to be tossed from any court in Texas. Right now, he wasn't thinking past the moment. All he wanted was a chance to question Truscott privately, away from all his men, their raucous singing, and cloying fog of smoke inside the Southern Cross.

"What do you think you're doing, Gary?"

"Putting you under arrest," Ryder replied.

"On what authority?"

"The U.S. Secret Service."

"Never heard of it," said Truscott, with a mocking smile, his fingers gliding toward the outer right-hand pocket of his suit coat.

Ryder jabbed his belly with the Henry's muzzle. "Move that hand another inch, you'll hear this plain enough."

"You'd shoot me here, in front of all my men?" Truscott was trying to be cocky, but he wasn't managing too well.

"You're coming with me, one way or another," Ryder said. "It's your call, either way."

"How are you planning to survive this?"

"Not your problem. Somebody starts shooting, you're the first to drop."

Truscott stared hard at him, apparently deciding that he meant it. "All right, then. Be quick about it, will you, for the sake of all concerned."

Ryder was backing toward the hallway he'd just passed through, calculated he was halfway there or better, when a drunken voice behind Truscott called out, "Cap'n? Wha's goin' on?"

That drew a few more from their off-key singing, to observe Ryder and Truscott. Even soused, they couldn't miss the rifle Ryder held pressed into Truscott's belly. Voices growled profanity. Hands flew to holstered pistols, and to knives.

"Stand easy!" Ryder cautioned, as the jangly piano music died. "You pull on me, I'm letting daylight through your boss."

"Bullshit!" one of them snarled, and whipped his pistol clear.

Ryder started to move, keeping Truscott before him to use as a shield, but the drunk fired a shot anyway, missing both of them by several feet. It was the break that Truscott needed, slapping at the Henry's muzzle, reaching back to snatch a bottle from the bar and lob it overhand toward Ryder. When Truscott struck the rifle, Ryder fired a shot by accident and heard a yelp of pain from someone in the crowd behind Truscott, then he was reeling as the whiskey bottle struck his shoulder, staggered him, and bounced away.

Truscott was off and running like a man who's seen his house on fire, the other members of the KRS ducking for cover from the unexpected gunfire. Ryder had their boss man in his sights, when someone fired another pistol shot and cut a jagged piece out of the bar immediately to his left, stinging his cheek with splinters as he dropped into a crouch and focused on the job of trying to survive.

How many men against him in the Southern Cross? He guessed it must be thirty-five or forty, anyway, and likely more. Most of them now had weapons drawn but didn't seem exactly clear on what they should be doing with them. Some reached out to Truscott as he passed them, sprinting for the nearest exit, but he struck their hands away and shouldered through their ranks, not taking time to rally a defense.

The man Ryder had wounded lay beside a table that was overturned, a couple of his friends hunkered behind it in the vain belief that it would stop a bullet. Ryder couldn't tell how badly the man was hit, and frankly didn't care. He was in danger from the men still on their feet, not one rolling around the floor, clutching his gut and bellowing in pain.

He ducked behind the near end of the bar, the only decent shelter in the room, as half a dozen pistols started firing, bullets gouging strips out of the floorboards, peppering the wall behind him, wild shots breaking bottles shelved behind the bar. He figured Truscott must be out and gone by now, but if he cleared the barroom fast enough, Ryder still had a chance to overtake him on his way back home.

One rule he'd learned about gunfighting: those who fired in haste—particularly in their cups—normally missed if they were any farther out than point-blank range. Of course, a stray shot was as deadly as an aimed one, if it clipped an artery or drilled a vital organ, so he couldn't calculate the odds of getting out alive.

What Ryder needed was chaos, and plenty of it.

Glancing toward the barroom's ceiling, he saw two suspended wagon wheels, fixed on pulleys to be raised and lowered, each with half a dozen oil lamps mounted equidistant from each other on its rim. If he could clip the ropes they dangled from and bring them crashing down, the lamps would likely shatter, spill their fuel across the wooden floor, and set the place on fire.

If he could make that shot, with pistols barking at him, enemies he'd never met before shouting their threats and curses, all intent on killing him.

Sweating, he raised the Henry, tried to hold it steady, index finger curled around its trigger, praying that the rifle wouldn't be shot from his hands.

Chance Truscott covered one full block before it hit him: if he ran away, how would his men, his Knights, ever have faith in him again? He was afraid, no doubt about it, but if he let *them* see that, he would be finished as their leader.

Was it already too late, the way he'd bolted from the Southern Cross, shoving his men aside to save himself? Maybe. But if he went back now and rallied them, led them to kill the traitor who'd deceived him earlier that evening, he could likely win their trust back. Spin some story about going off to look for help, and then deciding he was needed more among his men than fetching reinforcements.

That could work. But it meant going back *right now*.

Reluctantly, he turned and ran back toward the Southern Cross, breath wheezing in his lungs. His mind was racing, searching for a handle on the situation. Rodgers, or whatever he was called in fact, had said he worked for something called the U.S. Secret Service. True or false, Truscott thought he could use that to distract his men from any doubts or disappointment they might feel toward him, directly.

Paint it as another federal incursion on the sovereign State of Texas, once its own republic, now crushed under Yankee boots and likely to remain so, if a force of loyal native sons did not arise to sweep the blue plague from their soil. If Rodgers had credentials or a badge, it would confirm a charge of spies among them, undermining every aspect of the old traditions his supporters had been raised to view as part of God's eternal plan.

His courage was returning as he reached the Southern Cross—at least, until he heard the storm of gunfire echoing inside there. As he neared the bat-wing doors, the light appeared to shift in the saloon, immediately followed by a crash that shook the place. Men cursed and howled, more guns went off, and when he peered in through the nearest window, Truscott saw the place was burning now, its wooden floor a sea of spreading flames.

Stupid to go in now, he thought. *The place is burning. Anyone with any sense will make a break for it.*

But leadership and common sense were not always compatible. Sometimes a leader had to take a chance, risk everything, if he was going to inspire his men and hold their confidence. He couldn't urge them into battle, when a situation called for him to lead them by example. If he didn't joint the fight, those who escaped the Southern Cross tonight would carry two grim memories: their own fear, and his failure as their captain. They would shun him as a coward, maybe even seek revenge against him for deserting them.

Truscott drew his pistol—nothing big, a Colt Pocket Police revolver in .31-caliber, weighing just over a pound and a half—and moved forward against his better judgment, shoving through the bat-wing doors into the anteroom of Hell.

R yder had missed the wagon wheel's suspension line with his first shot but cut it with the second, while the raving drunks around him ducked and wondered what he had in mind. They found out seconds later, when the ring of lamps came plunging down and trapped one man beneath it, six lamps shattering on impact with the floor and spewing liquid fire. The man beneath it screamed and tried to wriggle free, his legs acrawl with biting flames.

Ryder couldn't get a clear shot at the second wagon wheel, but didn't think he'd need to. Panic swept the room, men's voices shouting, "Fire!" as if nobody else could see the spreading smoke and flames. A woman screamed, one of the upstairs girls, and Ryder hoped she'd make it out all right, but couldn't turn the fight into a rescue mission. He was focused on escape now, tracking Truscott and—

"Captain!" one of the shooters cried, over the din of general confusion.

And another, right behind him, hollered, "Cap'n! You come back!"

"Discretion," Truscott's deep voice answered, "dictates we evacuate this place."

"We got 'im cornered, though," a third man said. "If we can root 'im out real quick—"

"Indeed," Truscott replied, cutting his soldier off. "We cannot leave an enemy to possibly escape, then harm us further on another day."

That earned a rousing cheer, over the crackling of the fire, and Ryder braced himself for what he knew was coming. They would charge en masse and overrun him, kill him where he stood—or crouched, more like—and that would be the end of it. If he tried bolting out the back, they'd shoot him as he ran.

Unless . . .

He still had thirteen rounds left in the Henry, six more in his Colt without reloading. If he fought back hard enough, there was a chance that he could rout them. Not a *good* chance, but it beat his odds if he did nothing. And if he could turn the charge, there was a chance that he might reach the back door with a slim head start.

And Truscott?

Drop him if you can, he told himself.

It took another smoky moment, even with the place in flames, for Ryder's enemies to rally, summon up their nerve, and rush the point where they had seen him last. By then, he'd edged further behind the bar, gaining more cover for himself, and when he rose, his Henry shouldered, several of his would-be killers gaped at him in stark surprise.

Log them as drunk *and* stupid.

Ryder rapid-fired into the charging crowd, dropping two men in the front rank before he spotted Truscott, swung around, and nailed him with his third shot. Ryder saw his .44 slug drill through Truscott's cheek, then had no time to watch him fall or see if he was trampled by the others rushing up behind him. Blazing at his human targets like a madman, Ryder barely had to aim. The wall of angry flesh before him made a wasted shot impossible.

His fusillade tore through the ranks, causing a ripple that became a rout, the men he hadn't killed or wounded yet changing their minds about the wisdom of hurling themselves at a repeating rifle, while the building that contained them filled with smoke and threatened to collapse.

Their mass retreat began when someone cried, "The cap'n's

hit!" More voices joined the lamentation, and the charge broke ten feet short of a collision with the bar. To keep them moving, Ryder started lobbing whiskey bottles after them, each one exploding into bright flames as it shattered, setting fire to trousers, bodies, furniture—whatever was nearby.

Ryder took advantage of his adversaries fleeing toward the street, a couple of them smashing windows to leap through them when the flapping doors seemed too congested. No one noticed as he scuttled down the hallway to the back door, bursting through it, bleary-eyed and coughing from the dense smoke roiling through the Southern Cross.

The place was done, cooking away with Truscott and a number of his people still inside it. Ryder didn't plan to stay and watch it all fall down, particularly since that meant police, the fire brigade, and far too many other witnesses to suit him. Starting on the trek back to his boardinghouse, slapping his clothes to shed some of the smoky odor, he began to think about his next report to Washington.

What would he write? *Got tired of waiting, so shot up the place and burned it down.*

He wasn't sure that anything he'd done so far, in Corpus Christi, fell within the law. He could have said the same for Galveston, of course, and that turned out all right, as far as his director was concerned. He'd lost Tom Hubbard to the KRS, along with several freedmen, but that would have happened anyway, he guessed, whether he'd been in town or not.

The thing to work on now was moving forward. Ryder wasn't finished with the Knights, by any means. He'd only started, and his next move would be taking him into the hard heart of their territory, to disturb a hornets' nest.

He needed to be ready, or his bones—like those of Yankee soldiers in the Rebel song—would soon lie still in southern dust.

6

★ The train left Corpus Christi for Houston at nine o'clock on Friday morning. Ryder had passed a restless night, sitting up in his room at the boardinghouse, half expecting the police or sheriff's deputies to turn up anytime. He was relieved when they did not appear, managed to eat a double helping of the landlady's biscuits and gravy, then packed his gear and headed for the station two hours ahead of schedule, taking back streets all the way.

The railroad station had a fresh coat of paint, but the tracks were rusty and the train that pulled into the depot at half-past eight consisted of three passenger cars trailing a boxy prewar locomotive, its giant funnel smokestack out of all proportion to the boiler and the engineer's cab. In motion, he knew from experience, it would spew gray smoke and cinders, proven by the staining on the cars it towed.

They killed time while the locomotive took on fuel and water, but Ryder had his ticket ready and sat out that time in the last of the three aging passenger cars. His half dozen fellow passengers sat in the first car, treating themselves to the worst of the smoke and jolts from the journey, and he left them to it. Assuming they stayed on the rails, all three cars should arrive in Jefferson at the same time.

He had plotted the trip beforehand. The stretch from Corpus Christi to Houston covered 184 miles, at an optimistic top speed of twenty miles per hour. With at least one other fueling stop along the way, call it ten hours on the rails. At Houston, he'd be switching trains for the 218-mile journey to Jefferson, eleven hours minimum, not counting any stops along the way. A full day of rattletrap travel, but once he got used to the noise and vibration, Ryder supposed he could catch up on sleep from last night.

And what would his adversaries be doing, in the meantime?

He was leaving Corpus Christi's Knights of the Rising Sun in disarray, momentarily leaderless, but Ryder guessed they wouldn't stay that way for long. They didn't have his name, and Truscott—dead now—was the only one to whom he had identified himself as a federal agent. Beyond that, he assumed that general alarms would go out to other KRS chapters statewide, and the organization's headquarters in Jefferson should logically be first to get the news.

That meant he'd be walking on eggshells tomorrow, when his train arrived. The KRS might have a welcoming committee at the depot, watching out for strangers, maybe even with a general description of their target from survivors of the shootout at the Southern Cross. If so, he would be ready for them—or, at least, as ready as he could be in the circumstances. One man in a hostile city, where his badge was nothing but a bull's-eye, and he couldn't count on any help from local lawmen.

Perfect.

As he sat and watched the arid countryside roll past beyond his smudged window, waiting for sleep to overtake him, Ryder went back over what he'd learned about the Knights. Their "grand commander" was a former Rebel captain, Royson Coker, known to friends and enemies alike as Roy. He'd been attached to the First Texas Partisan Rangers, a cavalry unit organized by another Jefferson resident, Colonel Walter Lane, in June of 1862. The unit had seen its first action in Arkansas, then retreated into the Louisiana bayou country for a series of guerrilla engagements lasting until the Trans-Mississippi Department's formal surrender in May 1865. Colonel Lane had been pardoned and worked as a shopkeeper now, but Coker had apparently decided to continue fighting on his own terms, loyal to the Lost Cause.

No one could say how many "Knights" Coker commanded statewide, but the bulk of them were thought to live in Jefferson and surrounding Marion County, flush against the Louisiana borderline. They had already tarred and feathered the publisher of Jefferson's only Republican newspaper, running him out of the county with threats to do worse if he ever returned, and Ryder had reports of half a dozen freedmen murdered since war's end. Their "crimes" consisted of refusing to continue working for their former masters and, in two cases, of having the temerity to register as voters. Coker's men, it seemed, intended to preserve the antebellum status quo as best they could, and so far, no one from the county sheriff's office had restrained them.

Ryder wasn't looking forward to another one-man war against long odds, but he had taken on the job with both eyes open, and he'd see it through as best he could.

Or die trying, a voice inside his head retorted.

Maybe. But one thing that he *wouldn't* do was quit.

Two hours out of Corpus Christi, reasonably sure that he

was safe for now, the train outrunning any horsemen who might try to follow, Ryder closed his eyes and willed himself to sleep. He kept the Henry rifle wedged between his left leg and the window, right hand resting on the curved butt of his Colt Army revolver.

Just in case.

R yder's train arrived in Houston with two hours to spare before his scheduled departure for Jefferson on the Eastern Texas Railroad line. No one was waiting for him on the platform, a relief, and Ryder found a restaurant nearby, on Commerce Avenue, where no one raised an eyebrow at his guns or luggage. Hungry from his long ride north, he ordered steak with all the fixings. The waitress brought a slab of beef that could have fed two men, plus fried potatoes under gravy, mushrooms, and a heap of collard greens.

Ryder surprised himself, putting it all away within an hour, then examined downtown Houston for another thirty minutes, before hiking back to catch his train. It still amazed him, coming from the North, that no one in a city of this size thought anything about a man walking amongst them with a rifle, six-gun, and a Bowie knife on full display. Most of the other men he passed were armed with pistols, either on their hips or peeking out of shoulder holsters, and he would have bet some of the women had shooting irons stashed in their oversized handbags.

He wondered what would happen if a fight broke out, or someone tried to pull a daylight robbery. A scene of bloody chaos came to mind, and Ryder hoped that his imagination was exaggerating.

From what Ryder could see, it seemed that Houston was recovering from the war in fair style. He knew the city's economy had been hurt by a Union blockade of Galveston, in 1862, but Rebels had recaptured that port city early the following year, restoring the flow of commerce to some degree. Houston's Chamber of Commerce held the city together until General Lee's surrender, and there'd been no local skirmishing to damage any of the shops or homes, but postwar government seemed problematic. A newspaper he bought from a cigar store, near the railroad station, carried articles about the anarchy enveloping some rural parts of Texas since Appomattox, with local officers and U.S. cavalry incapable of keeping order.

There were bad days coming, Ryder realized. He wondered if his mission to East Texas would improve matters, or only serve to make them worse. He understood his duty, didn't want to second-guess it, but there was a human element to be considered, also.

Had he made things worse in Corpus Christi? Thomas Hubbard had been killed despite Ryder's best effort to protect him. Now his Josey was a widow and would wind up God knew where, assuming she escaped from Texas with her life. If Ryder had abstained from intervening that first night, if he had let the lynchers have their way, would it have spared Miss Emma and the others from a second lethal raid? Were two lives worth the dozen-plus eventually sacrificed, when he had wound up losing one of them regardless?

Ryder didn't know, and knew that pondering the question overlong would make his head ache, likely rob him of the sleep he craved. He couldn't turn back time, undo what had been done, and self-flagellation wasn't Ryder's style. He made mistakes, like any other man, and tried to learn from them.

Unfortunately, when he dropped a stitch in his trade, people sometimes suffered.

Sometimes died.

He thought of Hubbard: young, idealistic, off on a crusade to help the freedmen rise above their miserable lot. That quest had killed him, but would it have been successful if he'd lived? Ryder believed the odds were poor. A chasm yawned between the races, both in Texas and across the country, had divided them for some two hundred and fifty years, and showed no sign of closing. Race, religion, the economy, and rage over the war were all tied up together in a strangling knot which, Ryder thought, might choke the South to death if nothing changed.

But could it change? Would it?

From what he'd seen of how free blacks were treated in the North, before the war and during, Ryder saw no reason to be optimistic.

Still nobody at the depot appeared to be a KRS lookout, and Ryder took his seat in the second of four passenger cars. Three other travelers were already seated when he arrived— one he pegged for a salesman, the other two clearly a mother and child. A final rider boarded as the warning whistle blew, a rangy man whose coat was a couple of sizes too large, slouched hat riding low on a minimal forehead, his thick mustache drooping almost to his chin on both sides of a straight, thin-lipped mouth. He barely glanced at anybody else inside the car and took a seat three rows in front of Ryder, on the left side of the aisle.

Someone to watch? Or just another Texan riding on the cheap from one point to another, one job to the next? Ryder decided not to borrow trouble on a guess, but kept his weapons handy when the train began to move at last, leaving the depot with a blast of steam and smoke that drove onlookers from the platform, hands and handkerchiefs raised to their faces.

Ryder waited till they cleared the city limits, then slouched back and closed his eyes to rest. Eleven hours, minimum, before he reached his destination, and he couldn't say when he would have a chance to sleep again, in Jefferson. Other towns along the Eastern Texas line included Lufkin, Nacogdoches, Henderson, and Marshall, where the train would gain or unload passengers, say half an hour for each stop, to extend his time inside the railroad car. No time to grab a meal, but he'd make do.

A smooth ride was the best that he could hope for, and the odds of that were slim.

R oy Coker lit a slim cheroot, eyes narrowing against its acrid smoke as he reread the telegram from Corpus Christi. It was from the Nueces County sheriff, filling Coker in on grim events that had occurred during the night.

```
REGRET TO INFORM YOU OF SERIOUS LOSS
STOP CHAS TRUSCOTT AND OTHERS DECEASED STOP
SEARCH FOR THOSE RESPONSIBLE CONTINUING
STOP BE ON GUARD STOP
```

Coker scowled, crumpling the flimsy paper in his fist, and was about to drop it on the street when he thought better of discarding it, and tucked the telegram into his pocket. Careless errors could prove fatal, as he'd learned during the war.

He understood the friendly sheriff's need to be discreet. It wouldn't pay for an elected law enforcement officer to be caught fraternizing with a group of Rebel vigilantes, after all, no matter how the voters in his county felt about the Yankee occupation of their territory. Carpetbaggers and the bluecoats who supported them could build a case against him, probably remove him from office, perhaps lock him up on some kind of conspiracy charge.

The warning he'd received would have to do, for now. Coker would send a couple of his men to Corpus Christi on the next train out—quicker than riding, some four hundred miles overland, that could take them a week to arrive—if they weren't picked off in transit by redskins or border trash looking for drifters to rob.

In the meantime, he would have to wait and see what happened next.

"Search continuing" told Coker that the sheriff hadn't caught the man or men responsible for killing Truscott and his boys, however many might have fallen. Had the killers even been identified? Were warrants in the works for their arrest? It was the damned uncertainty that set his teeth on edge, like scouting in the wartime wilderness for Yankees, never knowing when the woods in front of you might blaze with musket fire and cut you down.

He had survived those years by guile, audacity—and, yes, a fair amount of luck. Shot twice, still carrying fragments of shrapnel from an artillery round in his scarred left thigh, Coker was a survivor. He'd overcome the limp—well, mostly—and it could have been a damn sight worse, if he'd been hit a few short inches to the right. That would have disappointed several women he could name, if he were not a gentleman.

Well, more or less.

There was a chance, though he regarded it as slim, that Truscott and his other men in Corpus Christi had embroiled themselves in something stupid and had died as a result. He couldn't put it past them, necessarily, but Coker had been cautious in selection of his field commanders, passing over slack-jawed yokels to select the kind of men who looked before they leaped, thought through a situation before taking any action that would be their own undoing. Granted, there were situations when you couldn't see too far ahead, but in those situations you took stock, decided whether to proceed or not based on potential for success.

"Not much to go on," said Lloyd Graves, his second in command, who'd read the telegram as Coker did.

"Not near enough," Coker agreed. "We need a couple pairs of eyes in Corpus Christi. Put them on the first train headed south."

"Will do."

"The sheriff is a friend of ours. Have them find out if he's got anyone in custody, or any suspects. Wire the details back to us, and make sure they're in code."

Graves nodded. "Satterfield and Kimes can handle it."

"I trust your choices. If this was something federal, we need to stay ahead of it. We've barely gotten started, and I don't want anything derailing us."

"Don't worry."

"Worry doesn't enter into it. I'm talking preparation. Strategy."

"I hear you."

"If the bluebellies are after us, we need to know it."

"If they aren't," said Graves, "they soon will be."

"Agreed. But we could use some warning, all the same."

"I'll have the boys look sharp for strangers asking questions. See if Travis can get anything from Corpus Christi, in the meantime."

Harlan Travis was the sheriff of Marion County and, incidentally, a loyal Knight of the Rising Sun. He took his duties seriously and would spare no effort when it came to sniffing out the order's enemies.

Between the sheriff's office and his own men, Coker thought that he could deal with most threats from outside the county—but he wasn't ready, yet, to fight another all-out war against the Yankees with the troops he had available.

Before that day came, *if* it did, the people of Texas and the other Rebel states at large would have to bind the wounds they'd suffered during four long years of war, forget their losses, and rededicate themselves to the crusade that had been stalled but never truly failed.

But first, he had to take care of the problem that confronted him.

Beginning now.

The run from Houston, northward, had more interesting scenery than Ryder's route from Corpus Christi had delivered. Lots of trees, to start with, on a landscape that rose and fell, so the train passed through tunnels of shadow, then burst into blinding sunshine without warning. There were no mountains here to match the Appalachians or the Smokies, but it made a welcome change from flat land bordering the Gulf of Mexico.

And there was more to watch for here, he realized. Not only wildlife on the tracks, which would be crushed and mutilated if it didn't move aside in time, but people watching from the forest shadows. Ryder knew that outlaws prowled the district. White, black, Mexican, it made no difference if they shot first or came upon you in the night and laid the sharp edge of a blade against your throat. And there were native tribes, of course: some Cherokees who hadn't made the trip to Indian Territory, Anadarkos who'd jumped the reservation, maybe even some Comanches driven from their normal range in West and Central Texas.

Sharp eyes watching as the train rolled past, leaving its trail of smoke.

Or was it only his imagination?

Ryder didn't like to borrow trouble, but his job had taught

him that the quickest way to die was to ignore the range of possibilities in any given situation. He had stayed alive this long by thinking first and acting second—well, most of the time—and he intended to survive this mission, too.

The railroad car he occupied was roughly half full, ample room for Ryder to avoid his fellow passengers. None of them appeared to pay him any mind, which suited him down to the ground. He kept his weapons handy without putting them on show, conforming to the rule for other travelers he'd seen so far. If there'd been any firearms confiscation in the Lone Star State, Ryder had yet to see the proof of it.

As far as he could tell, there were no guards aboard the train, unless the company had stashed them in the mail car. He had looked for soldiers, too, as they were boarding, without turning up a single Yankee uniform. Bandits could readily procure that kind of information, if they put their minds to it, which made the whole line vulnerable to attack.

Relax, he thought, *before you start to jump out of your skin.*

As if on cue, two horsemen materialized at the tree line outside Ryder's window, watching the train pass. They made no move to intercept it, simply sat astride their animals and stared until the locomotive and its trailing cars left them behind.

Nothing surprising there, he thought. This country must be full of cowboys, hunters, ranch hands—though, in truth, he hadn't spotted anything resembling a cultivated spread since leaving Houston. There had been no livestock grazing near the right-of-way, and nothing that suggested railroad crews performing maintenance. Until the riders showed themselves, he might have thought the territory was deserted, going back to nature in the wake of having track laid on its face.

Where had they come from? To the east, Louisiana sweltered, with its swamps and Spanish moss. Or maybe they had ridden down from Arkansas, its landscape mixing bayou country with the sort of forest Ryder saw flanking the tracks. They could be outlaws, what the locals called long riders, meaning that they constantly kept moving to avoid the law. They'd had a certain look about them, he supposed, though it could have been simple weariness or boredom. Maybe they were envious of people riding on a train, not getting saddle sores.

He tried sleeping again but couldn't get the hang of it, supposed it was impossible to store up sleep against a time when it could be in short supply. The rock and rattle of the train lulled Ryder, but it didn't put him out, only dulled his mind to a near-dozing level that felt like being drunk, without the benefits. He checked his fellow passengers from time to time, not staring, thankful that they all were seated farther forward in the car, with none behind him. That could change at any given stop, but Ryder thought he might shift toward the rear next time they pulled into a town, thus making sure that any other riders sat in front of him.

He didn't think the KRS could track him, much less put a shooter on the train who'd recognize him from the other men on board—but why take chances?

He had hours yet to think about what he should do in Jefferson, how he'd approach the main part of his task. It shouldn't be that hard to find Roy Coker, prominent as he was said to be, but Ryder didn't want to make it obvious, putting his quarry on alert after the bloody mess in Corpus Christi. Let him think it had been something local, coming back to snap at Truscott, with no reason to be up in arms.

From what he'd seen, though, it appeared the KRS was *always* up in arms. Any excuse to fight would do.

And maybe he could turn that to his own advantage, after all.

7

★ Ryder was dozing when the train shuddered and started slowing down. He cracked an eye, peered through the window to his left, and spotted nothing to explain it. As he shifted in his seat, shrugging the stiffness from his shoulder where he'd slumped against the window frame, he heard the whistle blow.

Three seats in front of him, one of the passengers who'd boarded back in Livingston turned to the lady he was riding with and said, "It's just a water stop, Marie."

From where he sat, the locomotive was invisible, but Ryder knew the drill. Railroads had stops for fuel and water placed along their lines at intervals of thirty miles or so, in case a train encountered problems and was running low. There'd be no settlement around the stop, out here, only a water tower with a chute the engineer or fireman could release and lower to refill the boiler, while the engine huffed and grumbled like a dragon caught up in a restless dream.

A roving crew would check the tower's water level every week or so, and drop more wood to feed the firebox.

How long would it take? He didn't know, but there was nothing to be done about it. Ryder cracked his achy shoulder, was about to settle back and close his eyes again, when one of the four women riding in his car gave out a little squeal.

Up front, the man who'd boarded last in Houston was on his feet now, turning to face his fellow passengers. He was smiling through his thick mustache and had a pistol in his hand, aimed vaguely down the center aisle.

"Ladies and gents," he said. "Sorry to interrupt your journey, but my friends and me have got some business with the Eastern Texas line today, and you're all part of it."

Friends, Ryder thought. *How many, and where are they?*

"What we're after, mostly, is the mail car," said the gunman. "Cash and such, you know. But we'd be stupid not to take whatever we can get, I'm sure you all agree. I'll come amongst you now, collecting. Just pretend you're sitting in your church on Sunday morning, giving to the Lord."

"That's blasphemous!" one of the men seated across from Ryder, forward, on the right side of the aisle, protested.

It meant trouble when the gunman's smile grew wider, as he faced the man who'd spoken, moving toward him. "Blasphemous," he echoed. "You some kind of parson, mister?"

"Just a Christian," said the other, still defiant.

"That makes one of us," the gunman said, standing beside the man who'd raised the challenge, looming over him. "O' course, you are entitled to your own opinion, but a smart man knows when he should keep it to himself."

And saying that, he whipped the muzzle of his six-gun in a short, swift arc across the seated fellow's face, slashing from right to left. Ryder saw blood speckle the nearby window, and a couple of the ladies yelped, surprised and frightened, as the injured man slumped over in his seat.

"Now, then." The gunmen beamed. "If no one else has anything to say . . . ? Nothing? All right. Get out your money, watches, any gold or silver jewelry you might be wearing." Reaching underneath his jacket, he produced a folded gunnysack and shook it open with his left hand. "Be generous and don't try holding out. As you can see from Mr. Big Mouth here, it's dangerous."

Ryder wished he knew how many other men were in the holdup gang, and where they were positioned. Were they in the other cars? Up in the locomotive's cab? Was someone waiting in the trees nearby, with horses for their getaway? He couldn't see the bandits riding on to Lufkin with their loot, where anyone could raise a shout and summon the authorities.

If there was anyone alive, that is, to do the shouting.

Ryder didn't know how many passengers were on the train, but suddenly, he had a sickly feeling. Wondered why the bandit hadn't bothered putting on a mask. Was he an idiot? Or did he plan on making sure there were no witnesses?

One pistol showing, which would leave him four rounds short for clearing Ryder's car, but he could have another one concealed. There was a chance, too, that the other members of his gang could help with mopping up. Why not, if they'd decided it was easier to stage a massacre than have to worry about being caught and caged.

He didn't *know* that was the plan, of course, but it was worrisome.

On top of which, he didn't feel like giving up his cash.

He reached under his jacket, as if going for his wallet, but he drew the Colt Army instead, holding it down and out of sight from where the gunman stood. He eased its hammer back, winced at the sharp click of the mechanism, but the bandit didn't seem to notice. He was talking to the woman named Marie, telling her to be quick about surrendering her wedding ring.

Ryder sat still and waited for his chance.

Mr. Mustache was within two rows of Ryder now, and one of those was empty. Ryder had considered how he ought to handle it: bracing the man and risking that he'd open fire, or simply shooting him and hoping that his first slug did the job. On balance, he'd decided it was safer, easier, to drop him where he stood.

But how?

A straight shot to the torso might not kill him outright, and there was a chance that Ryder's slug could exit from the target's back, fly on, and injure someone else inside the railroad car. The bandit's head offered a smaller target, but a miss would strike the wall or ceiling, rather than another passenger.

And if he made a clean head shot, the guy should fold without a fight.

Big *if.*

He'd have to place the shot precisely, minimizing any chance of a reflexive twitch between the bandit's index finger and his pistol's trigger. Even falling backward, Ryder knew the mustached man could still do lethal damage, hitting Ryder or another of the passengers who shared his car. Decisive moves had consequences, and he didn't want to make the situation worse than it already was.

Ten seconds, maybe less, before the gunman got to Ryder with his burlap bag, expecting cash. He was already turning from Marie and her companion when a shot rang out from the direction of the locomotive. The bandit grinned from ear to ear and said, "Sounds like the party's starting early."

Ryder shot him in the face, not taking time to aim as he would do in practice, on a firing range, but trusting muscle memory to place the .44 slug where he wanted it. Between the eyes was good, but when the dark hole suddenly appeared it was off-center, just above the target's right eyebrow. He was already toppling over backward when a spout of blood erupted from the wound and drew a crimson track across his startled face.

Now there was chaos in the car, and Ryder had to raise his voice, moving to stand over the dead man and relieve him of his pistol. "Everyone be quiet!" he commanded, glaring at the frightened faces that surrounded him. "Stay in your seats and duck down if you see somebody coming. I'll be back to tell you when it's clear to move around."

Adding *I hope,* to keep from tempting fate.

He moved along the aisle, a six-gun in each hand, and hesitated at the car's exit. There was a little window in the door that let him see into the next car, separated by the coupling, each car with a small platform for boarding, metal steps descending on both sides. Inside the middle car, he saw a shooter standing in the aisle, holding a scattergun and staring back at Ryder, wondering what had become of his associate.

He didn't think about it long before he raised the double-barreled weapon and let go. Ryder just had time to duck before the buckshot smashed through first one window, then the other, raining shattered glass on top of him, while women screamed and men cursed in the background.

Call it six or seven seconds to reload the shotgun, minimum, unless the shooter switched off to a pistol. Ryder used the time he had, shoved through the door, and leaped across the narrow gap between the cars, bursting through the second door to face his enemy.

The man was fumbling with a brass cartridge when he looked up and saw death coming for him. He dropped the shotgun then, too late, and started reaching for a holster on his right hip, tied down low for speed.

Too late.

Raising the captured pistol in his left hand, Ryder shot him in the chest and watched him fall.

He stepped in blood, moving to fetch the fallen bandit's shotgun and the cartridges he'd dropped as he was dying. Ryder glanced around the car, saw several of the passengers regarding him with fearful eyes as he reloaded, while the others made a point of staring out their windows, carefully avoiding Ryder's gaze.

"Who's armed?" he asked, of no one in particular.

Reluctantly, not knowing what they should expect, two of the men put up their hands.

"All right," he said. "Each of you take one door. No one gets in the car unless I'm with them to approve it."

He got nods from both men as they rose and drew their pistols, one moving to watch the door Ryder had entered through, the other trailing him to reach the north end of the second car, where Ryder stopped, repeating his surveillance of the last car through the doubled door windows.

This time, he didn't see a shooter in the next car, only passengers milling around and peering through their windows, trying to determine what was happening. Ryder left them to it, easing through the door, onto the narrow platform, moving toward its left side, where he craned to look around the car, up toward the locomotive and the water tower standing tall beside it.

Two men were standing on the ground, both aiming rifles up toward the engineer's cab. Behind the locomotive, Ryder saw the broad sliding door to the mail car was open. He ducked back, crossed the narrow platform, and leaned out to check the train's right-hand side. One bandit there, sitting astride a roan, holding the reins to six or seven other horses.

He had begun to wonder how they'd missed the gunfire, but he understood it now.

They weren't expecting any survivors.

Ryder had heard of train robberies during the war, a favorite trick of Missouri guerrillas led by William Quantrill and Bloody Bill Anderson. It stood to reason that the practice would continue into peacetime, and the quickest way to rule out testimony from eyewitnesses was to eliminate them.

Ryder wished he'd brought his Henry with him, but he hadn't thought about it in his rush to keep the gunmen from annihilating unarmed passengers. There was no time to go back for it now. He'd have to make do with the weapons he was carrying—and the advantage of surprise.

He left the solitary bandit with his horses, doubled back along the platform between cars, and checked the left side of the train again. One of the riflemen had disappeared, either inside the cab or in the mail car, which reduced the odds of Ryder being shot when he revealed himself. One man to face immediately, not as close as he'd have liked, but if he rushed the bandit . . .

Ryder dropped into the open, wasn't seen at first, his target either missing him or making the assumption that his friends would be the only people up and moving while the robbery was going on. He'd nearly reached the mail car when he raised the shotgun, sighted down its short barrels, and squeezed one of its double triggers.

Ryder didn't know what size of shot the cartridges contained, but he assumed that most would miss his target at the given range. Some found the mark, though, and the bandit staggered, dropped his rifle, clutching at his right arm where a splash of blood along his duster's sleeve revealed a wound. He turned to face the stranger who had shot him, reaching for a pistol underneath his coat, but was hampered by his damaged arm.

Ryder had reached the mail car now, was running past its open door, and saw movement inside. He fired the shotgun's second barrel through the doorway, aiming high, hoping to miss any railroad employees still alive in there. With any luck, the twelve-gauge blast would buy him time to finish off the outlaw he could see, then he could think about the rest.

Or else, die trying.

The bandit with the useless arm was cursing, reaching for his holstered pistol with his left hand, having trouble with the hammer thong that held it fast. Instead of waiting for him, Ryder drew his Colt Army and fired one shot from twenty feet, putting the gunman down.

He wasn't dead when Ryder reached him, but the wet sound of a sucking chest wound said that he was on his way. Ryder relieved him of the pistol, tossing it aside, then snatched the dying bandit's rifle—a Henry, like his own— and checked to verify it had a live round in the chamber as he turned back toward the train.

Emerging from the driver's cab, he saw the second rifleman he'd spotted earlier, a tall man with a bristling beard, descending with his own repeater pointed Ryder's way. There was no time to place a shot precisely, so he triggered three in rapid fire, pumping the Henry's lever action, hoping for a lucky hit to slow the bandit down.

His first shot missed, struck sparks, and ricocheted into infinity. The second tore into his target's hip, stunning the rifleman and throwing him off balance, while the third drilled through his shoulder, made him drop his Henry as he tumbled off the metal steps descending from the cab. The bandit landed on his face, the wind knocked out of him, and Ryder hurried over to him and slammed his rifle's butt into the outlaw's skull with every ounce of force that he could manage.

Dead or just unconscious? Ryder frankly didn't give a damn.

He saw the engineer above him, peering down, and tossed the bandit's rifle to him. "Check the other side," he ordered. "There's a lookout holding horses."

"Yessir!"

Ryder turned back toward the mail car, wishing that he'd taken time to count the waiting horses more precisely. Would he find one gunman in the open car, or two? In either case, how would he root them out?

Ryder eased closer to the mail car, ready with the captured Henry if the bandits tried to make a break for it. They'd likely come out shooting, in that case, and he would have to take his chances. On the other hand, if they stayed put . . .

A gunshot sounded from the driver's cab and echoed from the forest on the far side of the train. He hoped the engineer had plugged the gang's outrider, or at least had driven him away, then Ryder put it out of mind and focused on the task at hand.

The open door yawned at him, Ryder's angle wrong for spotting anyone inside the car. He stopped ten feet away and called up to the shadowed opening, "You're running short of friends out here, in case you hadn't noticed. Toss your weapons out, and you can live to see another day."

"And hang, you mean?" a mocking voice came back at him.

"I doubt it," Ryder said. "So far, your side's killed nobody."

"And we're supposed to swallow that?" the same voice challenged. "Who in hell are you?"

"Just on my way to Houston," Ryder said.

"That ain't no answer!"

"All right, then," said Ryder. "I'm the one who's got you covered. In another minute, I'll be locking up that door, and you can wait until the next town's sheriff smokes you out."

"Big talk!" a second voice replied. "We'd like to see you try it!"

Crunching footsteps at his back made Ryder look around. The engineer was coming toward him, looking rueful.

"Sorry, mister, but I missed the other one. He's gone, at least."

"That's good enough," Ryder replied. And to the bandits in the mail car, "Seems your lookout ran away and took your horses with him. Don't be counting on his help."

Silence, for half a minute, then the first voice said, "I guess that's it, then. Hold your fire. We're comin' out."

They came out shooting, one man leaping down behind the other, with a six-gun in each hand. The second bandit stumbled as he landed, jostled his companion, and the impact spoiled his aim. A bullet hummed past Ryder's face, and then all three of them were firing, laying down a screen of gun smoke.

Ryder guessed that he had five seconds, give or take, before one of the pistoleers got lucky with a wild shot, gutting him. He focused on the taller of them, hoping that the Henry he had captured had a full load in its magazine. If not . . .

His first round missed, in the excitement, but his second took the forward shooter underneath his chin, snapping his head back, floppy hat airborne with something wet and red inside it. Ryder didn't watch him fall, swung toward the second man, and saw that he was younger, likely in his teens.

So what?

The smoking pistols in his hands made him as old and dangerous as any other felon Ryder had confronted since he first pinned on a badge. A bullet neither knew nor cared who'd sent it on its way, or whose flesh it was mutilating when it found a target. Pistols didn't make men equal, necessarily. The act of killing did.

His third shot struck the young man just below his breastbone, in the spot Ryder had heard a surgeon call the solar plexus. Land a punch there, and you'd take the fight out of a man. A bullet did the same, but worse, drilling the liver, stomach, maybe angling down into a kidney, through the bowels, or burrowing straight through to the aorta. It was death, regardless, and he saw that on the final shooter's face as he stood over him, kicking his guns aside.

"You kilt me," wheezed the dying youth.

"A chance you took," Ryder replied.

"I never thought . . . You haven't seen my mama anywhere around here, have you?"

"No."

"I hope she gets here soon." The boy was crying now, whether from pain or grief it was impossible to say. "I need to tell her somethin'."

Ryder knelt beside him. "You can tell me."

"Shoulda listened to her. All the times she tried to tell me. Do you think he'll let me in?"

"Who's that?"

"The Lord. Oh, Christ, that hurts!"

"It won't, much longer," Ryder told him, seeing black blood from a liver wound. He gave the youngster ten or fifteen minutes, tops.

"Where's Amos?"

"Never met him," Ryder said.

"You didn't? He was with me in the car, just now."

Ryder glanced toward the mail car's open door and saw a grizzled old conductor, twice his own age, staring down at them. He figured Amos had to be the first man he had shot, out of the car.

"He's gone ahead of you," he told the dying man-child.

"Never shoulda let him get me into this."

"What's done is done."

"Like me. You see my mama . . . tell her . . ."

With a final wheeze, the kid slumped back and died, his message lost. Ryder shoved to his feet and found the engineer beside him, eyes bright with excitement, now that he'd decided he would probably survive.

"Mister, I don't know who you are, but—"

"Just a passenger," said Ryder. "How long till we're under way?"

"Huh? Oh. I guess . . . what should we do about the bodies?"

"Your call. There's two aboard the train, and four out here."

"Less trouble taking off the two, I guess," the engineer decided. "Anyhow, who wants to ride with stiffs?"

"There's still the mail car."

"Nope. Our contract with the gubment says nobody rides in there but Eastern Texas personnel."

"Well, there you go, then," Ryder said.

"You wouldn't want to help me get the others off?"

"I shot them for you," Ryder said. "That's where I draw the line."

"No problem. Nossir! You just go on back and settle in. We should be under way in five, ten minutes."

Ryder turned away, the engineer calling after him, "Hey! You forgot your Henry!"

"Isn't mine," said Ryder. "Keep it."

"Well, okay then! If you say so."

There'd be questions in the next town, a delay, but nothing that should carry over all the way to Jefferson. With luck, he could arrive as no one special, go unnoticed with the other disembarking passengers, and get back to his job. Forget the men he'd killed today, as if the incident had never happened.

As if none of them were ever born at all.

8

★ Another day was breaking as they rattled into Jefferson, the locomotive's whistle giving off one mournful note before it died away. A few minutes past six o'clock, and there were several passengers already waiting on the depot's platform, anxious to be out of there and headed somewhere else. They stood and waited for the passengers on board to disembark, but no one seemed to notice Ryder in particular.

There had been less trouble with the law in Lufkin than he had expected. Outlaws seemed to be in good supply throughout the district, and the local sheriff wasn't interested in retrieving any carcasses, once sun and scavengers had gone to work on them. He told anyone who'd listen that the Eastern Texas Railroad was responsible for cleaning up its own mess, and the engineer could tell that to the rangers, if he had a mind to.

As for Ryder, he was happy just to see the last of Lufkin and move on.

Not that the scenery improved in Jefferson.

It was a county seat, but still not much to look at, with a waterfront of sorts abutting the Red River, and a stockyard whose aroma fouled the air for blocks around. Ryder understood the river thereabouts was prone to logjams, but they didn't seem to stop the cargo barges getting through and dropping off the loads they'd carried from the Gulf of Mexico, along the Mississippi River to its major Texas tributary.

Jefferson was obviously growing, skeletons of shops and houses rising skyward, everywhere along the river, but they had a temporary look and feel to them. One careless match, and it could all go up in smoke—or Jefferson could fade away more slowly, like a hundred other boomtowns in the West.

First thing, Ryder went off in search of a hotel. He had a choice of four, downtown, and picked the cheapest of the lot after deciding that they all looked roughly equal in accommodations. It was called the Bachmann House and stood four stories tall on the west side of South Polk Street, five blocks north of the river.

Checking in, he paid for three nights in advance and signed "George Reynolds" in the register. The clerk was fairly young, late twenties, but his hair had started thinning out on top, combed over from the left in an attempt to camouflage the scalp beneath it. He was working on a mustache, but it wasn't going well so far. Ryder imagined that his earnest mood would dissipate with time.

His room was on the third floor, facing shops across the street. Ryder was tired, although he'd slept most of the way from Lufkin into Jefferson, a restless kind of sleep. He wasn't going back to bed in daylight, though, and hunger soon won out over fatigue. Heading downstairs, he walked two blocks before he found a restaurant and ordered breakfast from a menu written on a chalkboard: ham and eggs, with fried potatoes, biscuits, and black coffee.

His fellow diners didn't look much different from those he'd seen in Corpus Christi or at other stops along the railroad line. Some of the men were better dressed, in three-piece suits with coats of varied length, their shoes and cuffs powdered with dust from unpaved streets. Others were rustic in appearance, flannel shirts and denim trousers over heavy boots, most of them sporting knives and pistols in their belts. The women, a minority, wore dresses buttoned to the throat and caged in crinoline below, a challenge when they sat, to keep the hoops from rising indiscreetly.

Ryder took his time with breakfast, drawing out the meal and letting coffee refills bring him back to life. He'd put the shooting on the railroad line behind him, pushed it out of mind, and saw no reason he should mention it the next time he reported back to Washington. As far as that went, he would have to couch whatever messages he sent in cryptic terms, trusting the chief to work out what he meant, since Ryder couldn't tell who might be reading cables sent from Jefferson.

He was in Rebel territory now, where some men still denied the outcome of the war, and few were pleased with its results. His cover as a cattle buyer ought to serve him well enough, in the short term, but he had yet to think of any means for getting close to Royson Coker's Knights. The other side of that coin was a more direct approach, but with the local law presumed to be in Coker's camp, that posed its own decided risks.

See how it goes, he thought and left his money on the table, with a tip he thought would please the waitress, without making her remember him. The city was awake now, bustling, and he went to find out what it held in store.

I need a beer," Wade Stevens said.

Ardis Jackson frowned at him. "It's barely nine o'clock."

"Don't care what time it is. I'm thirsty."

"You're hungover," Caleb Burke said, not quite grinning.

"Makes you thirsty, don't it?" Jackson challenged.

"Jesus H., you drunk enough last night to pickle half a dozen men," Burke said.

"And I suppose you're a teetotaler?"

"I never said—"

"You two are givin' me a headache," Jackson growled.

"Looks like I ain't the only one hungover," Stevens answered, smiling.

"Wanna get some breakfast?" Burke inquired.

"God's sake, don't mention food right now," Stevens complained.

"Nice slab o' greasy bacon, with some redeye gravy on the side. Maybe some grits along with that."

"Goddamn you!"

"I'm just sayin'—"

Jackson pushed up from the bench they shared, outside the barber's shop. "You children stay and play your games," he said. "I'm gonna stretch my legs a bit."

"Hey, Ardis," Burke said, "we're just funnin'."

"You're high-larious," Jackson replied. "Just leave me out of it."

"Awright, come back, for Christ's—Hey, lookee there!" Caleb was pointing to the far side of the street, a shapely woman browsing past shop windows. "Know who that is?"

"Sure do," Jackson said. "That carpetbagger's sister."

"Not bad-lookin', for a Yankee," Stevens said, his comment punctuated with a belch.

"No doubt she'll love your manners," Jackson goaded him.

"She might, at that. Just needs a chance to get acquainted."

"I never seen red hair like that before," Burke said. "Reckon it's natch'ral?"

"You could ask her," Jackson said.

"Might do that very thing."

"Go on, then."

"By my lonesome?"

"Think you need protection?" Stevens prodded.

"Caleb thinks that nigger-lovin' bitch might run him off," Jackson suggested.

"Aw, to hell with both o' you," Burke snarled. He left his seat and crossed the narrow sidewalk, stepped into the street.

"Go get 'er, boy!" cheered Stevens.

"Think I'll see how this plays out," Jackson decided.

Stevens got up from the bench. "Hold on. I'm comin', too."

They waited for a passing wagon, Burke well ahead of them before the way was clear. A painful pulse behind his eyes made Jackson grimace as he hurried to catch up.

"Man gets a move on when he's motivated."

"You mean randy," Jackson said.

"That, too."

"Hungover like he is, I bet his head splits open when she slaps him."

"*If* she slaps him."

"Think she won't?"

"Who knows with Yankee bitches?"

Burke had reached the sidewalk by the time Jackson and Stevens got halfway across the street. He moved to intercept the woman, standing in her way, thumbs hooked behind the buckle of his gunbelt. She ignored him for a moment, or perhaps was unaware of his proximity, as she looked startled when she turned to go along her way and found him standing there.

"Smooth, ain't he?" Stevens asked.

"Like sandpaper," said Jackson.

In another moment, they were on the sidewalk, flanking Burke. The redhead, Jackson saw, was even better-looking close up than she had been from across the street. She stood there, fidgeting and giving him ideas, while Burke turned on his charm.

"Ma'am, you look good enough to eat," he said, flashing a yellow smile, verging on brown.

"Excuse me, please," she said, keeping her eyes downcast.

"Leavin' so soon? We ain't even acquainted yet."

"Please, let me pass."

"She's real polite," Burke said, to no one in particular. "I like the way she keeps on sayin' *please*."

"Bet she says that a lot," said Stevens, getting in the spirit of the thing.

"I don't want any trouble," she declared.

"Trouble? What trouble? No one said—"

"You've had your fun," a strange voice said, behind them. "Now step off and let the lady pass."

The three men turned as one, regarding Ryder with expressions ranging from surprise to vague amusement. One he took to be the leader of the trio asked him, "Who'n hell are you?"

"A man whose daddy taught him to show women some respect," Ryder replied.

"A Yankee!" said the grubby-looking fellow in the middle, picking up on Ryder's accent.

"That's right," he granted. "Fairly new to Texas, but it keeps surprising me."

"How's that?" the first one who had spoken asked.

"Before I left, somebody told me all you southern boys were gentlemen. Looks like they got it wrong."

"You oughta go about your business, Yank," the third man growled.

Ryder allowed himself a smile. "You don't know what my business is. Could be a teacher, for example."

"Yeah? What do you teach?" the spokesman asked.

"Today, it's manners."

"Meanin' what, exactly?" asked the fellow in the middle.

"That's a joke, I take it."

"Uh-uh."

"Then you're dumber than I thought," said Ryder.

"I don't take that kinda talk from any man, much less a bluebelly!"

Ryder considered that, nodding. Spoke past them, to the woman, saying, "Ma'am, you need to step inside that shop behind you."

"Why's she need to move at all?" their mouthpiece asked.

"Because I'd hate to shoot a woman accidentally," Ryder replied.

They seemed to see his Colt and cross-draw holster for the first time now, the short one in the middle blinking at him, while the others frowned.

"A teacher like yourself should learn to count," the one on Ryder's right proclaimed. "There's three of us, and only one of you."

"I noticed that." And to the redhead, once again, "Go on now, ma'am."

The middle man reached back to clutch one of her arms, a stupid move that took his gun hand out of play. "She wants to stay and see me make a Yankee dance," he said.

Instead of arguing the point, Ryder whipped out his Colt Army and struck the little man a slashing blow across his face. He felt the nose break, saw his adversary suddenly release the redhead's arm and sit down on the sidewalk, hard, forcing her to retreat a step. Blood spurted from his flattened nostrils, leaving purple splotches on an unwashed denim shirt.

The other two were reaching for their guns when Ryder cocked his pistol, letting one, and then the other, stare into its business end. When neither one pulled on him, Ryder said, "Maybe you're smarter than I gave you credit for. You want to finish this, or take your monkey here to get patched up?"

"You bought yourself a load of trouble, mister," said the leader of the pack.

"Okay, then." Ryder aimed his pistol at the speaker's face. "Let's settle it right now."

"My mama didn't raise no fools."

"I was about to ask if she had any children who lived."

"What's that supposed to—"

"Pull your pistol," Ryder said, "or pick your friend up off the sidewalk and get out of here."

The two still standing glanced at one another and decided not to risk it. Ryder kept his Colt in hand, its muzzle lowered now, and stepped aside to let them pass, with their companion slung between them, arms over their shoulders. Focusing as best he could, the one Ryder had slugged said something sounding like "Ah no zhu wan."

"That goes for all of us," the leader said. "We owe you one, and then some."

"Anytime you grow a backbone," Ryder said and watched them hobble off, the short one slung between them, slowing progress, till they reached an alley's mouth and ducked into its shade.

Ryder half expected two of them, at least, to spring back out with pistols drawn. He waited for the best part of a minute before holstering his Colt, then stood so he could see the woman and the alley both, at once.

"Thank you," she said. "That might have been . . . well, worse than it turned out to be."

"Ask Shorty how he feels about it in the morning," Ryder said.

That made her shudder as she answered him. "I hope I won't be seeing them again."

"I ought to introduce myself," he said but didn't get the chance.

"You, there!" a gruff voice called out from across the street. "Throw up your hands!"

Ryder turned to face a stocky figure, bandy-legged and barrel-chested, round face shaded by a wide-brimmed, high-crowned hat. He wore a pistol on his right hip, fingers curled around its grip, but had not drawn it yet. The star pinned to his vest glinted despite a layer of tarnish.

Ryder kept his hands down at his sides, asking the lawman, "What's the problem, Marshal?"

"Sheriff," he was instantly corrected. "Harlan Travis of Marion County."

"You're in the right place, then," said Ryder.

"I told you to throw up your hands!"

"And I asked you what the problem is."

Arriving on the sidewalk, Sheriff Travis kept his distance. "I just witnessed you assaulting three respected citizens of Jefferson," he said. "I'm putting you under arrest."

"Respected citizens?" Ryder could only smile at that. "I guess you've got a different definition for it, here in Texas."

"Listen, you—"

"Three blowhards, drunk at half past nine A.M., insulting ladies on the street and threatening a man who intervenes. Is that your kind of law and order, Sheriff?"

"You can tell it to the judge," Travis replied.

"I'm telling you. And if you're smart, it goes no further."

Smelling trouble, Travis cut a glance toward the lady and told her, "You can go about your business, ma'am."

"I will not," she informed him. "I'm a witness to the whole event. This gentleman—"

She hesitated, realizing that she didn't know his name, and Ryder had to think about how he should handle that. Give out the name he'd signed at the hotel, or use his own to match his federal credentials.

Well, he thought, *to hell with it.*

"Gideon Ryder," he told Travis. "And I've got a badge, myself."

Travis was frowning at him now. "Where is it?"

Ryder used his left hand, slowly, kept the right hand ready for his Colt as he drew back his coat's lapel to show the badge pinned on its inner lining.

"What's that say?" the sheriff asked him, squinting.

"U.S. Secret Service," Ryder said. "And let me guess: you never heard of it."

"Are you some kinda Yankee spy?"

"In case you missed it, Sheriff, that war's over. Lee surrendered."

"Some around these parts would argue that point with you."

"If they haven't learned it yet, they will, in time."

"Uh-huh. About this other deal . . ."

"You want to file a charge against me, Sheriff, go ahead. I'll cable the Unites States attorney, up in Austin, and he'll be here for the trial. You'll wind up looking like a fool, or worse, costing the county money for a case you're bound to lose. What I will *not* do is surrender and sit waiting in your jail, until a mob of yellow scum with sacks over their heads come and string me up."

The sheriff's face had gone from pink to red, verging on purple. Ryder knew his type, could sense his first resort was violence, but Travis managed to control himself somehow, lifting his gun hand clear, flexing the fingers as if they were paining him.

"I'm gonna check this out. Where are you staying?"

"Haven't made my mind up yet." Why make it easy for him, after all?

"I'm gonna keep an eye on you."

"And take care of that other thing."

"What other thing?"

"The bums who were harassing Mrs.—"

"Miss," the lady at his side corrected him. "Miss Anna Butler."

"I know who you are," the sheriff said, his eyes on Ryder.

"I've no doubt of that," she said. "Now, if we're finished here . . ."

"Those other three," said Ryder, not inclined to let it go.

"I'll look 'em up and get their side of it," Travis replied.

"And do your duty, as the law requires?"

"As I see fit," the sheriff said and turned away, clomping along the wooden sidewalk in his high-heeled boots.

"Some law you've got here," Ryder said, when he was out of earshot.

"If you want to call him that. He's little better than a thug, himself."

"In which case, I'd say that it's wise to stay away from him."

"But will he stay away from you?" she asked, half smiling.

"If he's smarter than he looks."

"I wouldn't count on that."

"Miss Butler, may I see you safely home? Assuming that you're finished with your shopping for today?"

"All this has put me off. And yes, Mr. Ryder, you may."

G lad you could make it, Sheriff."

"Came here straightaway, soon as I got your message," Travis said. "You've heard from them, I take it?"

Them being the three who'd caused the trouble, Caleb with his nose mashed flat and now taped over, as if that would help it any.

"We've been talking, that's correct," Roy Coker said. "And now, I'd like to hear your part of it."

"These three decided that they'd have some fun with Anna Butler."

"The carpetbagger's sister. We've been over that," said Coker.

"But they didn't count on someone steppin' in to call 'em on it."

"Once again, I've heard that bit."

"O' course, they didn't stick around to find out who he is."

"Don't make me guess, Harlan."

"Name's Ryder. Gideon, he says."

"A judge from the Old Testament," said Coker. "Did he have a Hebrew look about him?"

"Not that I saw."

"Judge? He weren't no judge I ever saw," said Jackson.

"I was citing scripture, Ardis. You won't know it, but the name means 'mighty warrior' or 'destroyer.'"

"What name?"

"Lord preserve us." Coker turned back to the sheriff. "So, if not a judge, what is he, then?"

"Comes from the government. In Washington, I mean. Showed me a badge from somethin' called the U.S. Secret Service."

"Which confused you, I suppose."

"Well . . ."

"It was organized in July of this year. A kind of national police force, but with limited responsibility. At least, they *say* it's limited."

"So, not a spy, then."

"Only inasmuch as all police spy on the common citizen."

"I never did."

"Of course not, Sheriff. Now, as to his business . . . ?"

"Didn't say."

"And you were too absorbed to ask."

"Abthorbed," said Caleb, trying on a grin for size. "Tha's Harlan."

"Keep it up, you want a jaw to match that nose," the sheriff warned.

"Ya doan thcare meed."

"All of you, simmer down," said Coker. "You can kill each other when we've done our work in Jefferson and finished cleaning up the state. Meanwhile, I want to know about this mighty warrior in our midst."

"Who's that?" asked Jackson.

Coker felt the color rising in his cheeks. "That would be Agent Ryder, Ardis."

"Oh, right."

"Can you focus long enough to find out where he's staying? Put some eyes on him and find out where he goes?"

"Will do," said Jackson, making no move to stand up.

"Right now would be the time."

"Yessir!" He bolted for the door, spurs jangling, half surprising Coker when he opened it without a hitch.

Coker turned back to the sheriff, saying, "Harlan, this could be a problem for us."

"I can handle it."

"No doubt. But I'm concerned that if you do, there may be repercussions from the federals."

Travis frowned at that. "What's repo-cushions?"

"Trouble," Coker answered, swallowing an urge to slap Travis and send him back to grade school. "If a lawman like yourself, or any of your deputies, does anything to interfere with Agent Ryder, we could be ass-deep in bluecoats. And we don't want that, do we?"

"No."

"Exactly. So I'll deal with him, and you will carry out a full investigation, satisfying all concerned."

"I will?"

"At least, on paper."

"Oh. I get it. Whatcha got in mind?"

"I'll have to think about it," Coker answered. "First, we'll find out where he's staying, then come up with something suitable."

"Ah cad haddle im," Burke interjected.

"All evidence to the contrary, Caleb," said Coker. "You have had your chance. Now give your nose and mouth a rest. I'll try someone with more finesse."

Burke muttered something unintelligible.

"What was that?"

"Nuddin."

"As I suspected. You may go."

When he was left alone with Travis, Coker said, "I know it's difficult for someone like yourself, a man of action, to be eased aside. But trust me, Harlan, this is for the best. You're too important to be jeopardized."

He almost choked on that bit, but the sheriff swallowed it, nodding along as Coker spoke. "Okay, I see that. But if you need me for anything—"

"You'll be the first to know."

"Awright, then. If we're done . . ."

"We are, indeed."

Travis went out and closed the office door behind him. Coker took a glass and bottle from his desk drawer, bottom right, and poured himself a double shot of whiskey. Being lubricated helped him think, and he had plans to make.

Charting the final hours of an enemy from Washington.

9

★ Ryder and Anna Butler walked six blocks due east from South Polk Street, passing locals who regarded them with various expressions ranging from suspicion to outright distaste. Since he was new in town and hadn't met a one of them before, Ryder supposed that their hostility was meant for his companion—and, by logical extension, anybody else who deigned to walk with her.

So be it.

Every block or so, he paused to look behind them, watching out for any of the gunmen he had rousted earlier.

"You think they'll follow us?" she asked.

"No sign of them so far."

He didn't say that there might be no need for them to follow. If she was notorious in Jefferson, an object of antipathy, the thugs likely already knew where Anna lived, giving the chance to go ahead and lie in wait. Or maybe, after being shamed in public, with the sheriff now involved, they would be smart enough to bide their time.

Maybe—though *smart* wasn't the first description Ryder thought of, when he pictured them.

Not smart, but no less dangerous for that.

"Miss Butler—"

"Call me Anna, please. You saved my life, remember."

"Likely not your life."

"My honor, then. More than the so-called gentlemen of Jefferson would do."

"You don't have lots of friends in town, I take it."

"Well, not *white* friends, anyway." She watched his face and asked him, "Does that shock you?"

"I don't shock that easily."

"I'm glad to hear it, Mr. Ryder."

"Gideon."

"That's better."

"What I meant to ask is if you're down here on your own."

"Oh, no. There's Abel."

"And he is . . . ?"

"My brother. We're with the American Missionary Association. You may have heard of it?"

"The New York abolitionists?"

"Not all from New York," she corrected him. "But, yes, that is the group I mean."

"What brings you south, now that the slaves are freed?"

"In theory, they are free," she said. "Reality is something else entirely. Our goal, for the AMA, is to establish schools. Did you know that before the war, it was a crime to educate black men and women held in bondage?"

"Sounds familiar."

"First, ban them from learning and imprison anyone who

tries to teach them, then use ignorance as an excuse for keeping them in servitude."

"Doesn't sound fair, I grant you."

"Not fair? It's diabolical!"

"Were you a teacher, back at home?"

"Training to be," she said. "My brother is a minister."

"So, healing hearts and minds."

"If we can get the chance."

"And people hereabouts are stopping you."

"By any means they can devise."

"I can't promise to clear that up for you," Ryder admitted, "but I'll do the best I can."

"You've done enough," she said, then stopped and told him, "Here we are."

The house was small but well kept, freshly painted sometime in the past six months or so, new-looking shingles on its sloping roof. Someone, likely the woman at his side, had cultivated flowers in two beds below windows facing the street, and while the yard was sandy dirt, it had been raked to keep it smooth and free of jutting stones. A knee-high picket fence enclosed the yard, with access through a swinging gate.

They passed through, Anna pausing long enough to latch the gate behind them, then proceeded to the house. Before they reached its porch, a man emerged to greet them, dressed in shirtsleeves and suspenders. He resembled Anna, though his face was masculine enough that no one would have called him pretty.

She performed the introductions. "Abel, this is Mr. Ryder. Gideon, my brother, Abel."

"And what brings you here?" asked Abel Butler.

Anna answered before Ryder had a chance. "He helped me out of trouble. Coker's men again."

"Are you all right? They didn't—"

"More rough talk, as usual," she told him. "Calm yourself."

"They need a hiding," Abel answered, through clenched teeth.

"They got it. Well, one of them did," she answered, smiling up at Ryder. "And he sent the sheriff packing, too."

"It seems that we are in your debt," said Abel. "Please, sir, come inside."

Within, the house was every bit as clean as its exterior. It might have been prepared for a white-glove inspection, nothing out of place that Ryder saw, and no dust visible on any surface. The only sour note he spotted was a bullet hole, high up on the parlor's north wall, in line with one of the street-facing windows.

"A token of appreciation from the KRS," Abel explained. "We've just replaced the windowpane."

"The KRS," Anna began to say, "that's—"

"I'm familiar with them," Ryder said. "In fact, that's why I'm here, in Jefferson."

"Not one of them?" Abel was instantly suspicious.

"Just the opposite," said Ryder. "I'm investigating them."

He showed his badge again, and Abel read the small inscription.

"Secret Service? Yes, I've heard of that, I think."

"You're one in a million."

"But what can you do, if the sheriff won't act?"

Ryder shrugged. "That remains to be seen. I had some luck with them in Corpus Christi, earlier this week."

"Did you arrest them?"

"Not exactly."

"What, then?"

"Let's just say they seemed discouraged when I left."

"This is their headquarters," said Abel. "If you found a way to crush them here . . ."

"I'm working on it," Ryder told him. "And I'm hoping you can get me started with some information."

I checked all the hotels in town. There ain't no Ryder booked at any of 'em," Ardis Jackson said.

"I see," Coker replied. "And what else did you try?"

"What else?"

"Describing him, for instance. To the clerks?"

"Yessir, I did do that. They got a fella stayin' at the Bachmann House sounds somethin' like him. Calls hisself George Reynolds, I believe it was."

"You're not sure?"

"No, that's right."

The same initials, Coker thought. *He's not so clever, after all.*

"And did the clerk inquire why you were asking?"

"Told him I was working for the sheriff, and he oughta keep it quiet."

"You surprise me, Ardis. That's good thinking."

Jackson beamed, delighted with himself.

"You didn't actually *see* him, though?"

"Boy said that he was out somewhere."

"We'll need a confirmation," Coker said, "before we move against him. Punishing the wrong man could rebound against us."

"Uh-huh." Jackson's normal blank expression had returned.

"One of you needs to keep eyes on the Bachmann House. Make sure this Reynolds is the man we want. Not Burke, of course. That busted mug of his stands out a block away."

"I'll see to it."

"But carefully," said Coker. "Verify the man's identity and come straight back to me. Do *not* try anything yourself."

"I reckon I could take him."

"Let's recall this morning, Ardis. How'd that go?"

"He cheated."

"Mmm. Imagine that."

"He wouldn't have to see me comin'."

"Let me say this one more time. You are to watch, and then report back. Nothing else. You understand?"

"I hear you." Sullen.

"And."

"I'll do just like you say."

"Should you forget, I will be mightily displeased."

"Yessir. Who's gonna take him, then, if you don't mind me askin'?"

"I was thinking of Chip Hardesty."

"He's got that Sharps."

"Indeed, he does."

"No worries about gettin' close."

"You read my mind."

"Okay, then."

"I'm so glad that you approve."

"Well, sure."

An awkward, silent moment passed, then Coker asked, "Is there some reason you're still standing there?"

"Huh? Oh, nossir. I'm just goin'."

"Adios, then."

"Good one. Talkin' like a Messican."

Coker watched Jackson close the door. It was a struggle sometimes, dealing with the quality of men he had available. They were passionate enough about the cause, but when it came to brains . . . well, many of them would not bear a close examination. Most were poorly educated, which he understood. It was a function of their social standing. On the other hand, the KRS seemed to attract more than its share of village idiots. Which made him wonder sometimes, in the dead of night, whether his fight was doomed to fail.

Faith made the difference, of course. His Bible told him that God Almighty had set the races apart. Adam's seed were the masters, while Cain's were the hewers of wood and drawers of water, ordained to be servants forever. No earthly king or president could violate that standard with impunity, as Mr. Lincoln had discovered to his sorrow. On the one hand, there was man's law, sometimes useful, often foolish and misguided. On the other, God's immutable commandments.

Royson Coker saw himself as one of God's elect, a man apart, born to the struggle between light and darkness in a world gone mad. If he could not restore the antebellum order to his state alone, then he would have to trust the Lord for help. And when had He denied a faithful servant's plea for aid?

But God helped those who helped themselves. And Coker had a plan in mind that might eliminate the need for thunderbolts from Heaven. He had Chip Hardesty, a master of the Sharps .52-caliber rifle who had distinguished himself as a sniper at Round Mountain, Shiloh, Murfreesboro, and Chickamauga. He'd picked up a limp at Lynchburg, hip-shot, but it had not spoiled his aim.

Before he sicced Chip on a target, though, Coker was bound to make sure that he had the *right* target. Initials could turn out to be a mere coincidence, although he doubted it in this case. Once he knew for sure that this Ryder and Reynolds were one and the same, he could take the next step. Until then . . . well, an accidental killing of some random stranger was the last thing Coker needed now, with Washington prying into his business.

And what about killing a federal agent?

That would bring more scrutiny upon him, surely, but it had been part of Coker's plan from the beginning. Every rebellion had to start somewhere, and no war was fought without killing. He would not repeat the grave mistake of the Confederacy, though. There would be no pitched battles, no massed formations or batteries of field artillery. He meant to wage an irregular struggle, emulating the Mexican *guer-rilleros* who, in turn, had learned their style of fighting from Apaches.

Hit, retreat, slip back to strike again, and so on, till your enemy was frazzled and exhausted, ready for the final coup de grâce. His first move, Coker now decided, would be the elimination of the scout sent down from Washington to build a case against him.

Was this Ryder, Reynolds, call him what you liked, responsible for Coker's recent losses down in Corpus Christi? Did he have a hand in wiping out Chance Truscott and the local Knights? It seemed unlikely, on the face of it, that any lawman acting on his own could take such forceful action.

On the other hand, Coker had no faith in coincidence.

He would eradicate this enemy and be prepared to deal with any others whom the Radicals might send against him. It was in his nature to survive and triumph.

Why else had the Lord put him on Earth?

Y ou seem to know a lot about the so-called Knights," said Abel Butler.

"Most of it, I picked up on the road," said Ryder. He did

not intend to mention Corpus Christi or the killings there, uncertain how the Butlers might react. Abel was something of a pacifist, and Anna . . . well, he didn't want her looking at him as a killer, if he could avoid it.

"Coker is the man in charge. You got that right," Abel went on. "He was some kind of officer in the rebellion and still sees himself that way, telling his soldiers where to go and what to do. They're rabble when you get down to it, though. Controlling them's a trick he hasn't mastered yet."

"The three who stopped your sister on the street," Ryder suggested.

"As a case in point. I doubt Coker would send them to harass a woman, more particularly as you say they were intoxicated. There's a chance he may impose some kind of discipline on them, when he finds out."

"The sheriff will have told him," Anna said. "He rushed off like his shirttail was on fire."

"We're in a kind of war here," Abel said, "although it wasn't meant to be. I aim to see the freedmen get their due. Coker stands on the other side, believing Appomattox was a fluke and he can still restore the South's peculiar institution. Failing that, he wants to see Negroes kept in subservient positions by whatever means are presently available. Cheap labor, if it can't be absolutely free, and God forbid they ever get the vote."

"Nobody's mentioned votes, that I've heard," Ryder said.

"It's coming. You can bank on that," said Abel. "It will change the country, possibly the world."

"I guess you've never been accused of thinking small," Ryder remarked.

"I have my failings," Abel granted, "but that isn't one of them."

"Abel's a dreamer," Anna said. "He always has been."

"And there's nothing left to dream of where you come from?" Ryder asked them both, together.

"Oh, New York has ample problems of its own," Abel agreed. "There's Tammany, the Irish, the Chinese. No doubt you heard about the draft riots in '63."

"Heard of them, and observed them," Ryder said. "I was a U.S. marshal then, guarding the federal court."

"A tragedy. So many lives lost, and the property destroyed, simply because one race disdains another."

"Not the first time," Ryder ventured. "Likely not the last."

"But it can *change*," said Anna, wide-eyed with the strength of her conviction. "Don't you see that?"

"What I mostly see, in my profession, would be people doing all the wrong things for the worst of reasons," Ryder said.

"That must be terrible."

He shrugged. "You get used to it."

"Lord, that's even worse!"

He changed the subject. "You appear to have experience in dealing with the KRS. If you can think of any information that would help me bring them down," said Ryder, "I'd appreciate it."

Abel frowned. "I hadn't thought if it in those terms, but we have been logging information, filing it away. Names of the members we've identified or have good reason to suspect, their jobs and addresses."

"That could be useful."

"I've made copies," Anna said, then turned to face her brother. "Abel?"

"Why not," he replied. "If it can help to stop them."

"Just a minute," Anna said and hurried from the room.

"She gets excited, as you see," said Abel, once he reckoned she was out of earshot. "It's a blessing and a weakness, all wrapped up in one. The passion, and the frequent disappointment."

Ryder didn't have an answer at his fingertips for that remark, just nodded, and another moment took the pressure off, as Anna came back with what looked to be a diary in her hand. She passed it to him with an earnest smile.

"It's all in here," she said. "As if we'd just been waiting for you to appear."

"Well . . ."

"I'm serious," she said and looked it. "You're like—what, Abel?—a gift from Providence!"

"Nobody's ever called me that before," said Ryder, with a rueful smile.

"Perhaps they didn't recognize it."

Abel grinned and told him, "When she gets this way, there's no point arguing."

"Hush, you!" she chided him. "I'm serious."

"We see that, Anna."

"You will come to supper, won't you?" she asked Ryder. "I mean, if you have the time and it's convenient? We should thank you properly, for helping me. For helping *us*."

"I'd be obliged," he said. "What time?"

Ardis Jackson loitered in an alley catty-cornered from the Bachmann House, smoking and killing time. No one who passed by on the street appeared to notice him, or if they did, gave any sign of recognizing him.

So far, so good.

He had been waiting for the best part of an hour, still no sign of Reynolds, Ryder, or whatever he was called. The bastard who'd humiliated him and left poor Caleb with a nose his mama wouldn't recognize. The worst part had been facing Mr. Coker, telling him the story, feeling like an idiot.

No, that wasn't right. The worst part was the fear he'd felt while looking in the Yankee stranger's eyes, knowing that one wrong move could get him killed. Jackson had been a bully all his life, had learned it from his daddy, and he usually got away with it. A pistol and some attitude could sway most folks, convince them that they ought to go along with him and save themselves a peck of trouble. It was even better when he had a few more boys to back him up, one reason he had joined the KRS, aside from his belief in what they stood for.

But it hadn't worked that morning.

Jackson felt as if they'd started strong, then everything went sour in a heartbeat. They'd been telling off the stranger, then, next thing he knew, Caleb was on the ground and spouting carmine from his blowhole, damn near crying like a baby, leaving Jackson staring back into the coldest eyes he'd ever seen, bar none.

He could have died there—would have, if he'd dared to make a move in the direction of his pistol. He could see it plain as day, the stranger's Colt Army blasting a keyhole through his forehead, blowing out his candle before Jackson even had a chance to draw.

He'd nearly wet himself, had been relieved to turn and scuttle out of there with Caleb hanging off his shoulder, fleeing like so many others had gone running off from him in better days.

And that was something he could not forgive.

He rolled another quirley, struck a match to light it, all the while watching the hotel and the street in front of him. It struck him that he might be waiting at the wrong spot, but he had his orders. Mr. Coker had commanded that he stay and watch. The last thing Jackson could afford to do was traipse off, chasing second thoughts, and miss his man entirely.

But if he showed . . . then, what?

Again, he had his orders: scurry back and tell the chief. No one had mentioned thinking for himself, taking a potshot at the stranger while he had a chance. It would be counter-manding Mr. Coker, almost like defying him, and retribu-tion could be swift. It could be *fatal*, come to that, but Jackson still felt that he owed the Yankee something for his personal embarrassment. Maybe, if he could spot the man, he'd have a talk with Mr. Coker, get permission to attempt the job himself, instead of calling in Chip Hardesty.

Maybe.

A wagon rumbled past, trailing a plume of dust, and nearly ruined everything. When it was gone, Jackson saw Mr. High-and-Mighty strolling up to the hotel, no way of telling where he'd come from. If the wagon had been any slower, he could easily have slipped inside the hotel and Jackson would have missed him.

Never mind the *if*s, though. It was him, no doubt about it, pausing in the doorway, looking up and down the street, then entering the lobby. For a second there, Jackson was worried that the stranger might have seen him hiding in the shadows, maybe glimpsed a gray plume from his cigarette, but then he turned his back and disappeared into the Bach-mann House.

Jackson was trembling, and it made him furious. He felt a sudden urge to rush across the street, bust in, and blaze away before his enemy could mount the stairs. Backshooting didn't bother him a bit; in fact, he favored it, if truth be told. What stopped him was the fear that Ryder-Reynolds might be waiting for him, standing in the middle of the lobby with his Colt drawn, lined up on the door, waiting for Jackson to appear.

That couldn't be. Could it?

Another moment, and he knew he'd lost his chance. He dropped the quirley, crushed it underneath his heel, and doubled back along the alley, not about to take a chance on being seen from the hotel. Ten minutes, give or take, and he would be in Mr. Coker's office, making his report. Doing exactly what he had been told to do. No one could fault him there.

No one, that was, except himself.

Screw it.

Living was better than the only known alternative, and maybe Mr. Coker would reward him for his service. Let him watch, perhaps, when Hardesty took down the Yankee spy— or even lend a hand somehow, if that were possible. Serve as a lookout, maybe even play the role of bait, luring the Yankee out where Chip could drill him with a single shot.

He went in through the back of Coker's place, the old Red Dog saloon, and made a beeline for the office, with its PRIVATE sign tacked to the door. He knocked and waited, fidgeting, until the deep, familiar voice said, "Enter!"

Rushing in, he stood before the massive desk and blurted, "Boss! It's him!"

10

★ Ryder had hours to kill before his supper with the Butlers, and he used the time as best he could, making the rounds of Jefferson, showing his badge and asking questions of the locals. Most of them refused to talk or pleaded ignorance; a few seemed to be wishing they could help, but made no secret of their fear. The only one who spoke to him at any length was a middle-aged barber, glad to tell a Yankee that he'd lost two sons in battle for the Stars and Bars, to keep Texas the way it was before the War of Northern Aggression.

Leaving there, Ryder was glad he hadn't asked the barber for a shave.

He had received no answers to his questions, but that hadn't been the point. After his run-in with the sheriff, he assumed that his identity would be made known to everyone in town. His best angle of attack, in Ryder's estimation, was to make his adversaries nervous, agitate them to the point that one or more of them began making mistakes.

That was a risk, of course, potentially a deadly one. As he had seen in Corpus Christi, Coker's "Knights" were not the kind of men who sat around debating problems. They were men of action—far from heroes, but at least willing to join a mob—and once they started letting fear or anger take control, it weakened them.

He only hoped it didn't kill him first.

Anna had told him to come back at six o'clock and bring his appetite. It wasn't noon yet, but it felt like ages since he'd eaten breakfast. Ryder heard his stomach growling as he left the barber's shop and started looking for another place to eat. A small lunch, nothing that would ruin supper for him after Anna took the time to cook.

Thinking of her troubled Ryder. She was certainly attractive, and intelligent to boot. Her passion, when she spoke about the freedmen and their rights, was plainly evident. Religion played a part in that, he understood, but it was still beyond him how a woman of her station in society would travel far from home, putting her life at risk for people she had never met, in a society that marked her as an enemy.

The brother, he could understand. Men went off on crusades. But women?

Ryder thought of Josey Hubbard, widowed, far from home. Had it been loyalty to Thomas that compelled her? Or was Ryder slighting women with his narrow-minded view of how they felt, thought, acted in their daily lives?

Granted, he didn't have a great deal of experience with members of the so-called weaker sex. He'd been around, of course, mostly with working girls at various saloons, but they were obviously different. The wives he'd met in Washington, and on his former travels as a U.S. marshal, had been straitlaced for the most part, standing in the shadow of their menfolk, keeping any stray opinions to themselves unless they dealt with housework, decorating, and the like.

Had he been wrong in most of his assumptions, all along?

That train of thought was making him uncomfortable, so he cut it off and listened to his stomach, telling him it needed fuel. Across the street, he saw a place called Howland's, with a sign in its front window advertising FAMOUS CHILI. Crossing at his own risk, weaving through the horse-drawn traffic, Ryder kicked some of the road's dust off his boots and went inside.

A waitress seated him and handed him a menu. When he asked what made the chili famous, she just smiled and told him, "Judge that for yourself."

"I will," he said. "And can I get a beer with that?"

"Sure can." She flashed another smile that told him Sheriff Travis hadn't been around to warn the city's cooks and servers of the viper wriggling in their midst.

The beer came first, lukewarm but palatable. Ryder barely had a chance to sip its foam before the waitress brought a steaming bowl of chili to his table, set a spoon beside it, and moved on.

One bite told Ryder why it might be famous, heat from fire and spicy peppers joining forces to assault his senses. By the second bite, his eyes were tearing up and heady fumes had cleared his sinuses. He thought the taste might be addictive, if the first bowl didn't lay him out.

Ryder slowed down and took his time, not rushing it, flagging the waitress for another beer when he had drained the first one. Time was what he needed now, to plot his moves—except that Ryder didn't have a move in mind.

He'd handicapped himself, coming to Anna's aid that morning. Not that he regretted it, but he'd revealed himself before he had a chance to build a case of any kind against the KRS. Nothing he'd seen in Corpus Christi tied Roy Coker to the bloodshed there, which meant that Ryder had to wait and watch for any move his adversaries made, an opening he could exploit to his advantage.

In the meantime, he would pass an evening with the Butlers, glean more information if he could, and go from there. At least he'd have a pleasant hour or two before the job closed in on him again.

And after that?

He couldn't say, but found the outlook grim.

Somethin' you oughta know, Sheriff."

"What's that?"

"Damn Yankee's goin' here'n there, all over town, askin' about the Knights."

"I know that, Cletus."

Standing with his chest puffed out, the barber looked confused now. "Huh? You know? And whatcha gonna do about it?"

"Askin' questions ain't against the law," Travis informed him. "If it was, I'd have to lock up every gossip in the city."

"Yeah, but this is diffurnt."

"For a fact, it is. Still not illegal, though."

"So, you don't plan on doin' nothin'?"

"What I plan to do, and what you need to know, are two entirely differ'nt things."

"So, you're just gonna let him go around and—"

"If he breaks the law, I'll be on top of him. Until then . . . well, he's just another citizen."

"He damn sure ain't no Texan!"

"And you're welcome to remind him of that fact. Without breakin' the law yourself, o' course."

"I guess I set 'im straight, all right," the barber said.

"Oh, yeah? I hope you ain't been talkin' out of turn."

"You know me, Sheriff."

"True. That's what concerns me."

"Hey, now."

"And it won't please Mr. Coker if you're spillin' things that ain't nobody's business, 'less they're in the brotherhood."

"I never would!"

"See that you don't," warned Travis.

"I just come to tell you—"

"And you told me. Best go back and see if someone's waitin' on a shave."

"This is the thanks I get for helpin'?"

"Thank you, Cletus," said the sheriff, with exaggerated courtesy. "Now go on back to work. Act normal. Play dumb if the Yankee comes around again."

The barber went out, grumbling. Travis thought that playing dumb would not require much effort on his part, then started worrying about what Cletus might have told the Secret Service man already. Shutting up had never been his strong suit, but whatever he'd let slip, it was too late to take it back.

Travis supposed that he should talk to Mr. Coker, but he didn't relish getting lectured for a second time that morning. Coker had his own plans under way, and it was best not to disturb him when his mind was gnawing on a problem. Travis would be there to clean up afterward, a lawman's dreary lot in life.

Back before the war, he'd been a small-time rancher, not averse to buying steers whose brands were altered, driving them to Mexico for sale. It wasn't quite the same as rustling, and no one had ever caught him at it, but if anyone had told him he would be the county sheriff after Appomattox, Travis would have given them the horselaugh.

It was funny how times changed—except he wasn't laughing now.

He hadn't needed Cletus to alert him that the man from Washington was circulating around Jefferson, asking questions. Travis had followed him, keeping his distance, staying out of sight, and followed up by talking to some of the merchants Ryder had interrogated. Most of them were standing firm, the rest too scared to buck the KRS. Leave it to Cletus, with his big mouth, to be a fly in the ointment.

Travis wasn't sure how Coker planned to deal with the investigator. Maybe it was better if he didn't know, in case he had to put his hand on a Bible one day. Not that he'd ever shied away from lying, when it suited him, but lying under oath before a federal judge could land him in a prison cell, and Travis didn't plan on serving time.

He thought about alternatives, not getting far beyond the thought of lighting out for parts unknown, but he'd been born and raised in Marion County, couldn't imagine fitting in anywhere else. And he believed in what the Knights were doing. Sure he did. Why not? Things had been fine before the war, when darkies knew their place and toed the line. During the war, he'd volunteered to lead the local slave patrol, which kept him out of uniform and paved his way to being sheriff. There had been no insurrections while he was in charge, unlike some other counties he could mention, where the fabric of society had started to unravel.

No, he wouldn't run. Not yet, at least. Maybe, if things began to fall apart and he could only save himself by pulling out. Until then, though . . .

The Yankee worried him, there was no use denying it.

He had a badge and guts to back it up. If push came to shove, he could probably call on the bluecoats to help him, but how would that sit with the citizenry? Would that spark the uprising necessary to expel an occupying army?

Or, the better question: having dodged one war, was Travis itching to enlist and fight another?

Food for thought, but it was sour in his mouth.

Whatever Coker planned, he hoped it worked.

And that it happened soon.

I t's not a problem, then?"

"One Yankee? No, I shouldn't think so."

"Good," Coker replied. "We're tracking him. If you could deal with him tonight . . ."

"I need to get a look at him beforehand," said Chip Hardesty. "Be no mistakes, that way."

"Of course. Harlan can point him out for you."

"The sheriff knows about this?"

"Nothing in the way of details. But he's one of us, regardless."

"Always thought he was a little soft, myself," said Hardesty.

"He didn't fight, it's true. Still, he's been useful."

"If you say so."

"Will it be the Sharps?"

"What else?"

"Your signature."

"I don't fix what ain't broken."

"Very wise. You understand, this may result in a . . . disturbance."

"Bluebellies?"

"It's possible."

"We both know they ain't bulletproof."

"If it comes down to that, I'll count on you."

"Whatever is required," the sniper said. "I ain't too spry these days, but I still get around awright."

"I've noticed. Which reminds me of another job I have in mind."

"The carpetbagger and his woman?"

"Well, she claims to be his sister, if it matters."

"Not to me."

"We know they've been in contact with this agent out of Washington. No doubt, they've told him everything they know or may have guessed about the brotherhood."

"We should have put 'em down first thing, instead of waiting."

"That was my mistake," Coker acknowledged. "Waiting for the town to make its feelings known, encourage them to move along."

"I guess it didn't work."

"And now, I leave it to your expertise."

"I'll handle it."

"No qualms about the woman?"

"First thing that they told me in the service: enemies are enemies, whether they're wearin' skirts or trousers. Course, I knew that, going in."

"You are an inspiration to us all."

"I heard about the fellas this guy buffaloed."

"They've learned a valuable lesson," Coker said.

"Maybe they weren't cut out for soldierin'."

"These days, we need whatever able-bodied men may be available."

"Long as they don't get in my way."

"I guarantee it," Coker said.

"I'll scoot along and see the sheriff, then. You want to know before it happens?"

"Not required. I trust you, Chip."

Nodding, the sniper rose and left the office. Not exactly *scooting*, with that limp of his, but he did well enough. Coker imagined Harlan's face when Chip turned up demanding help to spot his target, had to smile a bit at that, but couldn't see the sheriff raising any serious objection. Travis knew which side his bread was buttered on and wouldn't last another month in town if he began to buck the brotherhood.

All falling into place, he thought, albeit earlier than he had counted on. His people were war-weary, sick to death of loss and changes in their lives, dictated by a bunch of bureaucrats beyond their personal control. He'd thought it might require a year or more for them to risk another battle with the Yankees, but events had overtaken him. As in the great war just completed, Coker knew he must adjust, adapt, and persevere.

With that in mind, he opened the top right-hand drawer of his desk and removed the pistol he kept hidden there. It was a LeMat revolver, designed and manufactured in New Orleans, carried by wartime Confederate officers including Generals P.G.T. Beauregard and Jeb Stuart. The .36-caliber weapon featured a nine-round cylinder, giving him three up on Samuel Colt's six-shooters, but the kicker was a second barrel, offset from the first, that delivered a sixteen-gauge charge of buckshot. The pistol's maximum effective range was forty yards, though it could kill by accident out to a hundred. Close in, where it mattered, it was devastating.

Coker checked the pistol's load, made sure that its percussion caps were firmly seated, then removed its shoulder holster from the lower right-hand drawer and slipped it on, testing the leather straps to make sure they were properly adjusted. He had gained a little weight since last he'd worn the rig, but it felt fine. The three-pound pistol, holstered, drew his shoulder down a bit, but with his rigid military bearing, Coker guessed that it would cause no lasting strain.

A fast draw from the shoulder harness could be problematic, so he reached into the top drawer of his desk again and found the knife he used occasionally as a letter opener. It was a French switchblade with engraved ivory handles, S-shaped cross guards, and *Châtellerault* etched along one side of its razor-edged six-inch blade. In an emergency, Coker could draw the knife from a side pocket of his coat, snap it open, and strike at a foe in two or three seconds flat.

Practice made perfect, as they said.

Not that he planned on facing the Washington agent himself. Far from it. He had Chip and other soldiers to perform such tasks, while he directed them. The war had taught him that, while fighting men revered a leader who would actually *lead* them, it was dangerous in the extreme. Besides, he'd set his sights beyond the struggle, focusing on politics, where men with bloody reputations often failed to make the grade.

There was a new world coming, and if Coker meant to run it for the white man's benefit, he had to stay alive.

Ryder was early, even though he hadn't planned to be. He'd found another barber who agreed to trim his hair and shave him, didn't seem suspicious in the least about his northern accent, but he kept the Colt Army handy, in case things went awry.

Once he'd survived that episode, Ryder went off in search

of flowers for the lady of the house. That took a while, but he eventually found a small shop selling posies for a dollar and decided they were worth it. Then he had to worry that the blooms would wilt before he reached the Butlers' house, but they surprised him, holding up all right.

"They're beautiful!" said Anna, as she took them from him, on the doorstep.

Ryder couldn't think of anything to say, so bobbed his head and followed her inside, where Abel offered him an aperitif. That proved to be a glass of whiskey, which was a surprise, considering the pair's affiliation with a well-known missionary group.

"We're not fanatics, Gideon," he said. "I hope we didn't give you that idea."

"I hadn't thought about it," Ryder lied. "But now that you mention it . . ."

"As I believe my sister told you, we're involved in teaching freedmen for the AMA, not saving souls."

"And how's that going?" Ryder asked.

"Slowly. No one will rent us classroom space, so I'm negotiating for a plot of land. We'll build our own school, if it comes to that."

"May not be popular," Ryder suggested.

"With the KRS, I'm sure it won't be. We have good support among the freedmen, though. They'll help erect the structure, if we ever find the proper place."

"You mean to build it right in town?"

"Ideally, but at this point, I suppose we'll take what we can get."

"And what you get is supper," Anna told them both. They trailed her to the dining room, where she'd placed Ryder's flowers in a small vase, making it the table's centerpiece.

"Something smells good," Ryder remarked.

"I hope you like fried chicken."

"Always have," he granted.

"Also yams, green beans, and fresh-baked bread."

"I'm not worth that much trouble," he advised her.

Anna smiled and said, "I'll be the judge of that."

They sat with Abel at the master's place, head of the table, Anna at his right hand, Ryder to his left and facing her. The food smelled heavenly and didn't let him down on taste. After he'd complimented Anna on her culinary skill, Abel returned their conversation to Roy Coker and his Knights.

"I understand from AMA reports that groups like his are popping up in all the former Rebel states," he said. "They aren't connected to the KRS, as far as I can tell. Most sound like local operations, Confederates who can't believe they lost the war."

"Or won't accept it," Anna said.

"We hear a lot of that," her brother added. "Some will tell you that they never lost a major battle. Lord, you'd think they never heard of Gettysburg, Shiloh, or any of the rest."

"People are funny that way," Ryder said. "They remember what they want to and forget the rest."

"That bodes ill for our future, don't you think?" asked Anna.

"Hard to say," Ryder replied. "My job leads me to see the worst in people, but I still keep hoping they'll surprise me."

"Well, if I were you," said Abel, "I would not count on a great surprise in Jefferson."

"They're rock-ribbed Rebels, most of them," Anna agreed. "The handful who don't share those views are too frightened to speak their minds."

"Why stay someplace where they feel terrorized?" asked Ryder.

"It is still their home," she said. "For some, the only one they've ever known."

"Call that a choice, then," Ryder said. "If they're content to live in fear, just for familiar scenery, I can't see any hope for them."

"It isn't them we care about, primarily," said Abel. "As you understand, the freedmen are our first priority. They've been oppressed too long to suffer any more delays."

"You've got a long, hard road in front of you," Ryder replied. "I don't see many native Texans lining up on your side."

"Not at present," Abel granted. "But we hope to change their minds, in time. Once they discover that their former slaves are human beings, that they share the hopes and dreams of any other soul, well . . ."

"I'm convinced," said Ryder, pushing back his empty plate. "Between the two of us, I'd say I've got the easy job."

"But it's so dangerous!" Anna protested.

Ryder shrugged. "You live with danger every day, among these people. When I'm done, my chief will send me somewhere else. You'll still be here, trying to change a way of life that's put down roots."

"We won't give up," she said.

"And I admire that. Now, I think it's time for me to go. Thank you for—"

"Wait!" she interrupted him. "You can't run off without dessert."

"Well, if you mean to twist my arm . . ."

She brought out apple pie and coffee. Like the meal that went before, it was delicious. Ryder told her so and won another smile. They made small talk, avoiding any weighty subjects while their time ran down, and Ryder finally excused himself with thanks to both of them. They saw him to the door, and as he started down the sidewalk, he glanced back to catch a glimpse of Anna watching from a window.

Ryder felt the tug of an attraction, but the time, the place, the woman with her open heart and high ideals—none of them fit the life he led. If he let something grow between them, it would feel too much like stealing from a child.

Distracted, Ryder missed the broken sidewalk slat in front of him and stumbled, almost going down. He caught himself, then heard the sharp crack of a large-bore rifle shot, the slug already past before the echo reached his ears.

Instinctively, he dived into the nearest patch of shadow, reaching for his Colt.

11

★ **C**hip Hardesty cursed bitterly and hurried to reload his Sharps. He rarely missed a shot, couldn't recall when he had ever failed to drop a man this close to him, and chalked it up to pure bad luck.

Still no excuse.

He pulled down on the rifle's trigger guard, opened the breech, and shoved a paper cartridge in. The sharp edge of the breech's rolling block snipped off the rear end of the cartridge, as Hardesty advanced the Maynard tape primer, seating a copper cap filled with mercury fulminate into position for firing. He was fairly quick about it, years of practice on his side—but when he bent back to the rifle's sights, his man was gone.

Gone *where*?

That was the question. There were shadows all around that might conceal him, houses standing far enough apart to let a runner slip between them, hedges ringing several of the sparse front yards. He had been counting on a one-shot kill, but now it had become a hunt.

Bad news for someone with a game leg, up against an able-bodied enemy.

Hardesty took a chance, aimed more or less where he'd last seen the target, squeezing off another shot that echoed through the streets of Jefferson. He pictured neighbors cringing in their homes, ducking for cover, then a muzzle flash across the street forced him to drop and grovel as a pistol bullet hummed past, overhead.

Reloading was more difficult while lying belly-down, but he'd grown used to it in combat. Simple motions, hurried without being rushed, a crucial difference in killing situations where a hasty move, a single slip, meant death.

The rifle was his favorite, although it couldn't match a six-gun's rate of fire. For that, if he was forced to work close in, Hardesty had an old Colt Walker Model 1847 tucked under his belt, gouging a kidney as he lay prone on the ground.

He had to glance down at the Sharps, couldn't reload it in the dark by feel alone, and lost track of his adversary as he cranked the tape primer forward, its scorched paper strip dangling over the rifle's receiver. Hardesty thumbed back the hammer, eyes straining into the night for a scurry of movement, feeling as if he'd gone blind.

Where in hell was the Yankee?

Why in hell hadn't he asked for more shooters to help him?

Too late. After three shots, he knew someone had to be fetching the law. Not bad news, necessarily, what with the sheriff behind him, but Hardesty knew it was better to just slip away if he could, try again under better conditions next time. He hated disappointing Mr. Coker, but he didn't fear

the boss man when you got right down to it. If Coker tried
to punish Hardesty over a twist of fate, he'd better think
again.

No movement yet, across the street, and he was easing
backward into deeper shadows, lurching to his feet on one
good leg, when Ryder fired again. This time, the bullet
notched Hardesty's hat brim, nearly took it off his head. He
fired reflexively, a wasted shot, then started running at the
best speed he could manage, hampered by his wobbling
stride as he reloaded on the move.

Footsteps closing behind him told Chip that the Yank
was in pursuit. Again, he cursed his own pigheaded pride
for making him insist that he could do the job alone. He
wasn't finished yet, though. One leg might be gimpy, but he
still had one or two tricks up his sleeve.

The sniper's first shot had been close, the next two rushed
and off the mark, but Ryder wasn't taking any chances
with a buffalo gun. Large caliber meant large wounds, and
the thought of trusting a physician in a town where most
folks would be glad to see him dead did not imbue Ryder
with confidence.

He would be cautious, to a point, but didn't plan to let
the rifleman escape. If he could take the man alive—

Rounding the corner of a cottage where his would-be
executioner had vanished, Ryder saw another muzzle flash
and pitched face downward in the dust. The slug hissed by
where he'd been standing a split second earlier, and then the
shot's reverberation stung his ears. Ryder returned fire, three
rounds left before he had to switch out cylinders, and he
could hear the sniper running for it.

Ryder knew the difference between a Henry's sound, or

one of Colt's revolving rifles, and the noise made by a larger weapon, like an Enfield, a Lorenz, or a Sharps. The big rifles were single-shot, the first two muzzle loaders, but he guessed this was a Sharps, if it could be reloaded on the run. An expert with a Sharps could manage eight to ten shots per minute in ideal conditions, dropping targets out to five hundred yards or better, but a footrace with an adversary who was firing back negated some of any shooter's skill.

Some, sure. But would it be enough?

Depends on how you play it, Ryder thought. *Keep pushing him and hope he makes another dumb mistake.*

Ahead of him, the running footsteps faltered, then quit altogether. Ryder stopped dead in his tracks, dropped to a crouch, and waited for a shot that didn't come. The sniper was recovering from his initial failure and would be more dangerous than ever now. Arresting him might be impossible, and while he'd hoped to quiz the shooter, squeeze some answers out of him by any means required, Ryder would pick survival over information if he had to choose.

The silence, stretching out, began to make him twitchy. Slowly, cautiously, he started edging forward, cringing at the sounds his boot soles made on dirt and gravel. Barely breathing, he advanced, and when the next shot came, instead of falling prone, he flattened up against a nearby wall.

The Colt bucked in his hand, no realistic hope of drawing blood, but he could keep his quarry running, maybe run him down. A stumble in the dark, at speed, could be nearly as bad as getting shot. Maybe he'd twist an ankle—break it, better still—and lose his weapon, giving Ryder time to overtake him.

Wishful thinking.

Ryder's man was off and running once again. He hurried

after, ears straining to catch another break in stride that meant the man had stopped to fight. It was a risky game, but Ryder couldn't tolerate the thought of letting him escape.

At the next street, he paused, listened, then dared a look around the corner of another bungalow. Saw nothing to his right, then glimpsed a loping figure to his left, one leg dragging a bit behind the other, running northward. Was the sniper wounded, after all? If so, it must have been dumb luck on Ryder's part.

Lungs burning from the chase, he swallowed hard, then set off in pursuit once more.

"That's gunfire!" Anna gasped. "Abel?"

"I heard it."

"Someone's after Gideon!"

"We don't know that for sure."

"But what else could it be, so close?"

He knew she must be right. His hesitation shamed him.

"All right," he replied, retreating toward his small bedroom.

"Where are you going?"

He returned a moment later, with the Colt Paterson he kept under his pillow. The pistol made for lumpy sleeping, but it also gave him partial peace of mind.

Seeing the gun, his sister stepped in front of him. "Abel, you can't—"

"Can't what? Go out and help the man who risked his life for you?"

"You don't know where they are, much less how many."

"I've heard two guns, one of them a rifle. And we're wasting time."

"But—"

Abel stepped around her, reached the door before she had a chance to grab his sleeve. "Lock up behind me," he instructed. "Don't let anybody in unless I'm with them.

Anna hesitated, seemed about to ask what she should do in case he never made it back, then swallowed it and nodded. "Please be careful."

"Always am," he said and ducked into the night.

Another rifle shot gave him direction, crossing underneath one of the city's streetlamps, quickly leaving it behind and jogging into darkness. Sounds could be deceiving in the city, more so after nightfall, but he had a fair sense of direction and paused every thirty yards or so, to get his bearings.

Only now did Abel stop and wonder what he planned to do if he found Ryder and the man or men trying to kill him. He'd been driven from the safety of his home by a desire to *help*, but what did that mean?

He was not a coward, but he'd never fired a shot in anger at another human being. Granted, he had thought about it many times since settling in Jefferson, surrounded by hostility, and had decided he could kill if need be, to protect his sister or himself. But *thinking* it and *doing* it were very different things.

What if he froze and could not pull the trigger when it mattered? What if he found Ryder dead or dying and was left to face his unknown enemies alone?

No, not unknown.

He might not know their names or recognize their faces, but they would be some of Coker's men, beyond all doubt. Ryder had earned their enmity that morning, helping Anna and defying Sheriff Travis. This was how they paid their debts, like yellow jackals in the night.

A sudden flush of anger strengthened his resolve. Abel

picked up his pace, just as another rifle shot rang out, immediately followed by a pistol's bark. He took the latter sound to mean that Ryder was alive and fighting back—not only that, but chasing down the man or men who'd failed to kill him on the first attempt. Encouraged, Abel homed in on the sound, ignored a sharp stitch in his side, and concentrated on the chase.

Worst damned mistake I ever made, he thought, then shook it off. His worst idea had been allowing Anna to come with him, when he left New York for Texas—or, perhaps, the act of moving south at all.

Here's what your stupid conscience gets you into.

Mortal danger, courtesy of helping out his fellow man.

Cursing himself with every step, he ran through darkness, frightened of whatever he might find, more terrified of what awaited Anna if he died.

Don't die, then, Abel told himself and nearly laughed aloud at the outrageousness of his conceit.

Chip Hardesty stumbled and fell, kept his grip on the Sharps, but lost most of the skin on his knuckles to save it. When he cursed, it had a whining tone to it that made him hate himself—and hate his Yankee adversary all the more.

What should have been a simple job had turned into a nightmare, a humiliation, and he saw now that it just might get him killed. He wasn't giving up yet, having never learned to quit, but he was worried, and it troubled him.

In the battles he had fought, some of the war's bloodiest actions, Hardesty had never truly been afraid. He'd marched off into combat thinking the Confederacy would claim victory within a few short weeks, and once that bubble burst, he had resigned himself to the fatalistic understanding that he might be called upon to sacrifice himself. Having accepted that, seeing the cause as something greater than himself, he had been more or less at peace. A tough shot still required his concentration, made him nervous in its way, but when the blue tide clashed with gray and men were dying all around him, he had simply buckled down and done his job.

Tonight was different.

This single combat, one man up against another, wasn't what he'd trained for or experienced while he was still in uniform. It was supposed to be an execution, not a running gunfight through the streets of Jefferson. To that extent, he had already failed, and felt the weight of grim knowledge with each step he took.

That didn't mean that he was beaten, though. He simply had to get his mind right, find a vantage point to shoot from, and for God's sake do it right next time.

Simply? He almost laughed at that, but it was hard enough just breathing while he ran, his bum leg barely functioning.

He cursed the wound, the changes it had made in how he lived. Some people claimed to see it as a badge of honor, but to Hardesty it was a curse. Some Yankee who he'd never even seen or had the chance to kill had made him limp for life, goddamn his rotten soul.

He stopped to rest and listen for a second, straining to pick out the sound of his pursuer. Their exchange of shots was waking people, bringing light to windows on the streets they ran along. Soon, Hardesty supposed, there might be others in the mix, armed men worried about their families, with no idea of who was who in the original engagement. If he met the sheriff in his flight, that would be a relief and an embarrassment rolled into one. If someone took him for a bandit in the dark and shot him . . . well, he'd simply have to take that chance.

Hardesty's horse was at the livery, a long eight blocks away from where he hunkered in the dark, waiting to kill a man he didn't know. Retreating any further now, unless he found a way to shake the Yank, would not be a solution to his problem. He would be exhausted by the time he reached the stable, with the damned relentless agent still behind him, and he didn't want to die smelling of horse manure.

He'd smelled worse in his time, of course: a battlefield, for instance, corpses bloating in the summer sun, believing he'd be one of them before another killing day was done.

Had that day come for him, at last?

He had no time to think about it now, heard someone coming, and was drawing back the hammer on his rifle when a voice behind him barked, "You, there! Lay down your gun!"

Abel Butler was winded, felt like someone had been sticking needles in between his ribs. Each time he stopped to catch his breath, another gunshot echoed through the dark streets, drawing him along in his pursuit of shadows. Sometimes he was close, or thought so, then the sounds retreated, leaving him behind.

He was disoriented now, knew vaguely the direction in which home lay, and his sister waiting, but could not have walked directly to it on a bet. The good news was, he didn't have to. Not until he'd done his best to help Gideon Ryder, anyway.

And where in hell was he?

Somewhere southeast of where Abel was standing, he believed. Sounds were deceptive in the night, particularly those that echoed from the dark façades of silent shops and homes. If Ryder and the man or men who hunted him weren't following the streets, they could be anywhere. His hope of finding them at all was dwindling when he heard a scuffling sound of awkward, lagging footsteps just beyond his line of sight.

Someone advancing, or retreating? Abel knew the only way to answer that was to creep forward, find out for himself, and put a stop to this, if possible.

The wooden sidewalk creaked beneath his feet, and Abel sidestepped onto sand. He clutched the curved butt of his Colt so tightly that his knuckles ached, worried that he would drop it if he let his grip relax at all. His hands were trembling badly, making Abel worry that he couldn't hit a barn door when it counted, but his only choice was clear.

He must proceed, for Anna's sake, and for his own.

He crossed a barren yard, its dry grass crunching underfoot, and edged along the east wall of a square two-story house. As he drew closer to the corner, Butler heard a rasp of tortured breathing, as from someone near exhaustion. Ryder, or somebody else?

Butler held his breath and peeked around the corner, saw a man half-crouching, the long barrel of a rifle rising over his left shoulder.

So, not Ryder, then.

What should he do now? Butler saw three choices open to him. He could turn and flee, then struggle living with himself, bearing the scorn in Anna's every look. He could attempt to make it easy on himself, shoot his opponent in the back. Or he could do the only honorable thing, giving the man a chance to save himself.

Considered in those terms, it was no choice at all.

Butler stepped out of hiding, pistol leveled in a firm

two-handed grip, and used his most commanding voice to
say, "You, there! Lay down your gun!"

Ryder heard the shout, could almost place the voice, and
then two weapons fired as one, the rifle and a pistol.
Cursing reached his ears as he moved forward, following
his Colt Army.

Two rounds, he thought, *and then I'm empty.*

Never mind. If it took more than two, up close, he was
as good as dead.

Ryder reached the shooting scene to find the man he had
been chasing, seated on the ground now, reloading a Sharps
rifle. He was having a hard time of it, one arm apparently
unwilling to cooperate. Across from him, some twenty feet
away, a second man was lying on the ground, clutching his
head with one hand, scrabbling with the other for a pistol
he had dropped as he went down. The face, though streaked
with blood, was recognizable as Abel Butler's.

Ryder put it all together in a flash, saw Butler rushing out
to help him when he heard the first gunshots, meeting the
sniper somehow as the chase had circled back toward Butler's
home. He could as easily have missed the shooter, passed
along another street and never even glimpsed him, but coincidence or fate had put the two of them on a collision course.

Ryder could not assess his new friend's injury without
closer examination, but he had no time for that. His first
priority must be the rifleman, disarming him, preventing
any further damage.

"Drop it!" he commanded, and the sniper craned around
to look at him.

"This little prick a friend of yorn?" he asked.

Ryder ignored the question. Said, "Lay down the rifle."

"S'pose I don't?"

"Then you're a dead man."

"See your point. Awright, then. Here it goes."

He set the Sharps down carefully, as if afraid of causing any damage to it, then his hand whipped back and swung toward Ryder, brandishing a six-gun. Ryder fired without a second's hesitation, saw his bullet drill a dark hole through the rifleman's right cheek, then blood was spurting from the wound as he collapsed into a rumpled heap.

Ryder moved forward, freed the pistol from the dead man's grip, then kicked the Sharps away. He turned to Abel next and found him sitting upright, more or less, one hand still plastered to the left side of his head.

"You got him?" Abel asked.

"You helped," Ryder replied.

"I didn't mean to." Sounding dazed. "If he'd have dropped the rifle when I told him . . ."

"Let me see that wound," Ryder instructed, prying Abel's hand away.

There was a shallow gash, an inch or so above his left temple. The wound was bleeding freely, but it didn't seem life threatening.

"Lucky you winged him," Ryder said. "Another couple inches to the left and you'd have been a goner."

"Christ, it hurts!"

"We need to get that cleaned and bandaged. It should heal all right, but you'll be having headaches for a while."

"So much for good Samaritans."

"You did okay."

"It doesn't feel that way."

"Is there a doctor you can trust?"

Abel began to shake his head, then groaned and answered, "No."

"I think Anna can patch this up," Ryder suggested. "Can you walk?"

"I think so."

"Let's get moving, then."

"The sheriff will be coming."

"Let him wait. He took his sweet time turning out."

"He'll try to blame me."

"And I'll set him straight. Don't let it worry you."

"Easy to say. We have to live here."

"Do you, really?"

"Gideon—"

"Come on, now. Anna will be worrying."

It seemed a long walk back, Ryder supporting much of Abel's weight and watching out for other shooters all the way. Along their route, men and a smattering of anxious women had emerged from their respective homes, talking about the racket, lowering their voices into whispers as the two men passed.

The sheriff shouldn't have a problem finding Butler now. Ryder decided on the spot to stay with him—and Anna—until Travis came around to question them. He'd set the lawman straight, and that should be the end of it.

Or would have been, except for Coker and his gang.

You're next, he thought, as Anna rushed out of the house to meet them, tears of worry spilling down her cheeks.

12

★ **A** nd you say he fired at you, before you killed him?"

"Third time that you've asked me that," Ryder replied.

"I need to get it straight," the sheriff said.

"Go back over the route we traveled. Look for damage from the shots we fired at one another. Work it out."

"About that damage . . ."

"Bill it to the sniper."

"Chip wasn't a rich man."

"So, you're on a first-name basis?"

Travis reddened. "Nothin' wrong with knowin' my con-stishients."

"Some more than others, I suppose."

"What're you gettin' at?"

Ryder shrugged. "You knew the three drunks who were after Miss Butler this morning. Now, seems like you're friendly with this shooter."

"*Friendly* would be stretchin' it. I knew him, sure," Travis admitted. "And he weren't no troublemaker, that I ever heard."

"Just lost his mind, I guess," Ryder replied. "Decided he should shoot a total stranger on the street for no reason at all."

"That's your side of it."

"If you have evidence to contradict me, file a charge. That's how the law works, Sheriff."

"You don't have to tell me—"

"But we both know you don't have a case. Isn't that right?"

"I reckon time'll tell."

"Meanwhile, your buddy's getting ripe. You'd best convey him to the undertaker."

"Bein' handled as we speak. How long you aim to stay in Jefferson?"

"Until my work's done."

"And your work is . . . ?"

Ryder showed his badge again and told the sheriff, "Secret."

"Hocus-pocus," Travis sneered.

"Nothing for you to fret about, in that case."

"I ain't frettin'."

"What about your friend?"

"Which one? I got a lotta friends."

"Roy Coker's who I had in mind."

"Unless you're dumber than you look, you'll stay away from him."

"Or . . . what?"

"Nothin' from me. I'll leave that between you and him."

"After you run and tattle to him."

"Damn your—"

"Sheriff!" Anna scolded him for swearing.

"Sorry, ma'am. This fella gets my dander up."

"I'd rank that as a weakness," Ryder said.

"Say what you want. I might surprise you."

Ryder smiled. Said, "I sincerely hope you prove me wrong."

"I had enough of riddles for one night."

"Don't let us keep you, then."

"I'm gettin' to the bottom of all this," said Travis.

"Something tells me that you're near the bottom now," Ryder replied.

The sheriff went out in a huff, telling the men who'd waited for him in the yard that they could go on home. Anna had balked at letting them inside her house, and that had set the tone for all that followed.

Ryder waited for the yard to clear, then said, "I should be going, too."

"What if they circle back?" she asked him. "What with Abel laid up in his bed."

"I'd stay," he said, "but it would set your neighbors talking."

"We may live next door, but they're not neighbors," Anna told him.

"Still."

"You're right, of course. The AMA insists upon propriety—or its appearance, at the very least."

"Sounds like some preachers I'm acquainted with."

"I take it that you're not a man of faith?"

"I've had to get by all my life," Ryder said, "without help from some old invisible man on a cloud."

"You've never seen a miracle?"

"Not one I'd recognize as such."

"That's sad."

"I'll have to take your word for it. And I should probably be getting on."

"No, wait." She caught his sleeve as he was rising from the sofa, to detain him. "I haven't thanked you properly for bringing Abel home. Saving his life, I mean."

"His injury was my fault, in a way," Ryder replied.

"But with your own life in danger—"

"It's what I get paid for. The people I deal with—most of them, at least—don't hail from what you'd call polite society."

"Roy Coker, for example."

"Haven't met him, but I hope to, soon."

"Just know that I'll be praying for you, Gideon."

He shrugged and said, "It couldn't hurt."

Outside, the sheriff's posse had dispersed, but as he crossed the Butlers' yard, Ryder saw one man standing in the shadows, just beyond their fence. He drew his Colt and aimed it at the faceless stranger, without slowing down.

"Hold up there," said the sheriff's voice. "I think you've killed enough men for one night."

"Depends on what you had in mind," Ryder replied.

"Thought you might like to meet the man in charge," said Travis.

"What, that isn't you?"

"Come on with me, and learn somethin'," the lawman said.

"You lead the way," Ryder instructed him. "And keep both hands where I can see them."

The Red Dog?" Ryder asked, as they approached the two-story saloon.

"It's just a name," said Travis.

"I expected something more Confederate. The Merrimac, let's say. Maybe the Slave Market."

"Your jokes don't sit well here in Jefferson."

"What makes you think I'm joking?"

"Either way, a smart man doesn't start a conversation with no insults."

They were at the bat-wing doors by now. Ryder could smell the scent familiar from every saloon he'd ever patronized: stale beer, tobacco smoke, sweat generated by the booze or lust or gambling fever. Instead of a piano, Coker had a three-man brass band backing up a banjo player perched upon a stool.

The sheriff led him through the Red Dog's barroom, all eyes on them as they passed, around the south end of the bar and down a hallway, to a door marked PRIVATE. Travis knocked and waited for a voice inside to say, "Come in."

They entered, Travis leading, while a tall man rose behind a desk. The boss man wore a satin vest, dove gray, over a crisp white shirt, trousers to match the vest. His hair was long enough to hide the collar of his shirt, slicked straight back from an oval face wearing a Van Dyke style of beard. He moved around the desk, offered his hand, and said, "We meet at last. Roy Coker, and I take it you're the famous Agent Ryder."

"I hope not."

"You don't crave fame and fortune?"

"Wouldn't mind the fortune," Ryder said, on impulse. "But with fame, all kinds of people try to rob you."

"Isn't that the truth? Sheriff, feel free to leave us."

"Are you sure? I don't mind—"

Coker's eyes went cold. Travis swallowed whatever he had planned to say and left the office, making sure to close the door behind him.

"Harlan can be useful, but he's not the sharpest chisel in the toolbox," Coker said, smiling.

"I meet a lot of dull ones," Ryder said.

"I would imagine so."

"Comes with the territory."

"Which, in this case, happens to be Texas. More specifically, Marion County. May I tempt you with a drink?"

"No, thanks."

"So, straight to business, then. What brings you here?"

"My work."

"A mission for the fledgling Secret Service, I've been told. But more specifically . . . ?"

"Investigative work."

"Is there some reason why we can't speak candidly?"

"Beats me. Is there?"

"I'm hoping you can trust me."

"I just met you."

"Still—"

"And trust is something that I find in short supply, these days."

"May I be frank, at least?"

"Feel free," Ryder replied.

"You spend a lot of time with carpetbaggers."

"You have someone watching me?"

"Despite its recent, rapid growth, Jefferson is still a small town at heart. Word gets around."

"Apparently."

"It seems to me you've traveled far, to spend your time with strangers in our midst."

"Free country, since the war. People can travel where they want to, drift or put down roots."

"You understand, I'm sure, how *sensitive* the common

Texan is right now, to matters touching on the racial situation."

Ryder frowned. "Are you a common Texan?"

"Born in New Orleans, as it happens, but my family moved here when I was still a suckling. Texas is my home."

"I meant the 'common' part."

"I do my best to rise above the herd, without losing the common touch."

"Sounds like you've got an eye on politics."

"It's crossed my mind. But at the present, while we're occupied by foreign troops, that's not an option."

"*Foreign* troops?"

"We were a nation, as you know. First, the Republic of Texas, then a part of the Confederacy."

"I believe you skipped a step between the two."

"One of the U.S. states, of course. Until the government in Washington betrayed us."

"By opposing slavery?"

"The war was based on economic issues, not some sudden urge to free the Africans. You must know that, at least. Slavery was enshrined in the original constitution. Article Five protected foreign trade in slaves."

"Till 1808," Ryder said.

"While Article Four, Section Two, forbade white citizens from aiding runaway bondsmen. My Lord, Article One, Section Two, permits slaves to be counted for purposes of determining representation in Congress."

"Bound to be repealed, now that you've lost the war."

"Did we?"

"The last I heard."

"Great issues aren't decided in a day, a month, or in four years."

"You think the Rebel states will rise again?"

"It's not rebellion, when you're fighting for principles the country was founded on to begin with."

"We'll have to disagree on that," Ryder replied.

"In which case, let me ask you whether you're investigating me."

"I've had my hands full since I got here, dealing with your men."

"*My* men?"

"Slip of the tongue. I mean to say dumb crackers starting fights they're not prepared to win."

"Another man might take insult at that."

"Glad he's not here, then." Ryder rose and started for the door. "Next bunch you send, tell them I'm at the Bachmann House."

"I own it," Coker said. "You may sleep peacefully beneath its roof."

"Appreciate it. You wouldn't want to see it damaged, after all. It's likely not your style," said Ryder, one hand on the doorknob, "but if you decide to finish this like men, the two of us, just let me know."

Travis had been waiting in the barroom. He returned when Coker summoned him and took the chair directly opposite, sitting with hat in hand. The sheriff had a sour look about him, and he clearly was not looking forward to their chat.

"He's not amenable to reason," Coker said, without preamble.

"Huh."

"That means he won't negotiate."

"What did you offer him?"

The question was impertinent, but Coker chose to answer it. "We never got that far. He has the smell of abolitionist about him."

"Well, then."

"Hardesty was quite the disappointment."

"Overmatched, I guess."

"Indeed. We'll need to try a new approach, next time."

"More men?"

"And smarter," Coker said. "No more clumsy mistakes."

"I thought Chip was the best we had."

"I hope not, since he failed us."

"I can put the word out. Get a bunch together, maybe take him out tomorrow."

"You're forgetting something."

"What's that?"

"Jesus, man. We've got a rally scheduled for tomorrow, noon."

"Oh, right."

"I don't want any more disturbances before then. Understood?"

"I hear you."

"Make it crystal clear to anyone you speak to. If they spoil the rally, I'll be holding you responsible."

"I'll wait till after, so there's no mistake."

"Good thinking."

"Is the other thing still happening?" Travis inquired.

"What other thing?"

"You know. After the rally."

"Given the results desired, the answer would be yes."

"Okay. And I'm not s'pose to interfere."

Coker restrained an urge to roll his eyes. "That's right. Because you don't know anything about it, Sheriff."

"Course not. How would I?"

"And when the first reports come in . . . ?"

"Takes me some time to raise a posse, swear 'em in and all. They'd have to fetch their guns from home."

"Exactly."

"I was thinkin', though."

Never a good sign, Coker thought. And said, "Thinking? About what?"

"Bluebellies. We got the garrison outside of town. They might jump into this."

"I'm counting on it."

"Oh?"

"We need a spark to set this county and the state on fire."

"It could mean killin'."

"Every war means killing. You know that."

Travis was nodding. "Sure, I know. But folks elected me to keep the peace."

"Did they? And what peace would that be? The one imposed from Washington, where black and white are equal? Do the people who elected you want field hands voting? Knocking on their doors to see if little Mary can come out and play?"

"Who's little—?"

"I'm referring to their daughters, damn it!"

"Right. Okay."

"So, are we clear? No trouble with this Yank before the rally or what follows after. When that's done, have people standing by to deal with him. Before the smoke clears would be best. Tie all the loose ends up into one knot."

"Got it."

The sheriff didn't move, so Coker asked him, "Why are you still here?"

"Huh? Oh. Just going."

"Saints preserve us," Coker muttered, as the door closed, "from the shoddy tools we have to use."

The Bachmann House was quiet by the time Ryder arrived. A bell above the front door jingled as he entered, and a sleepy-looking clerk emerged from somewhere in the back, blinked recognition of a paying resident, and wandered back the way he'd come.

Upstairs, Ryder listened outside his door and checked the keyhole for scratches, then passed inside and locked the door again, behind him. No one had been snooping through his things, as far as he could see—not that he'd left them anything to find. His telegrams from Washington were burned as soon as he had read them, and he had no other written orders for his job in Jefferson. The guidelines had been vague, which left him ample elbow room, but also furnished rope enough to hang himself if he got careless.

On his way back from the Butlers' place, he'd seen posters on several of the streetlamp poles, announcing a KRS rally tomorrow, at noon. Remembering the last one he'd attended, Ryder thought there was a good chance there'd be trouble, either with the local Union garrison or from the Knights themselves. He knew exactly where the troops were quartered, on the northern edge of town, and planned to visit their commander in the morning, introduce himself, and see if they could make some kind of an arrangement to cooperate in an emergency.

And failing that?

Then he was on his own. Again.

Before he went to bed, Ryder sat down to clean his Colt Army, keeping the Henry rifle handy just in case. He switched out cylinders, reloaded five spent chambers on the

one he'd used that night, and stowed it in a pocket for tomorrow. Next, he checked the Henry on a whim, found everything in working order, and finally tested the Bowie knife's
edge on his thumb. Still razor sharp and ready for the ulti-
mate emergency, if he ran out of lead before a fight was done.

What fight?

That was the rub. He never knew, until one started.

Lying back, the Colt beneath his pillow, Ryder let his
thoughts return to Anna Butler and her brother. Mostly Anna,
it was true. She seemed so out of place in Jefferson—or what
he'd seen of Texas, generally—that he wondered how she
stood it. If their places were reversed, Ryder imagined he'd
have run back screaming to New York and never crossed the
Mason-Dixon Line again. That she remained to labor in her
brother's cause spoke volumes about Anna's courage and the
bond between them. She was in it all the way, and any adversaries would be forced to drag her out feet first.

Sadly, from what he'd seen in Corpus Christi, Ryder
didn't think that prospect bothered Coker and his Knights
at all.

Some southern "gentlemen" they were.

The more he saw of Texas, Ryder realized it was a world
apart from anything he'd known back East. Its cities,
although some were fairly large, could not compare for size
and crowding to New York or Philadelphia, even to Baltimore or Washington. The open spaces pleased him, and the
weather he'd experienced so far, but people were the same,
unfortunately, anywhere that Ryder traveled.

They were greedy, bitter, bigoted, and violent, whether
you found them in the nation's capital, Manhattan's Five
Points slum, or on the open plains. Not everyone, of course.
From time to time, he got a nice surprise from someone like
the Butlers or the Hubbards, but they seemed to be in a

minority, and they were usually victims of the others, those he was assigned to hunt and bring to justice.

Ryder took that strange, depressing fact of life into his dreams when sleep arrived at last, tossing and turning on his narrow bed through the small hours of the night.

I know what Mr. Coker said. He ain't the one got buffaloed in public. Didn't get his nose broke, neither, far as I can see."

Burke nodded in agreement, muttering, "Thash right."

"So, are we gonna take it lyin' down, or do somethin' about it?" Ardis Jackson asked his friends.

"Do thumpin," Burke agreed.

"I don't know," Stevens said. "This ain't only from Coker. Sheriff Travis said—"

"That bag of wind? You know he only does what Coker tells him," Jackson sneered.

"The same as us, I reckon," Stevens answered.

"Nossir! There's a difference. We's free men, ain't we? *Knights*, we claim to be. The only one a Knight takes orders from would be a king. King Coker. Do you like the sound of that?"

"He started up the KRS," Stevens reminded him. "We all agreed on him as leader."

"Then he needs to *lead,* goddamn it! What's he done to make things right for Caleb, here? For any of us? Sends Chip Hardesty to do the job and gets 'im killed. What good is that to anybody?"

"Loss a good man," Burke chimed in.

"Not good enough," said Jackson. "Now, we's s'pose to let it go and wait some more. For what? Until the damn bluebelly dies from old age?"

"Maybe Mr. Coker's thinkin' of the soldiers," Stevens offered.

"Mebbe so. We don't know, cuz he never tells us what he's thinkin'. All we get is go here, go there, do this or that cuz he says so. We ain't in the army no more, case you missed it."

"I know that." Stevens sounded irritated now.

"So, if we's fightin' for a cause, we should be *fightin'*, not sittin' around and waitin' all the time."

"This thing tomorrow—"

"Helps the boys let off some steam. I unnerstand that. But it don't accomplish nothin' in the long run. Scare some darkies, shoot a few. It's fun, o' course, but who's the enemy? Bluebellies, carpetbaggers, and the radicals behind 'em. They's the ones we should be fightin', if we're gonna make a difference."

"Dan rye," Burke growled, agreeing with him.

"How we gonna fight the army when we ain't an army?" Stevens challenged. "You just said—"

"I *know* what I jus' said. The point is, I'm fed up with takin' orders when they make no sense and get us nowhere."

"Okay, then. So, what's your big idea?"

"Take down this spy from Washin'ton our own selves. He's the one insulted us and made us look like rubes. Don't ask no one's permission, neither. We jus' up and do it."

"When?" asked Stevens.

Jackson drained his whiskey glass and topped it up again before he answered. "Not tonight," he said. "After the thing with Chip, he'll be expectin' somethin' else. Tomorrow's better, when the sheriff and his deputies are all distracted."

"How we gonna fin' 'im?" Burke inquired.

"We know where he's stayin'," said Jackson. "Jus' watch

the hotel, follow him when he leaves. Once the rally breaks up and the boys get down to business, he's ours."

"Jush da tree ob ud?" asked Burke.

"How many do you think we need?" asked Jackson.

Burke shrugged, raised a hand to touch his mottled face. "He purdy fass."

"I seen him draw," Jackson replied. "I don't plan meetin' him head-on."

"Thash bedda," Burke said. "Got mah shoggun rethy."

"Are you in, or not?" Jackson asked Stevens.

"Hell, you know I'm with y'all. I jus' don't like surprisin' Mr. Coker."

"What's he gonna do about it, once we're done? Thank us, is what."

"Or kill us."

"Bullshit! I'm expectin' a promotion."

Stevens nodded, clearly skeptical, then asked, "How do we set the watch?"

"He's tucked in for the night. The rally's not till noon, but we should watch him from the time he leaves the Bachmann House. How bout we meet up there at six o'clock?"

"Right there, at the hotel?" asked Stevens.

"No, he'd see us. Over cross the street, that alley by the lawyer's office and that dress shop. We can watch from there, no problem."

"Six o'clock," said Stevens, woefully. "I need to get some sleep, then."

"May too," Burke agreed.

"Go on, then," Jackson said. "But don't be late. Our honor's ridin' on the line."

13

★ **R**yder had a facility for losing track of dreams when he awoke. Some people suffered disappointment, waking, when their dreams blew out the window like a wisp of smoke, but Ryder figured he was lucky. He had passed a fitful night and had a long new day ahead of him. The last thing that he needed was anxiety conjured from somewhere in the depths of his unconscious mind.

He washed his face, got dressed, and went downstairs to use the privy in the hotel's fenced backyard. A dozen windows overlooked the yard, but Ryder wasn't bashful. Anyone who cared to watch him come and go was welcome to the pleasure, though he watched the window curtains for a hint of movement, keeping one hand near his Colt.

Relaxing of a morning didn't mean he was a fool.

For breakfast, Ryder tried a café called The Ruby. He had seen it twice in passing and was lured by the aromas from its kitchen. He ordered ham and scrambled eggs with grits, a southern oddity that he'd grown fond of since he'd been in Texas. Thick toast and a mug of strong black coffee finished off the meal.

When he was finished, Ryder asked his waitress for directions to the livery. She gave him three choices, and Ryder picked the nearest stable, located a quarter of a mile from his hotel. The morning wasn't hot yet but was clearly on its way, and he enjoyed the walk. Some of the locals Ryder passed regarded him suspiciously; others pretended not to notice him at all. He'd known that word of last night's violence would make the rounds, but having total strangers focus on him in a town the size of Jefferson defied coincidence.

He wondered now if someone—Sheriff Travis, possibly—was marking him deliberately. That would be no surprise, considering the sheriff's ties to Coker and the KRS, but it could be an obstacle to Ryder as he followed his investigation. As a Yankee in the midst of Rebels, he had started at a disadvantage. Now, he hoped to even up the odds a bit.

The stable smelled of fresh paint and manure, a heady combination on a day that promised to be scorching by high noon. The man in charge was stocky, ginger-haired, and freckled, somewhere in his early thirties, muscular from shifting bales of hay and handling animals five times his weight. He was affable enough and readily agreed to rent Ryder a horse, providing that he paid a full day's rate up front.

Ryder had half a dozen animals to choose from, all appearing strong and healthy to his less-than-expert eye. He chose an Appaloosa gelding for its coloration, which the hostler said was called a roan blanket with frost—meaning its neck was mostly brown, the rest a mix of brown and white as if it had been through a storm of chocolate and powdered sugar.

"I call 'im Traveler, after the stallion rid by Gen'ral Lee. O' course, *his* horse weren't gelded and were mostly white."

"It suits him, anyway," said Ryder.

Ryder chose a trail saddle, designed with comfort of the horse and rider as a top priority, its rigging made of brass to ward off rust and leather rot. When Traveler was saddled up, he had the hostler add a rifle scabbard to the getup, for his Henry.

Playing safe.

Last thing, he got directions to the local Union garrison, northwest of Jefferson, two miles beyond the city limits. Ryder paid and left, thinking he'd got more than his money's worth.

He rode back to the Bachmann House, noting that people seemed to pay him less attention now that he was mounted. It was strange, but Ryder didn't try to work it out. He fetched the rifle from his room, secured it in its scabbard, and began his journey at an easy pace.

W hern he gwan?" asked Caleb Burke.

"The hell should I know?" Stevens countered. "Nobody said nothin' about trailin' 'im if he left town."

"Ardish ain't gwan lige us losin' 'im."

"You'd best run on and tell 'im, then."

"Canned run. Id huts mah node."

"How long you gonna lean on that crutch? Go and ask 'im—"

"Ask me what?" Ardis surprised them, coming up behind them on the sly.

"The Yank picked up a horse from Jamison's and headed out of town," said Stevens.

"And neither one of you saw fit to follow him?"

"We didn't think—"

"No *we* in dis," Burke interrupted.

"You didn't think," said Jackson, with a sneer. "The story of your life, Wade."

"Hey, now."

"Where's he headed?"

"Um, I couldn't tell you that."

"And you don't think it might be useful if we knew?"

"Well, sure, I guess."

"You see him ride out?"

"Sure did!"

"Which way was he headed?"

"North from the hotel."

"How long ago was this?"

"Ten minutes. Mighta been a little more."

"You've still got time to track him, then."

"Track him? Jus' me?"

"Hands off. To find out where he goes and who he talks to."

"Oh, well, sure. I can do that, I guess."

"So, what'n hell are you waiting for?"

Stevens departed at a loping run, to fetch his horse and try to catch up with the Yankee agent. Jackson hadn't warned him to be careful, hoping it was understood between them, but he worried now that he was taking too damned much for granted. Stevens didn't have the nerve to jump the Yank himself, alone, but what if he was spotted and their quarry turned on him? It would be like Wade to run blindly, in a panic, leading the Yankee straight back to Jackson.

That's what I get for using idjits.

"Huh?"

"Nothin'," said Jackson, unaware that he had voiced his thought aloud.

And now I'm talking to myself. Jesus.

"You gwan ted Mr. Coker bow dis?"

"When I'm feel like it. How long the sawbones reckon you'd be talkin' like you gotta buncha marbles in your mouth?"

"Din't see none."

"Didn't see a doctor?"

"Nuh."

"Still hurts, though?"

"Ya dab right."

"Well, lemme fix it." As he spoke, Jackson reached out, gripped Caleb's nose between his thumb and forefinger, twisted, then yanked it straight—well, *straighter*—with a sudden jerk. Burke howled in pain, drew starts from passersby, but no one stopped to ask him if he needed any help.

"God*damn* it, Ardis!"

"See, you sound better already," Jackson said. "What's that worth to you?"

"Boot up your ass."

"Damned ingrate."

Jackson left him whimpering and went in search of a saloon. He hadn't had a drink so far that morning, and his nerves were wearing thin. On top of going behind Coker's back to kill the Yankee, now he had to worry about *losing* him, before they had the chance. Five hours yet, before the rally started, and he was supposed to be there with the other Knights, hearing their leader's speech and hooting up a storm. When that was done, they had the other thing.

A little trip to Colored Town.

Sounded like fun, all right, but Jackson's mind was

focused on the Secret Service man, and what he planned to do to him.

A little taste of sweet revenge.

Abel Butler's headache had retreated overnight. It still throbbed dully on the left side of his skull, but he no longer felt as if his head was going to explode.

Small favors.

He had never come so close to death before, much less to being murdered, and the shock of it had shaken him. Seeing the fear in Anna's eyes, on top of being hurt himself, had prompted him to reconsider what he'd taken for a righteous calling when they left New York for Texas.

It was easy to be ardent for a cause when you were sitting in a well-appointed home, twelve hundred miles from where the trouble was occurring. Once you had bridged that distance, though, and found yourself surrounded by a city full of people who despised you, offering your life up as a sacrifice for other folks who didn't understand or trust you, things were different.

Abel was starting to believe that he had made a serious mistake—and worse, that he had dragged his sister into it, placing her life in jeopardy.

"You're looking better," Anna said, as she set breakfast down in front of him.

"I'm feeling much better," he exaggerated.

"I've heard nothing yet today, from Gideon."

"Were you expecting to?" he asked, eggs poised before him on his fork.

"Not necessarily. But after last night, I supposed . . . well, I don't know."

"Don't tell me that you're falling for him."

"What? Of course not!" Anna managed to look angry and to blush, at the same time.

"You know he won't be staying, Anna."

"And are we?"

The question startled him. "What do you mean?"

"You almost died last night, Abel. That crazy man almost blew out our brains."

"We both knew it was dangerous. We talked about it, back in Syracuse."

"Talking about it's one thing. Living it is something else entirely."

"Are you frightened?"

"Yes! Aren't you?"

He swallowed his eggs, along with his immediate response. Admitting nothing to his sister, Abel said, "The point is not to let your fear immobilize you. You remember Edmund Burke?"

"Not personally."

"Please be serious."

"All right. Which quote is it this time?"

" 'All that is necessary for the triumph of evil—' "

" '—is that good men do nothing,' " she finished for him. Adding, "Or women."

"Exactly. We are on a mission, helping the less fortunate. Some evil men oppose us, but we have the strength of Providence."

"I don't feel very strong. Last night was horrible. Yesterday morning, with those men out on the street—"

"You feel a debt of gratitude to Mr. Ryder, certainly. I understand."

"It's more than that."

"How could it be? You've barely known him for a day."

"I fancy I'm a decent judge of character."

"The man's a killer."

"If he wasn't, you'd be dead now."

"And he's a policeman."

"So?"

"Their work corrupts them, rots their minds and souls. They see the very worst of other men and women every day. It gets inside them. Gnaws away at their capacity for caring."

"When did you become an expert?"

"I have more experience. I'm older—"

"Two years!"

"And you've led a sheltered life."

"I'd like to have it back," she said, voice softening.

"I've thought about that. If you wanted to go home—"

"And leave you here? Ridiculous!"

"It's something to consider. You could help the AMA in other ways, with mailing, or—"

"Become a *secretary*."

"Something to consider."

"I've considered it. The answer's no."

"If you would just—"

"Eat up," she said. "Your breakfast's getting cold."

The garrison wasn't what Ryder expected. He'd pictured the kind of stockade shown in Beadle's Dime Novels: a wall made from tree trunks, all sharpened on top to repel climbing foes, with log structures inside, and corrals for the horses. Instead, he was looking at tents pitched in rows on dry ground, with a cluster of picketed animals off to one side, what the Texans called a remuda. He counted five blue uniforms on guard duty, each with a musket and fixed bayonet.

The one who stopped him was a kid, late teens or early twenties. He demanded Ryder's name and business, studied Ryder's badge, and frowned when Ryder asked to see the officer in charge.

"Can't leave my post, sir. And you can't go in alone."

"That's a conundrum."

"Huh?"

"Could you call someone else to walk me in?" asked Ryder.

"Well, I guess so. Wait right here."

"I promise."

Ryder waited, still astride the Appaloosa, while the sentry walked a few paces away and called out for the sergeant of the guard. An older, larger man in uniform appeared, this one with fading yellow chevrons on his sleeve to designate his senior rank. The sergeant took his turn peering at Ryder's badge, then asked him, "What's your business with the captain?"

"To discuss affairs in Jefferson," Ryder replied.

"Uh-huh. Well, I don't know if he'll see you, but it costs nothin' to find out. Follow me."

Ryder dismounted, led the Appaloosa by its reins to reach a tent significantly larger than the others. While he waited, wishing there was shade, the sergeant paused outside the open tent flap and requested leave to enter. It was granted, he went in, and came back moments later to tell Ryder, "Sir, the captain is available."

The tent had shade, but it was *hot* shade, and the slight breeze he had felt outside was banned here. Ryder found himself confronted by an officer midway in age between the sergeant and the sentry, wearing striped trousers and boots, his blue coat draped across a camp chair near his cot.

"You've caught me out of uniform," the captain said.

"I won't tell if you don't."

"We have a deal. Captain Legere," he said, reaching for Ryder's hand. "And you are?"

"Ryder. Gideon. I'm with the U.S. Secret Service."

"So my sergeant indicated. Wishing to discuss affairs in Jefferson, I understand."

"That's right."

"How do you find the city, Agent Ryder?"

"It's all right, I guess."

"It's a pesthole," said Legere, with sudden vehemence. "My men are treated like pariahs by these Rebels. They'd be spat on, if the locals weren't afraid of being pricked with bayonets."

"You've had some trouble with them, then."

"Nothing *but* trouble, from our first day here."

"Are you familiar with an outfit calls itself Knights of the Rising Sun?"

"Indeed I am. Is that your business?"

"More or less."

"Feel free to round them up and take them all away. They're rabble of the lowest order and mistreat the coloreds terribly."

"What have you done about it?"

"Done?" The captain almost smirked. "I've followed orders, sir. And to the letter, may I add. Those orders are precise: observe and intervene, if called for, should any incident appear to threaten civil order or incite rebellion."

"So, you've made arrests?"

"Of whom? For what?"

"Of KRS members, for the abuse of freedmen that you talked about."

"Oh, that. It's not rebellion, and it doesn't threaten civil order. Truth be told, in this wasteland it *is* the civil order. Things like that I leave to Sheriff Travis."

"Who does nothing," Ryder guessed.

"Out of my hands, unfortunately."

"What would it take, exactly, for you to involve yourself?"

"A clear and present danger to the public peace, or to our garrison."

"And short of that?"

The captain spread his hands. "It sounds more like your jurisdiction than my own."

"Okay. I'm glad we had this talk."

"Feel free to come back anytime," Legere replied. "We're always here."

J ackson was right, for once. Wade Stevens hadn't had much trouble following the Yankee, once he stopped by Jamison's and found out that his man had asked directions to the Union garrison. There was a chance that he'd been laying a false trail, in case someone like Stevens tried to follow him, and Wade had ridden hard for fifteen minutes, lathering his roan before he caught sight of the Yank, still half a mile ahead of him. He backed off then, letting his quarry lead him at the very edge of visibility and hoping that he wouldn't turn around to look behind him.

Sure enough, he rode into the army camp. That couldn't be good news, a spy from Washington canoodling with blue-bellies. They must be cooking up some kind of plot against the KRS, or Mr. Coker personally, planning how to spread their damned race-mixing poison far and wide through Texas.

Stevens almost bolted then, uncertain whether he should spill the news to Jackson or go straight to Mr. Coker with it. He was leaning toward the former, since the boss man didn't even know they had the Yank under surveillance, when it hit him that he couldn't leave.

Not yet.

Ardis had ordered him to trail the agent and discover where he went. A part of that was done, but Stevens couldn't satisfy himself that this was all of it. Suppose the Yank went on from there to someplace else, and he'd gone back to Jefferson, not knowing what came next? For one thing, Ardis would discover he'd been shirking, when their target came back hours later. For another, Stevens didn't want to be the one who let his buddies down.

With that in mind, he stayed, scanning the countryside and picking out the only tree that he could find, a cottonwood, standing a half mile due west of the camp. From there, he could observe the garrison without much fear of being seen himself. He would have liked to be inside one of those tents with the commander and his visitor, eavesdropping on their plans, but that was just a daydream.

Twenty minutes after he went in, the Yank was back, riding his rented Appaloosa back toward Jefferson. He didn't glance toward Stevens, hiding in the shadow of the big old cottonwood, and faded into the distance before Stevens made a move to follow him back home.

What would he say to Ardis? Just the truth and nothing but. Tell what he'd seen and not embellish it with anything from his imagination. Ardis couldn't get mad at him over that.

Could he?

Ryder kept his eyes peeled on the ride back into Jefferson. He half expected to be ambushed on the way, but with the countryside so flat and open, snipers would have found no ready hiding place. At one point, halfway back to town, he had a sense of being watched and reined in, turned the Appaloosa back the way they'd come, to sweep the skyline, but he spotted no one on his trail.

Getting jumpy over nothing? Maybe.

At the livery, he helped unsaddle Traveler and gave the ginger man a little something extra for selecting such a fine, accommodating animal. From the reaction, Ryder thought he might have made a friend, but he knew better than to take such things for granted in a southern town.

His watch told him that he had time to catch an early lunch before the midday rally started. He'd developed a taste for Mexican since arriving in Texas, and now sought out a little restaurant two blocks from his hotel, called La Comida. Seated near a window, with his back against the wall, he ordered *tacos sudados*, with an enchilada, rice, and beans, washed down with dark beer, stronger than his usual. The spicy taco filling made his eyes water, but Ryder cleaned his plate and might have asked for more, if there'd been time.

The rally site was a patch of wasteland overlooking the Red River, south of town. Ryder had not scouted it beforehand, but he had no trouble finding it. He simply trailed the locals moving through the streets in that direction, muttering about the shame of Appomattox and the way that Washington was trying to destroy their state. It sounded like secession talk to Ryder, but they'd tried that route already and been soundly beaten for it. Coker's name was mentioned often, one man saying that he ought to be the state's next governor.

The crowd was mostly men, as it had been in Corpus Christi. Women weren't expected to participate in politics, since they were not allowed to vote and had their homes to tend. A few men strolling toward the riverfront were arm in arm with sporting ladies, but those nymphs du prairie were exceptions to the rule. Ryder observed, as usual, that nearly all the men were packing iron. He was relieved that none appeared to recognize or notice him.

The open rally ground was filling up when Ryder reached it, people milling in a space of some two acres. Near the river bank, a flatbed wagon had been parked, its team removed, and corner-mounted poles upheld a banner reading AWAKE! KNIGHTS OF THE RISING SUN. Two men with pistols tied down low were standing underneath the banner, sharp eyes studying the crowd and watching out for troublemakers.

Ryder didn't bother moving any closer. He was happy on the far edge of the audience, less interested in Coker's speech than how his audience reacted to it. It occurred to Ryder that he'd made himself a target by attending—that an enemy could slip a blade between his ribs in passing, and that no one in the throng was likely to assist him—but he stayed there, standing with his arms crossed, right hand within inches of his cross-draw holster.

He could feel the crowd becoming restless, as they will, when someone near the front ranks cried out, "Here he is! The man himself!"

14

★ **R**oy Coker loved talking to crowds. It thrilled him, seeing all those upturned faces, bright eyes seeing only him, some listeners standing with mouths agape, waiting for him to tell them what they should be thinking, saying, doing in their daily lives. He loved the power of manipulating others, moving them like pawns on a gigantic chessboard. He had first experienced that feeling while in uniform, commanding men whose very lives depended on his orders, and he hated General Lee for groveling at Appomattox, when they could have fought to the last man.

Maybe this time.

One of his Knights helped Coker mount the wagon bed. He stood beneath the banner that had been prepared for him and scanned the audience, spotting familiar faces close in toward the makeshift stage. Others were new to him, but all seemed avid, anxious to receive his message and adopt it as their own.

"My friends!" he called out, in a voice that needed no

assistance from a speaking trumpet. "Knights of the Rising Sun, and those among you who have yet to join our ranks, welcome!"

A rumble went up from the crowd in answer. Someone whistled near the back. A sporting lady, closer in, reached up to wave a lacy handkerchief. The faces ranged before him were all white, as he preferred.

As it was meant to be.

"Welcome to the beginning of a new day here in Jefferson, in Texas, and across the South," he bellowed. "Times are changing, as you all must be aware, but is it for the better? Are we moving *forward*, or are radicals among us dragging our society back into savagery?"

That raised a growl. Some fists were shaken, not at him, but at the *others*, enemies that few in Jefferson could name and none could reach. The pulsing anger of his people could have warmed the open ground if it were winter, and the middle of the night, instead of blazing noon.

"We've lost a war, they say," Coker reminded them. "*They* say we're beaten. Look around you, and you'll find our homeland occupied by enemies who tried to kill us, just a few short months ago. *They* claim they're helping us. *They* say we need to change, give up our ways, renounce our principles. But what do *we* say?"

"No!" a dozen voices answered and were answered in their turn by hundreds. *"No! No!! No!!!"*

He could have turned them loose at that point, but they didn't have a target yet, so he pressed on.

"No, indeed! *They* say that animals we once called property are now free citizens, our *equals*. They must vote, take part in government, decide where they will work and when. Where does it end, my neighbors? Will the hogs and chickens turn up next?"

That set them laughing, but it was a nasty kind of laughter, and mean-spirited. The kind Coker recognized.

"And once the pigs are in your parlor, will they ask about your *daughters*?"

Laughter turned to snarls, then, punctuated with more angry shouts of "No!"

"You're damned right, no!" he shouted back at them. A slick sweat beaded on his forehead, dampened Coker's nape. "As long as I'm alive, *I* say our race will not be muddied and degraded! *I* say we will not bow down before the radicals in Washington and be their silent slaves. We are the *masters* of this land and will remain so, as long as a red-blooded white man draws breath!"

More cheers. He scanned the outskirts of the crowd, looking for soldiers, but saw none. The bluebellies were wise enough to stay away from Jefferson, most days. They had supplies delivered to the camp and only came to town in small groups, to support the brothels. Off to the left from where he stood, Coker saw Harlan Travis and a couple of his deputies, thumbs hooked behind the buckles of their gunbelts, on alert for any trouble.

"When the time comes," Coker told his people, "we shall rise as one and reassert our claim to this, our homeland. We are not afraid of carpetbaggers, scalawags, or soldiers from the North—not even darkies dressed in blue!"

That got the hooting started, and a few shrill Rebel yells. Coker stood tall, basking in adulation, while his heart thumped solidly against his rib cage. He could sell these people anything, he thought. Make them *do* anything. He was about to test that theory, but they needed further motivation first.

"My brothers—"

"What about your *sisters*?" shrilled a painted lady, ten or twelve rows out.

He played along. "My brothers *and* my sisters, our oppressors think that we are beaten. That we have no spirit left in us, and we will do whatever we are told, regardless of the cost. I say they're wrong. What say the rest of you?"

"Dead wrong!" one of his Knights called back, on cue. Others took up the cry, until it rolled along the riverfront like a relentless tide.

Coker waited for it to ebb, standing with arms outflung as if he had been crucified. Silence returned by slow degrees. He waited, shoulders aching by the time the crowd was still enough to hear him speak again.

"But where should we begin?" he asked them. "What are we to do?"

Gideon Ryder felt the crowd stirring around him, tipping toward that balance point that, once exceeded, turned an audience into a mob. Last time, in Corpus Christi, troops had been on hand to quell the violent impulses and absorb the worst of them. He didn't want to see another riot, soldiers forced into the line of fire, but when he thought of the alternatives, they all looked worse.

He didn't know what Coker had in mind, but he—and all the others present—would find out, he guessed, within the next few moments.

"We have two plague spots in Jefferson today," Coker declared. "The first, you're all aware of. That's the Yankee nest outside of town. They don't belong here—they don't even want to *be* here, take my word for that—but tackling them means touching off a fight we aren't prepared to finish yet."

That "yet" hung in the air above the crowd, a dangling noose waiting for someone to step up and put his head in.

"Now, the other plague spot, most of you likely don't think about. It hasn't been that long ago that darkies knew their place, and that was in the cotton patch or working on the docks. Today is what they like to call the Year of Jubilo. You've heard the song? 'De massa run, ha, ha! De darky stay, ho, ho!' It's what they pray for, night and day."

More angry rumbling. The faces close enough for Ryder to observe were reddening, and not entirely from the sun. A man nearby, to Ryder's left, spat out the stub of a cigar and shook a clenched fist toward the wagon stage. Another had a long knife in his hand, upraised, as if to slash the sky.

Ryder relaxed his crossed arms just enough to let his right hand find the curved grip of his Colt Army.

"Today, *right now*, your rightful servants live together on the west side of this very city, doing nothing. Waiting for those forty acres and a mule the radicals have promised them. *Your* acres, since they never owned a scrap of dirt before, much less a house or farm. *Your* mules, most likely, while they're at it. You know damn well Congress doesn't deal in livestock."

"Bet your ass they don't!" a fat man bawled, away to Ryder's right.

"And when they come to take your land away, what will you do?" Coker demanded. "Will you run away like *massa* in their song, or will you stand and fight?"

"We'll fight!" the cry went up, at least a hundred voices strong.

"Or will it be too late by then?" asked Coker, from his wagon. "Will you look back from a pauper's shanty, wishing you'd done something on your own, before they got the nerve to loot your property and kill your sleeping children in their beds?"

The crowd was roaring now.

"You know the place I mean," Coker reminded them.

"Now, I can't tell you what to do. The Yanks would call it treason, string me up for it. But I believe you're *wise* enough to work it out yourself, and *strong* enough to do the job!"

Somebody fired a pistol in the air, then half a dozen more. From there, it was a stampede from the rally grounds and off along the nearest street, the mob in motion.

Headed west.

L ook, he's goin' with 'em," Ardis Jackson said.
"What for, you think?" Wade Stevens asked.
"Dunno, don't care. It make things easy for us, though."
"How's that?" asked Caleb Burke.
"The middle of a riot, who's to say how he got kilt?" Jackson replies. "Who'll even give a damn?"
"I get it." Stevens flashed a crooked grin.
"Then let's go *get* it!" Jackson said.

They stepped into the tide of bodies and were swept along, running to keep pace with the flow and working up a sweat. Of course, they'd been sweating before, but this just made it worse. Jackson felt vaguely sick, wished he'd laid off the whiskey that morning, but now his sweat smelled like red-eye. He wondered what would happen if he fell, deciding that the mob would likely run right over him and leave him in its dust.

Caleb was running to his left, mouth breathing even with his nose fixed, more or less. Stevens was faster, started pulling out ahead of them, then got snarled in the crush and couldn't make much headway. Jackson cursed him breathlessly for showing off, then cursed himself for dreaming up this half-baked scheme in haste.

How in hell were they supposed to kill the Yankee if they couldn't even find him in the middle of the riot that was shaping up? Jackson had lost sight of his quarry when they joined the mob and hadn't glimpsed him since. For all he knew, the man from Washington had ducked out one side or the other, left the group, and was returning for a nice rest at the Bachmann House. Why would he want to join a charge against the darkies anyway?

Unless . . .

What if he's after Mr. Coker? Jackson thought. The boss had treated him unfairly yesterday, but that made Jackson yearn to please him and regain his confidence, not see him gunned down in the street.

It hit him then. If he could rescue Mr. Coker from the Yank, it would be one of those sweet situations that you rarely saw in life. Two birds, one stone. Who could predict how Mr. Coker might reward him for a thing like that?

Jackson picked up his pace, although with difficulty, knowing that the best intentions in the world were useless if he missed the party. That would do him no damn good at all.

"You see 'im?" he called out to Stevens, wheezing.

"Well, find 'im, dammit!"

"How'm I s'pose to—"

Stevens tripped, almost went down, but Jackson caught him by one arm and used the last ounce of his energy to keep him upright, moving forward. "Jesus, watch your step!" he hissed, wishing that he could catch his breath instead of panting like a dog.

They had another five, six blocks to go, at least, before they got to Colored Town. Jackson had been out on patrol around the darky district more than once, but he had never had to run there from the river, and he never would again. This one time ought to do it, if he kept his wits about him and his aim was true.

Against his will, he started thinking of the things that

could go wrong. What if the Yankee wasn't out for Coker, after all? No problem, there; Jackson could fake it, once the man was safely dead. What if they couldn't find him? Or they found him, tried to shoot him, and they wound up hitting someone else?

What if they hit *the boss*?

"Shut up, goddamn you!" Jackson cursed his brain.

"I di'n't say nothin'," Burke complained.

"Not you. Just save your breath and find that Yankee spy!"

Y̲ou can't go out there, Abel!"

"What choice do I have?" he countered, wishing that his sister would not raise her voice. The throbbing in his head had not retreated far enough, as yet, to bear the volume of an argument.

"What choice?" Anna regarded him with something close to disbelief. "Stay here, of course!"

"There's going to be trouble with the KRS. I feel it."

"And suppose you're right. What can you do against a mob fired up on hate and liquor?"

"Stand my ground," he answered, stubbornly.

"It's not *your* ground!"

"Anna—"

"You shot a man last night. The sheriff would have locked you up, except for Gideon. If you go out again—"

"The sheriff doesn't care what happens to the freedmen. You know that, as well as I do. Someone has to help them!"

"We came south to help them learn and vote, not fight a war. The AMA would toss us straight out on our—"

"It's my duty!" he insisted.

"Why? You aren't a lawman. You have no official duties whatsoever."

"Anna, you, of all people, should recognize a *moral* duty."

"To be killed? To murder others?"

"It's not murder if you act in self-defense."

"Matthew 5:39," she replied.

Abel blinked at her. "What? You're not making sense."

"The words of our Savior," she answered. "Remember? 'I say unto you, That ye resist not evil: but whosoever shall smite thee on thy right cheek, turn to him the other also.'"

"We're not discussing a slap in the face."

"No, we're not. You were shot yourself, last night, if you've forgotten. Nearly killed."

"I'm fine."

"Then why do you keep wincing when I raise my voice?"

"Because you're shrill and grating on my nerves!"

"Abel, if you go out tonight and die—or if the sheriff holds you for a lynch mob—what becomes of me?"

"You leave this cursed place. Go home and start a decent life, a thousand miles away from savages and crackers."

"On my own?" Her eyes were brimming now.

While they argued, he was bent over the old Colt Paterson, confirming that all five chambers were properly loaded, spinning the cylinder, easing the hammer back and down with his thumb, staying clear of the trigger. Five shots wasn't much in the face of a mob, and there would be no chance to reload. It was a daunting prospect—frankly terrifying, in his present state—but he could not sit idly by while madmen pillaged a community of innocents.

"You'll be all right," he said, as if conceding that this night would be his last. "You'll find a suitor, never fear."

"A *suitor*?" Anna leaned across and punched his shoulder with her fist. "You think that's all I care about? My God, you don't know me at all!"

"I may not, but the neighbors will, if you keep shouting."

"Damn the neighbors! You are all the living family I have, and now you'd rob me of it, in defense of total strangers."

"They're not strangers. You know many of them."

"I'm acquainted with them, but I wouldn't say I *know* them. When we visit with the freedmen, there's a wall between us. Don't you feel it? Most speak only when they're spoken to, and even then they keep the answers short. I'm not convinced they want us here at all."

"Anna, we're white. They've been enslaved by white men since their grandparents were taken out of Africa in chains. You can't expect their trust to blossom overnight."

"And they have no right to expect that you will die for them!"

"They haven't asked me to."

"No. You're about to volunteer. But you are not their savior, Abel!"

"No. I'm just a man trying to do the right thing in a rotten situation."

He was on his feet now, pistol tucked under his belt, donning his jacket to conceal it. Anna tried to block the doorway, but he moved her, gently but firmly, to one side.

"Please, Abel! Please!" she begged him, weeping openly.

"I'll be back soon," he said and kissed her on the forehead. "Lock the door behind me."

It was hot outside. He could have done without the jacket, but the pistol made him anxious. Many men in Jefferson wore firearms anytime they left their homes, but Abel knew he was a special case. The sheriff might arrest him, even though there was no statute on the books forbidding him to travel armed. Jail could mean death, or at the very least, a beating.

He was frightened, couldn't lie about it to himself, but

Abel still saw no alternative. He could not face himself tomorrow, or in years to come, unless he took a stand today.

C hasing a mob was thirsty work. Ryder wished there was time for him to stop at a saloon along the way, but from the look and smell of things, most of the men around him had already drunk their fill of courage by the time they reached the rally grounds.

Ryder wondered which of them were KRS members and which were simply Negrophobes itching for any kind of action. He decided that it didn't matter in the long run. They had taken sides with Coker to commit a massacre, which made it Ryder's business as he understood the job he'd taken on.

If things went wrong, Chief Wood might claim Ryder had overreached, despite the vague instructions he'd received. Too bad. It wouldn't be the first time he'd been fired for stepping out of bounds. If he lost his badge—his *second* badge—Ryder could always find another line of work that didn't make him deal with human scum.

But he was still in Jefferson today, and he had work to do.

They were within a block or two of what white locals normally called "Colored Town," if they were in a mood to be polite. The racket from the mob—shouting and cheering, some cretin with a bugle—must have warned the freedmen that a mob was on its way to visit them. A part of Ryder's mind hoped they would flee and leave their empty homes to burn, saving their children and themselves instead of fighting over property. The other part of him hoped they would stand and fight.

How else would lynchers ever learn?

Whatever happened, Ryder knew that he'd be in the midst of it, a target for both sides. If shooting started—*when* it started—he'd have no friends in the mob around him. Meanwhile, to the freedmen, he'd be just another white man with a gun, invading their home ground.

He felt a bloodbath coming, either way.

And he had no plan yet in mind for stopping it. How could he? One man in the face of hundreds, while the local Union garrison remained in camp, either afraid to mount patrols or too damned lazy. It all came down to him, and if the best that he could do was save a life or two along the way, so be it.

Ryder kept his mouth shut while the rowdies who surrounded him were chanting, hooting, cheering long blasts from the bugle. He was marking targets to the best of his ability, noting the weapons those around him carried, which of them seemed most belligerent and therefore dangerous. Once battle had been joined, of course, his random survey wouldn't matter much.

It would be each man for himself, then—at least until the mob identified him as an enemy.

A half block now, and those at the front of the crowd had slowed down, jabbering amongst themselves. Ryder had no idea what they were saying from that distance, but he drifted to his right, jostling across the flow of foot traffic, until he had a clearer view forward. From there, he saw a line of freedmen spread across the street, silent and armed with weapons ranging from long guns to hatchets and hammers.

Somebody in the middle ranks of the advancing mob yelled, "Niggers!" followed by another blast from the discordant bugle. Instantly, the crowd surged forward and a crash of gunfire echoed down the street.

15

★ **A**bel Butler heard the din when he was still three blocks away. Raised voices, rattling gunfire, and a bugle blaring wildly, tunelessly, before its noise was suddenly cut off. He nearly turned for home, but caught himself at the last instant, swallowed hard, and started running toward the mist of gun smoke rising at the far end of the street.

Madness.

He should be at the house with Anna. Better still, they should be back at home in Syracuse, content to mail out pamphlets for the AMA in their spare time. What had possessed him, coming to this godforsaken land? And what, in God's name, ever made him think that he could fight?

Too late.

He smelled the burnt gunpowder now. It overpowered the aroma of his own fear and sweat. Colt Paterson in hand, he reached the northern edge of Colored Town—and stopped short, as a freedman with a shotgun suddenly appeared, his double-barreled weapon aimed at Abel's face.

"Hold up there, buckra!"

Abel kept his pistol pointed at the ground, mind racing. Was the black man's face familiar to him? *Yes!*

"Isaac, you know me. Abel Butler. I've been working with your people for the past few months."

The former slave regarded him suspiciously, then let the muzzle of his weapon dip. "You ought not be here, Mr. Butler," he advised.

"I came to help."

Ahead of him, another three blocks down, a house erupted into flames. More gunfire hammered at his ears. Butler saw white and black men locked in mortal combat, punching, stabbing, hacking at each other.

"Came too late," Isaac advised him. "You should go back home."

Damned right, thought Abel. But he said, "My place is here."

Isaac considered that. Replied, "Gwan, then. I'm s'poseta keep watch here."

"God keep you," Abel said, and moved on toward the fight.

Behind him, Isaac called, "Don't think He cares much what goes on down here."

I hope you're wrong, thought Butler, as he put another block behind him, slowing, pistol cocked so that its folding trigger was accessible. He kept his index finger clear of it, afraid to waste a shot by accident when he had none to spare.

The odds seemed roughly even, number-wise. He knew that some two thousand freedmen and their families inhabited the neighborhood, and while that made them a distinct minority in Jefferson, the number who'd turned out to face the mob approximately matched that which had rallied to attack them. That would swiftly change, he realized, when word spread of a clash between the races. Once that happened, more whites would arrive to join the fray, driven by simple bigotry or by the fear of a rebellion that had haunted them throughout the war.

It was insanity, but Abel could not counsel them under the circumstances. He could only help where needed, do his best, until a blade or bullet cut him down.

Another half block in, and he saw two white men dragging a colored woman from the street, into a nearby alley, laughing as she struggled in their grip. The world went red for Abel then, all thought of Christian brotherhood forgotten, as he raced across the street to follow them.

Inside the alley, they were laughing, tearing at the frightened woman's clothes. He shouted, "Back away there, both of you!" and advanced to meet them, finger on his pistol's trigger now.

"The hell you want?" one of them asked him, obviously drunk.

"Stay put an' wait your turn." The other leered.

"Release her instantly," Abel demanded, pistol rising in his fist.

They did—and both reached for their guns at the same time. He shot the grinning maggot on his left first, saw blood geyser from a chest wound, then he spun to face the other, thumbing back his pistol's hammer for a second shot. The would-be rapist had his own gun out by then, but fumbled, nearly dropped it.

Abel let him get it right, then shot him in the face, surprised and shamed by how it pleased him.

He moved in to help the woman, but she lurched away from him. "No more!" she cried and ran off down the alley toward its far end, leaving corpses in her wake.

Abel stood watching for a moment, then she vanished, and he turned back toward the fight.

R yder was watching when the bugler took a bullet, blatting out one final note before he dropped the horn and toppled to the ground. No telling whether he was dead or only wounded, and if he were being truthful, Ryder couldn't have cared less.

The freedmen had unleashed one volley at the mob, then scattered, seeking cover, buying time to stoke their muzzle loaders for a second round. The mob was short on long guns, mostly packing pistols, but approximately half of those guns were revolvers, giving them an edge over the team defending Colored Town. That didn't always help, as Ryder saw when one of them was skewered with a pitchfork, screaming, but the rioters took full advantage of it as they charged to meet their enemies.

Ryder knew he must choose his targets wisely in the midst of chaos. Random firing would be pointless, likely suicidal. To be helpful in the present situation—if, indeed, that was a possibility—he had to be selective, acting with precision, keeping a cool head. Strike first, strike hard, and then move on.

But where to start?

A house was burning on the corner, half a block in front of Ryder. What had sparked the fire, he couldn't say. None of the mob had carried torches; possibly one of their bullets struck a lamp inside and splattered flames to wallpaper or curtains. He saw dark folk running from the house, carrying furniture, one of them staggered by a gunshot from the street. Smoke poured out through the open doorway, smaller tendrils snaking from beneath the eaves.

Ryder saw one of the rioters a few yards distant, lining up his pistol on the freedmen scrambling to save the contents of their burning home. He rushed across the pavement, swung his Colt Army against the shooter's nearly hairless scalp, and put him down. Scooped up the second gun to use as needed and ran on, unnoticed in the tumult.

Out ahead of him, but closer now, the neighborhood's defenders had reloaded for a second volley, peppering the mob and adding more smoke to the air. A white man off to Ryder's left went down, clutching his stomach, and another to his right cried out, clapping a hand against his bloodied face. He felt a bullet sizzle past his face, inches to spare, but couldn't single out its source with all the firing, shouting, dashing back and forth. An image came to Ryder's mind of Captain Legere relaxing in his tent, and he unleashed a string of bitter curses at the lazy officer.

"Hey, now!" a shrill voice scolded him. "They's ladies present!"

Ryder turned to find one of the brothel doxies grinning at him, missing one of her incisors. He was startled that she'd kept up with the mob, less so when she held up a cut-throat razor, sunlight glinting from its wicked blade.

"C'mon!" she urged him, fairly cackling. "You don't wanna miss the fun!"

Ryder considered slugging her, but she was off and running in an instant, cackling like a witch out of some fairy tale.

Cursing again, he started after her, deeper into the fray.

The hell's he goin'?" Ardis Jackson asked nobody in particular.

"How should I know?" Stevens answered back.

"I seen him clout that fella," Burke put in. "Don't know if he were one a ourn."

"Don't matter," Jackson said. "He's on our side today. Get after 'im!"

Ryder was well out in the lead now, putting space between them. To be fair, the riot helped him, all those other people ducking in and out in front of Ardis and his shadows, bullets flying everywhere, acrid smoke burning Jackson's eyes. He liked a fight as well as anybody, but it was an obstacle when he had work to do.

"I don't see Mr. Coker," Stevens said, sounding surprised.

"Course not," Jackson spat back at him. "He's stayin' out of it to keep his hands clean."

"Don't know what he's missin'," Burke said, then squeezed off a shot toward someone running on the far side of the street.

"Quit that!" Jackson commanded. "Do you want 'im seein' us before we's ready?"

"Sorry," Burke replied, not sounding it. "That were the biggest buck I ever seen."

"And you missed 'im, anyhow," jeered Stevens.

"Whyn't you shut up?" Burke challenged.

"Why don't *both* of you shut up," Jackson cut in, "or get the hell away from me."

That muted them, however briefly, and he concentrated on the Yank, running a zigzag line in front of them, some fifty yards ahead. He could have tried a pistol shot from there but didn't like his odds of hitting anything he aimed at. Wanted to get closer for a sure thing on the first try.

Jackson's lungs were aching. Too much smoking when he drank—which meant all day—and now fog of gun smoke mixed with smoke from burning houses didn't help. He wished that he could stop and rest, or just enjoy the riot with his brothers of the KRS, but he was on a mission that allowed no time for play.

Jackson saw the Yank run up behind one of the fellow Knights—it looked like Tommy Beamish from a distance, with his long hair and big gut—just as Beamish grabbed a little black kid by the hair and sent him sprawling, rushing after him and brandishing a hunting knife. The Yank got there before Beamish could strike, spun him around, and pistol-whipped him with a double stroke that dropped him like a sack of apples.

"Sumbitch!" Burke spat out, raising a hand unconsciously to touch his wounded nose.

"We'll pay 'im back, don't worry," Jackson wheezed. Hell of a time to suddenly develop breathing trouble.

"You all right?" asked Stevens.

"Shut your hole and get him!"

Stevens muttered something Jackson couldn't hear, but he'd have bet the farm it wasn't complimentary—if he'd had any farm to bet.

They'd closed the gap by half but couldn't get a steady fix on Ryder as he ducked and dodged around the battle-ground. They saw him shoot one of their brothers—only in the hip, as he was running down a couple of darkies—and he slugged another from behind while he was winding up to pitch a torch he'd gotten somewhere through the window of a little yellow house. The Yank seemed to have no idea that he was being hunted through the melee, which would work to their advantage.

If we ever catch him, Jackson thought and had another coughing fit.

A moment later, Ryder stopped to help some women who were shrieking in the dooryard of a house in flames. They acted scared of him at first, but then he calmed them down somehow and ran into the house through roiling smoke, returning seconds later with a squalling infant in his arms.

"Lookit the good Samaritan," sneered Stevens.

"Screw 'im," Jackson said and raised his pistol for the kill.

*T*hree shots left, thought Abel Butler. Then what would he do? The battle showed no signs of slowing down; if anything, its fury was increasing. Blacks and whites alike were laid out in the street, and something like a dozen homes were already on fire, the flames likely to spread from one cheap, dried-out structure to its neighbors. Three shots and he'd be unarmed, for all intents and purposes, as useless in the present situation as a circus clown.

He almost tripped over the shotgun lying in his path. He looked around for someone who might claim it, saw a trail of blood retreating toward an alley on his left and followed it no further. Scooping up the double-barreled gun, he checked its load and found only one barrel had been fired so far.

A small reprieve, at least.

Firing at anyone was perilous in the confusion, more particularly with a shotgun, where the charge would spread and might strike several people Butler hadn't planned on shooting. He would have to get in close, which didn't seem to be a problem at the moment, people rushing everywhere, sometimes colliding, sometimes locked in combat hand to hand.

Go where you're needed most, he thought. But where was that?

A scream brought him around to find a freedman thrashing in the street, a white man kneeling over him, a bloody hatchet raised to strike. Its first blow had already gashed the freedman's face, shearing most of a cheek away, and Butler thought the next would surely split his skull.

He aimed high, fired, and saw the hatchet man disintegrate. His hat went sailing, with a portion of his skull inside it, and the hand that clutched his weapon burst like ripe fruit falling from a height. The dead man slumped across his victim, smothering the freedman's ragged screams, as Butler dropped his empty shotgun, ran up to the huddled forms, and dragged him clear.

He didn't recognize the wounded black man through his mask of blood. Someone he'd never met, perhaps, or well disguised by pain and fear. The fear was winning out now, as the wounded man stared up at Butler.

"Why you help me, mister?"

"It's my duty. Can you stand?"

"Yessir."

"Then run, for Christ's sake, while you can."

Panting with exertion—or excitement?—Butler drew the pistol from his belt once more and looked for someone in special need of help.

Ryder was handing off the baby to its mother when the woman gasped and lurched, collapsing toward him. Ryder caught them both and saw the blood a heartbeat later, looking past the wounded mother and her bawling offspring, searching for the shooter.

What he found was three of them, one with a flattened, purple nose that helped him recognize them, even through the smoke. All three had pistols raised and aimed his way, heedless of any innocents who might be in the line of fire.

"Watch out!" he warned the sobbing women, couldn't

tell if any heard him, much less understood. Already on the move, he drew his Colt Army with five rounds in its cylinder and sent one of them toward the three men he'd encountered yesterday while they were hazing Anna Butler. Ryder missed, but he'd come close enough to worry them, making the three fan out as they returned fire in a hasty rush.

No hits on his side, but he went to ground, lined up one of the moving targets—Mr. Busted Nose—and tried to lead him, knowing that he had to fire ahead of where his man was when he squeezed the trigger. It was tricky, but he'd managed it before.

The Colt bucked in his hand, and Ryder saw his man go down, drawing his legs up as he crumpled to the ground, gut-shot. The wound might well be fatal, but that wasn't Ryder's problem at the moment. One man down and out of action, which left two still hunting for him in the middle of the riot.

The ones still on their feet had run in opposite directions, which made Ryder's work more difficult—and dangerous. He rolled out to his left and heard a bullet strike the dirt where he'd been lying, vaulted to his feet, and broke in the direction of a nearby house that wasn't yet on fire. More bullets followed him, but they were poorly aimed, if aimed at all.

Once he was under cover, Ryder caught his breath and tried to hatch a plan. His mind was racing furiously, making cool deliberation tough, but it was clear he had two basic choices: show himself and face the shooters or attempt to lure them off the street, into a trap.

He chose the latter, edging back along the south wall of the house, another home barely four feet in front of him, forming a narrow accidental alley. Ryder hurried, reached the small home's southwest corner, and paused there, crouching and peering through the smoke that veiled his path.

Four shots remaining in his Colt, and if he wasted them, there might be no time to reload.

It took a few long moments, but they came. The first one through the narrow gap didn't seem to like being the leader, creeping down the narrow strip of dirt in a half crouch, his pistol out in front of him, eyes squinting through the smoke and shadows. Ryder waited until both of them were in the funnel, then shot the leader, punching a blowhole through his chest. A jet of blood sprayed from the wound as he dropped backward, landing on his buttocks first, then toppling over to one side, his head wedged up against the nearest wall.

His partner turned to run, but Ryder didn't feel like letting him escape to try again some other time. His last shot drilled the fleeing gunman from behind, between his shoulder blades, and dumped him facedown in the dirt.

It was a moment's work to switch his pistol's empty cylinder for one already loaded. Ryder got it done, then circled back another way to reach the street, without treading on corpses of the newly dead.

The battle was continuing. He still had work to do.

Abel Butler thought the tide was turning. He could not have said exactly when it happened, or precisely how, but suddenly it seemed that armed black men outnumbered whites, as if they'd sprung up from the earth itself somehow. Or maybe it was simply that more whites had fallen in the battle, leaving them shorthanded at the end.

Whatever the case, he was heartened by the shift but staggered by the dead and wounded bodies scattered everywhere around him. When he tried to count the burning houses, he lost track, confused by smoke and the necessity of watching out for men intent on killing him.

He'd used the last rounds from his pistol on three lynch-ers. They'd been grappling with a freedman, rope already snug around his neck, trying to toss the free end up and over the limb of a street-corner tree when Butler took them from behind. He hadn't warned them, didn't try to chase them off, just shot them where they stood and lingered long enough to see their victim flee. One of them, he believed, was dead. The others could go either way, depending on if help arrived in time.

What help?

The sheriff hadn't turned up yet, likely delayed either by fear or prearrangement with the mob. The Union troops, for all he knew, were still in camp, heedless of what was hap-pening. Whatever next occurred, whether the tattered mob retreated or its members called up reinforcements from the city populace at large, the residents of Colored Town would stand alone.

Except for him.

The empty Colt tucked through his belt, Butler had found an ax abandoned on the field of battle. While a part of him recoiled at using it to hack through human flesh, survival took priority. He would not strike, except in direst need, but if it came to that he would not hesitate.

Some of the rioters were fleeing now, he saw, a number of them clutching bloody wounds but strong enough to run away. Freedmen did not pursue them, concentrating on the others who remained, still fighting in the streets. Those were increasingly outnumbered, waging a defensive struggle now. As Butler watched, one of them fell no more than ten yards distant, skewered by a pitchfork, then surrounded and blud-geoned until he went limp.

"You shouldn't be out here," a voice behind him said. He whirled, raising the ax, then stopped and staggered back a half-step as he recognized Gideon Ryder. "Where did you come from?"

"The rally," Ryder said. "Come on. I need to get you home."

"It isn't finished here," Butler protested.

"Look around. They're mopping up, and after last night, you don't want to be here when the sheriff comes."

"Why not?" Butler replied, but he could see the logic in it. Sheriff Travis wouldn't need a great excuse to lock him up, perhaps even charge him with murder. Witnesses could be procured, and blacks were barred from testifying in the courts of Texas under current law.

"Your sister's waiting for you, likely worried," Ryder said, tipping the scales.

"All right."

Butler was trailing him when Ryder paused and said, "You'd better leave that here."

"What? Oh." He dropped the ax and went on empty-handed, feeling suddenly defenseless with the empty pistol in his belt. Trying to think of what he should tell Anna, how much she could hear before she looked at him with fear and loathing in her eyes.

16

★ **R**yder was eating breakfast—sausage gravy over biscuits, fried eggs on the side—when Sheriff Travis found him and sat down across the table from him without waiting for an invitation. Travis had a weary look about him, as if he'd been up most of the night and hadn't been enjoying it.

"Coffee?" Ryder suggested. "This place makes it strong."

Ignoring that, Travis announced, "We need to talk about what happened yesterday."

"Simple. You proved you can't police your town. Or won't."

"Says who?" Face reddening.

"The evidence. You have a major riot and the sheriff's nowhere to be found."

"Says who?"

"Eyewitnesses."

"Niggers!" Travis spat the ugly word as if it left a foul taste in his mouth.

"Do I look black to you?" Ryder inquired.

"So, you were there?"

"Observing. It's all in my field report."

"I'll need to see that."

"Write my boss in Washington. He feels like it, you'll get a copy when he's ready."

"Smug bastard!"

To his right, an older couple huffed and gasped. Turning their way, Travis said, "I'm sorry, folks. Heat of the moment." Neither one looked satisfied by the apology.

"If you were there," Travis told Ryder, "you saw white men gettin' slaughtered by a bunch of savages."

"That how it looked to you from home, or sitting in your office?" Ryder asked.

"That's how it *was*."

"No question in your mind why all those good white folks wound up in Colored Town with guns, before the killing started?"

"Not the way I heard it," Travis answered.

"Oh? What, then? You think the freedmen went and *dragged* them over there, armed as they were, just for the chance to fight them?"

"Well—"

"And liked it all so much, they burned their own homes, just for fun?"

"You get white folks riled up, they don't just sit and take it."

"Not like you, just sitting on your backside while a lynch mob's running wild."

"I'd have them niggers locked up right this minute, if it warn't for you!"

"How's that, Sheriff?"

"Runnin' to call the bluecoats out, the way you done."

"I hate to tell you, but you're wrong again."

"Save it. I know you went out to the garrison."

"Your spy should tell you that was in the morning, hours before the KRS got fired up for a massacre."

"So what?"

"And for the record, their commander sent me packing. Said he doesn't meddle in civilian matters."

"Well, he's dang sure meddlin' now. As if you didn't know."

"It's news to me," Ryder replied. "And overdue."

"In *your* opinion."

"Just about the only one I trust."

"You got a narrow view of things."

"I think of it as knowing right from wrong."

"And you're the judge of that?"

"We all judge, Sheriff. Some of us just get it wrong."

"If I was you—"

"A lot of people would be disappointed. Is this where you tell me I should leave town?"

"I don't have authority for that."

"You're right."

"But I'd suggest it all the same, for everybody's sake."

"Who benefits, in that case?"

"You do. Leastways, if you call stayin' alive a benefit."

"That's my problem. Who else?"

"The whole town, way I see it."

"What you mean is, all the white folks who agree with you and Coker."

"That's the town," Travis replied.

"Is it?"

"I just said so. You might try cleanin' out your ears."

"Or you could get your eyes checked. All the time you've been alive—what's that, now, forty-something years?"

"I'm thirty-seven."

"Could have fooled me. Anyway, in all that time, you've been a member of the only race that mattered. You were always on the top rung of the ladder, looking down. But things are changing, Sheriff. Slowly, maybe, but they're changing. Colored folk are free now, and I'd bet your next year's salary that someday soon, they'll have the vote. Keep treating them like dirt, how likely do you think it is they'll vote for *you*?"

"Don't matter none," Travis replied.

"You're tired of playing lawman."

"Not just yet." And now he smiled. "Seems like they's tired a livin' here in Jefferson."

"How's that?"

The mocking smile grew wider. "What, you didn't hear? They're moving outta town, all them that's still alive."

The residents of Colored Town were leaving under guard. When Abel Butler heard, he rushed back to the scene where he had shot six men just hours earlier and found the army standing by in case of any further violence. They weren't simply protecting people and homes, however; they were aiding in an exodus.

Abel caught up with one of those whom he knew best, a former slave named Luther Hill who'd worked on a plantation west of town until the war's end set him free. His wife was common law, no formal marriage having been permitted under slavery, and they had two young boys, aged eight and five. When Abel found them, they were clearing out their modest home, next door to one that had been razed by fire. Scorch marks on the south wall of Luther's house revealed what a close call the fire had been.

"What are you doing, Luther?" Abel asked, without preamble.

"What it look like, Mr. Butler? Gettin' out while we still can."

"But this is *your* place. The first real home that you've ever had."

"*Was* our place," Luther said. "Now it's just kindlin', if the white folks take it in their heads to light another fire."

"But if you leave, they win!"

"And if we stay? If we get kilt, who wins? You wanna tell me that?"

"The army can protect you." Abel heard the hollow ring to that, before Hill gave it back to him.

"Like they pertected us last night? For all the good they do, they may as well go back up North, or off to fight the Injuns."

Abel looked around him at the partial devastation: homes in ashes, bloodstains in the dust, a greasy pall of smoke still lingering, tainting the very air he breathed. He couldn't argue with the man he thought of as a friend, couldn't promise any member of the black community would live in safety if they stayed in Jefferson.

"Where will you go?" he asked, at last.

"One thing the soldiers know about is pitchin' tents. They's settin' up a camp for us to stay awhile in, next to theirs. Figger they'll keep an eye on us until we think of someplace else to try."

"In Texas?" Abel pressed him.

"I been thinkin' 'bout the Injun Territory," Hill replied.

Abel knew the basics of it: organized in 1834, to hold the Indians displaced by white westward movement and various wars. Several thousand members of the Five Civilized Tribes—Cherokee, Chickasaw, Choctaw, Creek, and Seminole—had joined the Confederate army, fighting in several major battles against Union forces. Abel had never understood their choice, but knew the tribes kept slaves to work for them. And that the Union Army had rejected Indian recruits throughout the war.

"What would you do there?" Abel asked him.

"Farm, same as I been, but for myself this time. To feed my family, instead of makin' white men rich."

"And what about the red men, Luther?"

"Got nothin' against 'em, long as they leave me and mine alone."

"You know, they might not want to share their land."

"Who ever does? It ain't their land, though, if you think about it. It's the gov'ment's, and the soldiers there do more'n sit around in camp, from what I hear."

"Well, if you're set on it . . ."

"Ain't set on nothin' yet, but gettin' out of *here* before another mob comes back to finish what they started."

Abel nodded. "If there's anything that I can do to help . . ."

"You helped last night, and it's appreciated. Best thing you can do right now is clear on outta here. White folks in Jefferson got no love for you, as it is."

"I'll come to see you, in the new camp. Find out if there's anything you need."

Hill shrugged. "You wanna make the ride, we'll be there. For a little while, at least."

Feeling deflated, useless, Abel turned back toward his rented house on the far side of town.

How many dead, again?"

"Fifteen for sure," the sheriff said. "Another two or three may go before the day's out. Close to double that amongst the niggers."

"Christ!" Roy Coker shook his head disgustedly. "It was supposed to be an *easy* job. A *simple* thing. What happened?"

"Well, you know I wasn't there, o' course, like we agreed beforehand. Way I hear it told, the boys went in awright, to start with, but the bucks stood up to 'em and fought right back. That ain't the kinda thing white men are used to, Mr. Coker."

"Jesus wept. Most of those men were soldiers, and the rest were on the wartime slave patrols. How could they go in and have their heads handed to them that way, by a bunch of field hands?"

"Again, I wasn't there, but—"

"Never mind. It was rhetorical."

"How's that?"

Coker ignored him, changed the subject. "Did you see the Secret Service man?"

"Just come from him, at Latimer's. I tole him he'd be wise to get out, like you said."

"And?"

"Like you thought, he didn't buy it."

"So, we've got the same old problem."

"Got rid of the niggers, though," said Travis.

"Have we? Gotten rid of them?"

"They're leavin', like I said before. Bluebellies watchin' 'em pack up and all. Word is, they's gonna camp out by the garrison awhile, and then move on."

"Good news for us," said Coker. "Not so good for whoever receives them at the other end."

"Least we don't have to worry 'bout it."

"The mind's a strange thing, Harlan. As it broadens, you can see the world. But when it's narrow, you can't see beyond your nose."

Travis considered that, then shook his head. "Don't follow you."

"As I surmised. From my viewpoint, we still have two problems in front of us. The man from Washington is one; the other, our departing dusky nemeses."

"Niggers?"

"You're catching on. If they leave now, how are we to fulfill our destiny for Jefferson and Texas?"

"Huh?"

"We need them here, under protection of the Yankees. When they are eradicated, it will spark a conflagration— that's a fire, to you—that spreads across our state and through the late Confederacy. A rebellion that will make the last one pale beside it."

"Hold on, now. I don't think—"

"That's the best way, Harlan. Don't think. Leave that to your betters."

Travis wasn't dumb enough to miss the point of that, and while his face flushed crimson, he was wise enough to keep his mouth shut, swallowing whatever tart reply had come to mind.

"Sure, Mr. Coker. You're the boss."

"And your job, for the moment, is to keep the brethren calm. I'll let them know, through you, when time comes for another move against the coloreds. In the meantime, there's another spot of trouble you can help me with."

"What's that?" Anxious to please.

"The carpetbaggers. Butler and his so-called sister."

"Want me to lock 'em up?"

"For what?"

"I'll think a somethin'."

"No. But I want them removed from circulation. Can you handle that?"

"'Remove' mean kilt?"

"It does—but not in such a way as to attract more notice now, right after last night's trouble. If they were to disappear, say, taking their belongings with them, most folk would believe they'd gone back North, upset by all the harm they've done down here."

"So, I should try again to scare 'em off?"

"Harlan, sometimes I fear . . ." He stopped himself and changed directions. "No. Don't try to scare them off again. Make sure they vanish, preferably in the dead of night, but looking like they've run away. Don't kill them outright. I'd prefer to question them beforehand, find out more about who sent them south, and why."

"I'll see to it," the sheriff said.

"But carefully. Don't leave your muddy tracks all over this."

Travis glanced at his boots. "They ain't . . . oh, right. I hear you."

"You should start on that right now," Coker advised.

"Will do," the sheriff said and left.

Ryder watched the carts and wagons leaving, escorted by soldiers. Most of the freedmen were walking, some accompanied by wives and children, carrying their meager belongings by hand or strapped onto their backs. The houses that had not been burned or shot to pieces overnight now stood abandoned, causing him to wonder who would occupy them next.

He found Captain Legere observing from the sidelines and approached him. The expression on Legere's face telegraphed displeasure, but still managed to keep a civil tone.

"Agent Ryder. You're here for the finish, I see."

"The finish of what?" Ryder asked him.

"This social experiment. Shoving blacks and whites together by fiat and hoping it works. As you can see, it's failed."

"Because of them, you mean?" asked Ryder, nodding toward the file of refugees. "How about *them*?" This time, his eyes fell on the whites who'd gathered at a distance, jeering and cursing the homeless freedmen.

"I hold both sides culpable," Legere replied. "If God had meant the races to cohabitate, why did He draw a color line?"

"It's funny you should ask, since you just fought a war to win their freedom."

"I fought to preserve the Union, nothing more or less. I do find slavery abhorrent, but that doesn't mean I wish to see one race lifted above another."

"They've already tried that, with the whites on top," Ryder reminded him. "It seems to me that you support the same old thing."

"I beg your pardon!"

"Beg away, but it won't get you anywhere. You could have stopped the massacre last night, just by marching your men out of camp for a change. I'd say you stood aside and let this happen, either out of prejudice or so you wouldn't have to risk soiling your hands."

"You are entitled to your own opinion, sir, however ill informed. I would advise, however, against slandering a military officer."

"Slander means something false. I file reports with Washington on what I see and hear. If that rebounds on you, so be it."

"Call it extortion, then."

"Extortion, Captain? All I've asked from you is that you do the job you were assigned to."

"*You* do not decide my duties, Mr. Ryder. You have no idea what's written in my orders."

"So, it's natural that I'd inquire, when I'm reporting back to headquarters. If you're all squared away, you've got nothing to worry about."

Legere turned toward him, cheeks inflamed. "What *is* it that you want, precisely?"

Ryder nodded to the straggling line of freedmen once again. "These people have been driven from their homes. Some of them have lost family. They're in your hands now, till they find another place to settle. What I want is your assurance that you'll keep them safe by any means required, instead of resting on your laurels."

"I will do what I think best for every person in my care," the captain told him, through clenched teeth.

"Still leaves a lot of room for error," Ryder said. "I'll keep an eye on things, in case it starts to slip your mind."

"You realize I can't guard them forever?"

"Here and now's what counts. You start off owing them for what you didn't do, last night. How much you make up from now on depends on you."

"And if I keep them safe, as you request?"

"You'll have the satisfaction of a job well done."

Ryder turned on his heel and left the captain staring after him. He had no further time to waste on lazy men with puffed-up egos. Ryder knew enough of those back East, and everywhere he went he found a new crop waiting for him. Men who claimed they'd made it on their own, but nearly always had some "little people" laboring on their behalf. He had no argument per se with men of power and authority, but overlong exposure to their arrogance disgusted him.

Despite failing to burn out Colored Town, Roy Coker had achieved his primary objective. Jefferson's black population was in transit, headed somewhere else. Wherever they touched down, Ryder supposed there would be more whites with the same old attitudes, prepared to torment them.

He wished them luck and went back to his job.

A t lunchtime, Ryder found a little place downtown that offered Chinese food. He'd tried it once before, in New York City, but the offerings on that occasion had been mild. Whether this was a different kind of Chinese altogether or it had absorbed the influence of Mexico, it set his mouth on fire and made him order refills for his beer mug.

It was good, though. No denying that.

Ryder was nearly finished with his dumplings, rice, and spicy beef with vegetables, when Coker walked into the restaurant. He homed on Ryder's table, stood directly opposite, behind a vacant chair.

"May I?"

"You people love to watch me eat," Ryder observed. "Go on, sit down."

He sat. "I hope I haven't spoiled your meal."

"Not yet."

"I hope that we can talk about the late unpleasantness."

"Which one?" Ryder inquired.

"The recent race war, obviously."

"War, to me, means two sides fighting by agreement. Normally, you'd find them roughly equal. What I saw last night was an attempted massacre. It only evened out because the freedmen took your fellows by surprise."

"My fellows?"

"From the rally. From the KRS. Don't waste my time pretending that you're ignorant. I know better."

"Not ignorant," Coker replied, "but *innocent.* At least, until I'm proven guilty."

"Someone ought to work on that."

"I understand that someone is."

"Could be," Ryder admitted, sipping at his beer.

"And how is your investigation coming, Agent Ryder?"

"One thing that I've never liked is spoiling a surprise."

"I have the right to know who my accusers are."

"No, sir. The Constitution says you have a right to face them at your trial. There's nothing about giving you a list of names beforehand."

"So, a list, is it? That many?"

"You'll just have to wait and see."

"How can I resolve this whole unfortunate misunderstanding?" Coker asked him.

"For a start, disband the KRS."

"The First Amendment grants—"

"Free speech, free press, freedom to *peaceably* assemble," Ryder interrupted him. "I've read it."

"And we have the right to self-defense. When my men are attacked by savages—"

"That's all a crock of bull. I heard your speech and saw what happened afterward. You didn't have the nerve to join them, but you aimed those lynchers straight at Colored Town, like lining up a rifle shot."

"You give me too much credit, sir."

"I give you none at all. To me, you're nothing but a rabble-rouser. Slicker than most, I'll admit, but your patter's the same. 'Hate those people. They don't look like us. Get 'em, boys!'"

"You think that's what I'm fighting for?"

"I've only seen you talk, so far. Your men do all the fighting for you."

"Think of me as their commander."

"Which makes you responsible for everything they do. I'm glad you cleared that up for me."

Coker released a weary sigh and shook his head. "I'd hoped we could work something out between us."

"Glad to disappoint you," Ryder said.

"I hate to see an honest and courageous white man die for nought."

"I'm not dead yet. Your side keeps getting whittled down, though."

"My side, your side. We're the same. Why can't you see that?"

"If I did, I'd have to swear off mirrors."

"Very droll. I hope that you'll be able to retain your sense of humor in the days ahead."

"No worries there."

Coker stood up, leaned forward, hand extended. "Just in case our paths don't cross again," he said.

"No, thanks. I washed already."

"Pride goes before a fall," Coker replied.

"Bigger they are. I guess you know the rest."

He watched the vigilante leader leave the restaurant, turn left, and move off down the sidewalk, out of sight. Ryder supposed he'd lit another fuse, but that was fine with him. He'd spent enough time as it was, in Jefferson, and would be glad to see it end, with gun smoke or indictments.

There were still some innocents to think about, however, and he didn't plan to let them down.

17

★ "That's the house, down there," Wayne Henley said. "The green one with the white trim."

"I don't see nobody," Orville Deen announced.

"You wouldn't, if they's both inside," Ben Kyle replied.

"What if they're gone?" Jed Barnhart asked.

"We wait," said Henley. "Someplace out of sight, so we don't scare 'em off and have to chase 'em."

"I hate runnin'," Orville offered.

"You been on the run long as I've knowed you," Henley said.

"Not *runnin'* runnin', though. I *ride* from town to town."

"We gonna do this now, or what?" Ben prodded.

"Hold your horses."

"Didn't bring 'em," Ben retorted, sniggering.

"Like workin' with a bunch a kids," said Henley.

"Hey, now!" Deen protested.

"Never mind. Orville and Jed, you go around the back,

keep 'em from slippin' out that way. I'll take the front with Ben."

They checked their pistols—wasted time, since they were always loaded—then split up. Orville and Jed ducked down between two nearer homes and disappeared. Henley and Kyle proceeded down the sidewalk, bold as brass, and turned in at the front gate of the green home's little yard. They left the gate ajar, climbing two steps to mount the porch, and Henley rapped his knuckles on the Butlers' door, no urgency about it, keeping down the noise.

It took a minute, but he heard footsteps approaching from inside. Told Kyle, "Be ready now," and then the door was opening, a young woman confronting them. She was a looker, but suspicion drew her bee-stung lips into a frown.

"What is it, gentlemen?" she asked, sounding uncomfortable with the final word.

"Miz Butler?" Henley countered, flashing her a yellow smile.

"That's right. And you are . . . ?"

"Lookin' for your brother. Got a message for 'im. For the two of you, in fact."

"You'd better leave it with me, then," she said.

"He's not around?"

Suspicion shifted to alarm on the young woman's face. She gripped the door with her right hand, jamb with her left, prepared to slam it. "I expect him shortly. You can wait out there, if you've a mind to, or come back another time."

"Ain't very friendly," Kyle remarked.

"Good day to you," she said. The door began to close.

Henley was quick enough to get his foot in there before she slammed it, sending bright pain shooting from his ankle to his knee. He cursed and shouldered through the door, too strong and heavy for her to resist successfully. Inside, he shoved her back, leaving the round impression of a breast against his palm, while Ben hung back to close and latch the door.

The lady opened up to scream, then saw the pistol he was pointing at her. "If you're gonna squeal," he said, "make it a good'un. It'll be your last."

"Don't hurt me, please," she whined, starting a tingle in his trousers, down below.

No time for that, he thought. "Was that horseshit, about your brother bein' gone?"

She shook her head, afraid to speak.

"And when's he comin' back?"

"I can't be sure." Too late, she understood the risk in what she'd said. A solitary tear spilled down her cheek.

"Take it easy. We ain't here to fiddle with you. Someone wants to see you and your brother, have a word with both a you. If you know where to find him—"

"Sorry. No. He didn't say where he was going when he left."

"Goddamn it, Wayne! We ain't got time—"

"No names, you idjit!" Henley snapped at Kyle. "Shut up and let them others in the back."

"Reckon we'll have to wait a spell," he told the trembling woman. "See if he shows up. Might have to find some way to pass the time."

"Please, no." Barely a whisper.

"Hey, now, I'm just funnin' you. One a these rowdies tries to lay a hand on you while I'm around, I'll chop it off and stuff it where the sun don't shine." Quickly amending it to add, "On him, that is, not you."

"Who is it wants to see us?" she inquired.

"The man in charge," Henley replied. "Tha's all you need to know."

Ryder passed the hours after lunch collecting testimony from assorted residents of Jefferson. On his first pass, he'd noted those who didn't send him packing right away, determined to revisit them when he had time. Most were reluctant to discuss the KRS, but he appealed to them as Christian citizens, worked on their consciences, and took notes once they started talking, slowly, haltingly, until the words began to flow more naturally. Several of the downtown shopkeepers resented being pressured for donations to the Knights, others were simply sick of Coker acting like a tin-pot dictator. Their stories, pieced together, gave Ryder a picture of the way the KRS had grown to dominate the city, with assistance from the sheriff's office.

"Travis is no better than a thug, himself," one merchant said.

"I wouldn't give you two cents for the lot of them," another told him. "But they run the town. What can I do?"

"You ought to try the army," said a third. "Whatever you do, don't trust the law round here."

Ryder thanked each in turn and left them feeling worse than when he'd met them, some of them apparently relieved at having spoken, all now worried that their comments might get back to Coker or the sheriff. Ryder didn't plan on telling either subject of investigation what he'd learned, but in a town like Jefferson, he took for granted that their spies were all around him.

Too bad that people lived in fear of doing the right thing, while criminals lorded it over them and got away with murder. Ryder hoped to change that, but he wasn't giving any kind of odds that he'd succeed. His motivation, now, was split between an urge to help the victims he had met in Jefferson and grim determination that he wouldn't die in Texas.

Thinking he might have set his sights too high.

Before he started looking for a place to eat his supper, Ryder thought he ought to check in on the Butlers. They'd been through a rough couple of days, testing their faith and courage all at once. He wished they'd leave and go back home to safety, but he didn't think that that was in the cards. Abel was more determined than his sister to remain, but Anna talked her way around to seeing his side of an issue, even when they started out in disagreement. Ordinarily, that wouldn't matter much, but in the present circumstances it could get them killed.

Ryder was worried, too, about how Abel might be holding up after two shooting scrapes within as many days. From teaching, preaching, or whatever, he'd become a gunman in his own right, not quite boasting when he told Ryder he'd shot six men during the riot. That was heady stuff to someone uninitiated in the ways of violence. There was no telling whether it would break him down or send him on a path diverging from his southern mission, to a place he didn't want to go.

Same place where I live, Ryder thought, then shrugged it off.

He'd joined the U.S. Marshals Service on a whim, to seek adventure, maybe do some good along the way—and incidentally, to be excused from fighting in the war. He'd managed it all right, shot one man trying to invade the federal courthouse in New York, then plugged another to protect himself while tracking counterfeiters and was fired, when the assailant proved to be a politician's pampered son.

The way things worked in Washington—and everywhere, he guessed, to some extent.

Since switching to the Secret Service, he had done his share of gun work and confirmed it didn't cost him any sleep. He'd had no accidents so far, no wounded innocents. The men he'd shot, whether they lived or died, all had it coming under law. Ryder saw no cause to reproach himself or agonize over split-second choices he had made. But there were times, admittedly, when he wondered if he might be happier if he had picked another path.

Or had the path picked him?

"Shut up," he warned himself and set off toward the Butler place.

A bel Butler's feet were dragging as he turned in through the gate, closed it behind him, and proceeded toward the porch. The Colt felt heavy underneath his belt, more than its usual three pounds or so, as if the men he'd shot with it had somehow left their souls attached to weigh it down.

Stupid, he thought. *That's childish superstition.*

But he couldn't shake the feeling, even so.

His faith was all about the supernatural, things people chose to think and to believe in, even though they'd never see a speck of evidence before they died—and only then, if their selection of a faith had been the right one. What if they were wrong? What if they'd picked an ancient "holy book" that offered only parables and silly superstition?

What if Jews were right, and there was no Hell burning miles below his feet?

Might be a lucky break for me, thought Abel, as he climbed the front porch steps and stood before his own front door.

In Jefferson, they kept the door locked at all times, a simple matter of security. He had a key, but knocked upon returning home, so that he wouldn't startle Anna in the kitchen or the bedroom, entering too quietly. She always met him with a smile, no matter how her day had gone, and they were able to relax—or, at the very least, commiserate.

He knocked this time, waited, and saw her sweet face as the door eased open. No smile there, for once; a teary, worried look, instead, and he was reaching for his pistol when the door flew open wide, revealing two men he had never seen before, standing on either side of Anna, guns in hand. Two more were watching, farther back inside the house, also with pistols drawn.

"We'd like to do this peaceable," the gunman holding Anna's left arm said. "It's your call, either way."

"Who are you?" Abel asked him, tight-lipped from a mix of fear and anger.

"Messengers," the one who'd spoken first replied. "We got a invitation for the two a you."

"An invitation?"

"Step inside first, willya? We don't wanna draw a crowd."

He did as he'd been told and heard the door close at his back. The man to Anna's right reached out to pull the Colt from Abel's belt, saying, "You won't be needin' this."

"Will you be needing yours?" he asked.

"Not right away," the first man said. "Unless you force it on us, bein' stupid. Play your cards right, and you might come out okay."

Abel had no good reason to believe him, every cause to doubt, but there was nothing he could do about it at the moment. He would not risk Anna's life unless he knew their situation to be hopeless beyond any doubt.

"So, what's this invitation?" he inquired.

"Somebody wants to meetcha," said their spokesman. "Somebody important."

"And he couldn't come himself?"

"He's so important, people come to him," the second gunman said.

"Impressive. How is Mr. Coker, by the way?" asked Abel.

Both men flanking Anna blinked at him. The leader of the pack recovered first and cracked a smile. "You ain't as dumb as some folks seem to think."

"Thank you for that. What is it your employer wishes to discuss?"

"We don't get all the tidbits."

"Just the orders, eh? And where should we expect to have this conversation?"

"Where we's headed for, directly."

"And if we prefer to stay at home? What, then?"

"We got instructions to *persuade* you. Maybe startin' with your sis, here. She's a juicy little piece. I guess you noticed that already."

Abel didn't plan to punch him, knew the risks entailed by doing so, but rage took over as the gunman reached across to lay a hand on Anna's breast. The impact of his fist against the gunman's face was satisfying, made up for the sharp pain in his knuckles as he spun to meet the second nearest shooter, swinging this time with his left.

The target ducked it, swung his six-gun in a high arc, grazing Abel's forehead with sufficient force to stagger him. Abel reeled off to his left and met another pistol whipping toward his skull from that direction. This time, colored lights exploded in his brain like fireworks, then the world went black.

He found the front door standing open, didn't like the look of it, and kept his right hand on the cross-draw Colt as he stepped through the gate, moving along the walkway to the Butlers' porch. Before he climbed the steps, Ryder called out to anyone inside the house—a risky move, if enemies were waiting there, but better than surprising Abel, when he might be in a mood to shoot first.

No one answered.

Ryder drew his gun before he reached the open doorway, easier to offer an apology from that point on than risk his life, and felt a little foolish knocking with his free hand as his shadow fell across the threshold. Called their names again, louder this time, and still got no response.

Inside the parlor, he could see the signs of struggle: a small table overturned, a broken lamp soaking the floor with kerosene, which thankfully had not been lighted when it fell. He called once more, a waste of breath, and looked around for bloodstains—found some spatters on the floorboards near the entryway, but nothing serious—before he went to check the other rooms.

Nobody in the kitchen, with its small table and chairs for four. The bedrooms were immaculate, which eased his mind a bit for no specific reason he could name. A broom closet held only brooms and other cleaning articles, no bodies stashed away. He went out back to check the yard, and then the privy, but the flies in there were on their own.

Ryder went back inside the house and had a better look around. Inside the parlor, this time, he saw something sticking out from underneath the sofa. Bending closer, he made out an old Colt Paterson like Abel Butler sometimes carried, evidently dropped and kicked aside during a scuffle. That told Ryder all he had to know about the crime scene.

Abel and his sister had been taken. Whether they were still alive was anybody's guess.

He found the sheriff in his office, working on a sandwich big enough to choke a draft horse. Travis looked up from his food as Ryder entered, mouth full, asking him, "The hell you want?"

"I'm looking for a lawman. Know where I can find one?"

Travis bristled. "If you come here to insult me, you can turn around and—"

"Chew your cud and listen," Ryder snapped at him. "The Butlers have been kidnapped. Will you help me find them? Yes or no?"

"When you say kidnapped—"

"You know what it means. And something tells me you know who's behind it."

"Hey, now!"

"If you do, and something happens to them while you're snuffling at the trough, I'll see you tried as an accomplice."

"That supposed to scare me?" Travis asked him.

"If you're smarter than you look. You know about a murder in advance, being a lawman, and you do nothing to stop it, you're as guilty as the one who pulls the trigger. If it's rape—"

"Whoa, now!" When he spluttered, Travis spat small fragments of his sandwich out onto his desktop. "Who said rape?"

"You trust your cracker buddies to control themselves with Anna Butler?"

"You don't know a damn thing about—"

"What I *do* know, *Sheriff*, is that you're bound by the law to stop a crime from happening, or find the ones responsible if you can't get a jump on things. We both know you've been working with this lynch mob outfit Coker operates. That makes you an accomplice and conspirator. I'll see you charged, tried, and convicted. Failing that—"

"You can't just—"

"Failing that," Ryder repeated, leaning on his hands

across the littered desk, "I'll come back here and do the job myself."

Some of the color drained out of the sheriff's face. "The hell's that s'pose to mean?"

"Use your imagination, Travis."

"Christ! What kind of lawman are you?"

"One with nothing much to lose, if I can't find the Butlers while they're still alive."

Travis dropped his sandwich, spread his hands, a helpless gesture. "Whadda you expect me to do?"

"Your job," Ryder answered.

"That's pleasin' the folks who elect me, not some high-and-mighty federal from Washington."

"And saving lives?"

"The ones that matter."

Ryder felt a sudden chill, as if someone had spiked his veins with ice water. He fought an urge to drill the sheriff where he sat. Said, "Have it your way. Your life just stopped mattering to me."

He left the sheriff's office, Travis staring after him. Ryder supposed that he would run to Coker next, and warn him, but it didn't matter now. He planned to get there first, surprise the man in charge, and squeeze him till he gave the Butlers up.

Failing at that, if they were dead . . . then, what?

He'd have to think that through, decide what he could prove and what he couldn't, if he started filing charges. So far, he had nothing against Coker personally, only supposition that he'd pulled the strings behind various crimes while standing back to keep his own hands clean.

Which didn't mean he was exempt from punishment. Not necessarily.

But Ryder had to find him first.

He walked down to the Red Dog, circled round in back,

and found the back door wasn't locked. Remembering the way to Coker's office, Ryder slipped inside and made his way along a poorly lighted corridor to reach the door marked PRIVATE. He tried the doorknob, gingerly, and felt it start to turn. Dispensed with knocking as he barged in, Colt in hand.

The empty office sneered at him. He checked behind the door, found no one hiding there, and closed it. Ryder moved around the desk, sat down in Coker's chair, and started going through his drawers, no real idea what he was looking for. It didn't bother him, the prying, but as each drawer failed to give up anything of value, he could feel the tension building in his chest, behind his eyes.

Where should he look for Coker next?

He likely wouldn't bring the Butlers here, where anyone might see them and connect Coker to whatever befell them afterward. That would be clumsy, and from what he'd seen of Coker, Ryder didn't think he was a stupid man.

A bigoted fanatic, absolutely. Maybe crazy. Stupid, no.

He ought to check the Red Dog's barroom next. Coker might well be killing time there, waiting for the word from his cronies that Abel Butler and his sister were securely locked away. He wouldn't want to rush off, make a great to-do of it, in case some hostile witness made a mental note. The key was acting normal in the public eye, until you had no further need of guile.

Ryder was on his feet and moving toward the door when it swung open. Standing there in front of him, with a surprised expression on his face, a cowboy type he'd never seen before, revolver dangling from his hip. The stranger blinked at Ryder once, seemed just about to ask him something, but he'd wasted too much time. Ryder reached out to grab the collar of his shirt, propelled him toward the desk, and kicked the door shut as he turned to face the new arrival.

Who was reaching for his six-gun now, too late again. Ryder was faster, pressed the muzzle of his Colt Army against the cowboy's forehead as he thumbed the hammer back.

"Can't miss at this range," he advised.

"Awright! Le's not be hasty, here!"

"You want to live, I take it?"

"S-s-sure!"

"Then, when I ask you something, answer me straight off, and keep it honest. Otherwise, your life's not worth a nickel to me."

"Ask away," the cowboy said.

"Where's Coker?"

"Thought he was in here. He's who I come to see."

"For what?"

"I'm s'pose to tell him how the boys are doin', them got hurt in Colored Town."

"And if he's not here," Ryder prodded, "where would you look next?"

"A couple places." Starting to look crafty.

"Spit it out. You're running short on time."

"Okay! I'd ask the barkeep if he's gone to eat somewhere, then maybe try his house."

Ryder already knew where that was, having made a point to track it down soon after reaching Jefferson. "Where else?" he asked. "I need someplace he'd go to have a private talk with someone, where they won't be interrupted."

"Here," the cowboy said, then winced as Ryder poked his skull more forcefully. "Jesus! I don't know ever'thing about him, mister!"

"Then you're no damned good to me," Ryder replied.

And knocked him cold.

18

★ **B**oss oughta be here any minute now," Wayne Henley said. "He never likes to keep folks waitin'."

"That's considerate," the carpetbagger with the bloodied head replied, "for a kidnapper."

"I'll warn you now. Best watch your mouth when he gets here. The boss ain't got my sense a humor."

Now the woman spoke up, asking him, "Why are you doing this?"

"I told you that awreddy. Boss just wants to have a talk with you. Show you the error of your ways."

"Our ways?" the man came back at him. "Given the choice, you'd still have slavery."

Henley responded with a shrug. "Why not? Jus' think of all the good we done for darkies."

"Good?" The woman wore a shocked expression.

"Sure." He started counting on his fingers. "First, we brung 'em here from Aferca. We gave 'em jobs, good food,

someplace to stay outta the rain when they ain't workin'.
Saved their heathen souls for Jesus, if you're one of them
who thinks they got souls. Me, I ain't so sure."

Now she looked disgusted. "God, I don't believe this."

"That's 'cause you's from way up North. The only darkies
you see are the servants in your houses, all cleaned up and
dressed proper. The only thing you know about our life
down here is lies told by them abolitionists."

"We've seen enough firsthand," her brother said, "to
know that you're barbarians."

"See, that's the kinda thing you shouldn't tell the boss,"
Henley replied, then kicked the smart-mouthed captive in
the stomach, where he sat against the wall. "Could get your
ass in trouble, if you don't watch out."

"You brute!" the woman hissed at him.

"Keep talkin', missy. You ain't winnin' any friends, and
friends is what you gonna need, about the time boss man
gets done with you."

She glared at him but held her tongue this time.

"You know," he told her, smiling, "I can be the friendly
sort, I put my mind to it. I don't ask much, except a little
'preciation."

"You're disgusting!"

"Lotta women think so, when we start to get acquainted,
but they come around."

She turned away from him, cheeks reddening. It made
him smile.

The other carpetbagger didn't like it, though. "If you so
much as touch my sister—"

"What?" Henley demanded. "You gwan jump up here
and whip my ass? Seems like you tried that once already."

"If you're half a man, give me a second chance."

"Half stupid's what you mean to say, I guess. You think

I'm gonna loose your hands before I get the boss's say-so, you're the stupid one."

"What do you hope to gain from this, harming a woman and an unarmed man?"

"Gain ain't got nought to do with it," Henry replied, his temper heating up. "You seen how much we *lost* awready, in the war you goddamn Yankees started. Nothin' any one of us can do to get that back again, until the lot o' you is dead and off our backs!"

"You can't go back in time," the carpetbagger said. "What's gone is gone."

"Like you'll be, in a little while. Not sure about your sister, though. I might just—"

"Might just what?"

The deep, familiar voice made Henley jump. He hadn't heard the door open behind him, raging as he was against the carpetbagger. Now he spun to face the boss.

"It's nothin', Mr. Coker. Just havin' some fun, is all."

"What happened to your face?"

He raised a hand to touch his bruised right cheek, wincing. "They didn't want to come along at first."

"Which one did that to you?"

He blinked at Coker. Said, "The fella."

"Well, that's something, anyway. I see that you repaid him."

"Sure, we got a few licks in."

"And now you're starting on the woman?"

"Huh? Hey, no! I wouldn't—"

"Wayne?"

"Yessir?"

"Get out."

"Um, sure . . . if you don't need—"

"Get out!" Barely a hiss, this time, but carrying the menace of a coiled-up rattler.

"Yessir!"

He wasted no time getting to the door and through it, closing it behind him, careful not to let it slam, in case it sounded like a gesture of defiance. Henley had a sudden need for daylight and fresh air, to calm his churning gut.

Ryder got the Appaloosa back, same daily rate, and pushed it to a gallop on his way out to the Union garrison. Arriving there, he found the soldiers and freedmen working together, setting up tents on a dry patch of ground beside the military bivouac, neither side saying much to the other as Ryder passed by on his way to see Captain Legere.

The captain, as expected, wasn't thrilled to see him for the second time that day. The sigh that he released verged on theatrical. "What is it this time?" he demanded.

Ryder laid the story out as briefly as he could: the Butlers missing, obviously kidnapped from their home, likely snatched by Coker's Knights. The captain didn't yawn, exactly, but he didn't seem impressed, either.

"Likely? That's all you have for evidence?"

"If I knew where they were beyond a doubt, I'd spit it out."

Legere stared off beyond the new addition to his camp, under construction. "Well, it makes no difference, in any case," he said.

"How's that?"

"Kidnapping is a local crime, perhaps a state offense. Who knows, for certain, in this godforsaken territory? Either way, I have no jurisdiction."

"There are lives at stake," Ryder reminded him.

"And constitutional restrictions which you ought to be aware of, as a federal agent. Tell your story to the sheriff."

"He's a part of it!"

Legere turned back to face him, cocked one eyebrow. "Is he, indeed? And how would you know that?"

"Because I've dealt with him. Because he next to told me so."

"Next to? That's pretty flimsy, you'll admit."

"What is it, Captain?" Ryder challenged. "Do you hate this place so much you won't do anything to help its people? Are you worried about drawing notice to yourself? Afraid someone will ship you off to fight the Indians, instead of lounging here in camp?"

Legere's face colored, not from any heating by the sun. "You have the gall to ride in here and ask for help, then to insult me when I tell you it's beyond my legal obligation?"

"Damn your obligation! Get your nose out of the rule book for a minute. Help me save two lives!"

"At the expense of my career?" Legere frowned wearily and shook his head. "This town is volatile. You've seen it for yourself. A spark could set it off. I won't provide that spark by usurping the sheriff's powers, going door to door in search of two lost do-gooders who should have stayed at home."

"You're that determined not to budge? You'd let them die? Likely condemn the woman to a foul indignity before her end?"

"Texans are savages," Legere replied. "I can't fix that with eighty men—or eighty thousand, if it comes to that."

"You're useless," Ryder spat, turning on his heel, toward where his mount was tethered. "Have another cup of tea. I'll deal with it myself."

"I would advise against—"

"To hell with your advice. I'm doing this, and if I light that spark you're so afraid of, you can either put it out or watch it burn."

"Hold up!" Legere called, catching up to him with long, swift strides. Reached out to pluck his sleeve, then yanked his hand away when he saw Ryder's face.

"Don't waste my time, Legere."

"A word on strategy, since you appear to be a novice in the realm of martial law. I am required, under my orders, to provide assistance if the town is seriously threatened. If its normal daily operations are endangered by a lawless element, as in the case of an uprising or rebellion, I would have no choice."

"You missed one yesterday."

"A racial skirmish, nothing more. I need something . . . impressive. Something that would justify my intervention to restore the lawful order."

Ryder thought about that, frowned, and said, "I'll see what I can do."

Y ou've caused us all a world of trouble," Coker told his prisoners.

"What trouble?" Abel Butler asked.

"Meddling where you're not needed, much less wanted. Stirring up the coloreds, filling their woolly heads with impossible dreams."

"I still don't follow you."

Vague sadness settled over Coker. How could anyone be so demented without blatant evidence of injury? "You come down here from . . . where was it? New England?"

"New York," Butler corrected.

"All the same to me. You come to Texas, thinking you can make a herd of animals our *equals*. That we'll stand by idly while you hand them ballots, let them wreck the land and government our fathers fought and died to wrest away from heathen Mexicans and red men? Worse, that we'll allow them to commingle with our daughters? To pollute our bloodlines and destroy the race?"

"We came to build a school, that's all," the woman answered back. "What harm is there in that?"

"What harm?" Coker could only shake his head in wonder. "They were banned from reading under servitude because it stirs them up. They do not have the intellect or the discretion to reject ideas that may be harmful to themselves, or to the civilized society they serve. You've seen them, spoken to them. Do they not strike you as childlike?"

"Not at all," Abel replied. "You and your Knights strike me as brutes and cowards."

"I suppose we do. Up north, you push your coloreds into slums and let them starve or kill each other as they please. We in the South have walked another path, controlling their energy, guiding it into productive channels."

"Productive for *you*," said the woman.

"And what's wrong with that, if it serves them as well? We brought them here from Africa—a haven for disease, devil worship, and cannibalism—to house them here and civilize them at our own expense. You don't think we're owed something in return?"

"What are you owed?" Abel replied. "The bondage of their offspring spanning endless generations?"

Coker tried another angle. "You're an educated man, I gather. Have you studied history?"

"I have."

"Then tell me, what great empires have the colored people founded? What thing have they built, in all of history, that's worth a walk across the street to see? Who are their famous kings, outside of stinking jungle villages? White men are the explorers, settlers, builders, and inventors. How can you not see that?"

"The Chinese—"

"Celestials!" Coker cut him off. "We can't even be sure they're human. Slaves to opium, their nation overrun by Europeans with a mere handful of troops against their tens of thousands."

Abel Butler drew a deep breath, then replied, "I see a race in subjugation, through no doing of its own. The so-called benefits you cite—transportation in chains, infliction of an alien religion—are like brands on livestock, nothing that a human should endure. With help and care, I see them lifted up and educated to a point where they can join society as useful members or, if nothing else, create their own."

"I see that you're beyond redemption," Coker told him, almost sadly. Turning to the woman, he asked, "And do you share these misguided visions?"

"Not misguided," she informed him. "But the answer's yes."

"In that case, I'm afraid there's nothing to be done for you. Before your trial and sentencing, however, you may spare yourself unnecessary suffering by answering some questions that I have in mind."

"Questions?" Fear mixed with anger in the frown on Abel's face.

"I need more information on the group that sent you here, its aims and tactics, what it hopes to gain by agitating southern blacks to rise against their betters."

"We've been over that," Abel replied. "There's no conspiracy. Just Christian love."

"You choose the hard way, then. I'll make the

preparations," Coker told them. "If you truly recognize a god of any kind, this is your time to pray."

Back in town, Ryder returned the Appaloosa to the livery and asked its owner what provisions were in place to save the horses, in the case of an emergency.

"Emergency?" The hostler didn't seem to follow.

"Like a fire, flood, or tornado," he elaborated.

"Well, if time allows, I'd get 'em out, o' course. Got a corral out back to stop 'em scatterin' if somethin' happens to the barn, like fire. A flood or storm, now, that's another story. Bein' penned up wouldn't help 'em none, I guess."

Ryder stroked the Appaloosa's withers, saying, "But you wouldn't just run off and leave them here?"

The hostler wore a shocked expression on his face, maybe insulted. "Hell, no! They're my business, Mister. Some of 'em are more like friends, you know."

"I'm glad to hear it."

Ryder left him frowning, wondering, and took the Henry rifle with him as he left. He had no one to back whatever play he made, and time was running out on any hope of rescuing the Butlers. Ryder told himself there had to be a reason they were snatched alive, or else he would have found their bodies at the house. He didn't know the reason, couldn't work it out, and had decided it was best to give up trying.

He would focus on retrieving them, and let the *why* of it come afterward.

Coker's people might be looking for him after his intrusion at the Red Dog. Ryder didn't know the gunman who'd surprised him in the office, hadn't left his name, but once the shooter came around he could describe the man who'd slugged him. Coker wouldn't have a lot of trouble putting it together, and he'd have his people mobilized as soon as he worked out that he was being hunted.

So, how many men?

He didn't want to think about that, at the moment. Finding Coker was his first priority, on two accounts: to stop him doing any further damage to the Butlers, if it wasn't already too late for them, and to take Coker out of action as the brains and guiding hand behind the KRS. Removing one man likely wouldn't end the group, but Coker would be looking at a prison term for kidnapping—maybe a rope for murder, if he'd killed his hostages and Ryder got the evidence to prove it. Either way, he might prefer to bargain for a lighter sentence, giving up the men who'd killed or committed other crimes on his behalf.

A long shot? Probably. And Ryder had to be alive to make it work.

He passed by Coker's house, a waste of time, but making sure he'd covered all his options, just in case. Two kids were playing in the yard, a handsome woman hanging laundry on the line, a nice domestic scene. No common passerby would guess the master of the house was off somewhere, devising plans for murder and rebellion in the name of white supremacy.

He could have turned in at the gate, asked Mrs. Coker if she knew where he could find her husband, but the prospect set his teeth on edge. The lady must have known her husband's business, since he practiced most of it in public, and she likely sympathized with his ideas about the races. On the other hand, he questioned whether Coker would have filled her in on plans for a specific crime in progress.

No. He'd have to find his man some other way. Which meant grabbing another member of the KRS and squeezing him, hoping he knew where Coker and the Butlers were . . .

or causing a distraction that would bring the "grand commander" out in search of him.

Tricky, but Ryder had a couple of ideas.

Coker was getting down to business—tools laid out, his workmen at the ready, looking forward to it—when the sheriff interrupted him. One of his Knights came knocking first and told him Travis was outside, needing to speak with Coker in a rush. Already in a sour mood, he scowled and went to find out what the lawman wanted.

Travis had a nervous look about him, edgy, pacing like a caged coyote. Coker took his cue from that, turned off the scowl, and tried to keep his tone flat as he spoke.

"Sheriff, some kind of an emergency? I'm rather busy at the moment an—"

"That's why I'm here."

Coker couldn't recall the last time Travis interrupted him. In fact, he never had, before.

"Explain."

"Them carpetbaggers."

"What about them?"

"Ryder's lookin' for 'em."

"Is he, now?"

"Came by my office, talkin' about my duty to the law, some kinda bull. Was askin' me to help him look for 'em."

"And what did you say?"

"Put 'im off. Told 'im I wasn't buyin' into it."

"And then?"

"The sumbitch threatened me. Can you believe it? Said that if he couldn't make it stick in court, he'd do the job hisself. Came out and said it just like that."

"He is audacious," Coker said. And smiled.

"Did I say something funny?"

"No. But you present me with an opportunity."

"How's that?" The sheriff looked confused now, piling that on top of worried.

"Think about it, Harlan. What if you should change your mind?"

"On what?"

"Cooperating with our nemesis."

"I don't get that."

"The Yankee agent."

"What about him?"

Christ all Friday, he was thick. Sometimes Coker despaired of working with the meager tools he had been given.

"Think about it," he suggested. "Ryder comes to you for help. You turn him down."

"Tha's right. I did."

"Talking's not thinking, Harlan."

"Right. Okay, then."

"So, you turned him down, but now you've had a chance to think about it and you've seen the light."

"What light is that?"

"Your duty, as you mentioned. You've decided you should help him, after all. It's preying on your conscience."

"Is it?"

"You're still talking."

"Sorry."

"So, you find him and explain that you've decided to cooperate. In fact, you know exactly where the carpetbaggers are, and you can show him."

This time, Travis raised his hand instead of speaking, like an oaf held back in school so long he's older than the teacher.

"What?"

"He's gonna figger that's a trick, ain't he?"

"Unless he's dumber than a cactus."

"Well, then—"

"But I think he'll go along with you, regardless."

"Why?"

"Because he needs a pointer to the carpetbaggers."

"Yeah, but if he knows I'm lyin' to him—"

"You are still his best hope."

"I don't get it."

"*Think*, Harlan. If he believes you're helping him, he'll go along with you. If he suspects you're tricking him, he'll still think you know where to find the Butlers."

"Yeah, but—"

"There's a certain risk involved, I grant you. Ryder may not be inclined to ask you gently. If he starts in acting rough—"

"I take him?"

Coker had to smile at that, asking the sheriff, "Does that seem a likely outcome?"

"Well . . ."

"Let's try it my way, shall we?"

"Okay. Sure."

"If you come under pressure, make a show of stalling him, then let him see he's broken you. Tell him you know where he can find the carpetbaggers. Beg him not to make you go along."

"You think he'll fall for that?"

"Of course not. He'll insist you lead the way, which you, reluctantly, will do."

"I will?"

"And bring him to the spot where I have men await-ing him."

"The trap."

"You see? It's not so hard to figure out."

"Uh-huh. So what stops him from figgerin' it out?"

"Nothing. He'll come expecting trouble, but he'll find a good deal more than he can handle."

"Right. With me smack in the middle of it."

"Where, I'm sure, you'll give your all to help the cause."

"My all?"

"It means to do your level best."

"Oh. Right." If he was reassured, it didn't show. "So, where'm I leading him again?"

"Now that's the beauty of it," Coker said, smiling again. "Right here."

19

★ **R**yder saw the sheriff coming from two blocks away, hurrying north along Camp Street. Travis had a flustered look about him, redder in the face than usual, as if he'd lost something and was afraid he wouldn't find it. When he spotted Ryder, headed south, he hesitated for a second, then veered off to cross the street.

"Looks like you're hunting," Travis said, and nodded at the Henry Ryder carried in his left hand.

"You want something, Travis?"

"Yeah, I do. Been thinkin' 'bout our talk, a while back."

"And?"

The sheriff looked both ways along the sidewalk, heaved a sigh, and said, "It sunk in you were makin' sense. This thing with Coker's gotten outta hand. You still want help, I'm with you."

"Meaning what, exactly?"

Travis dropped his voice an octave, even though there

wasn't anyone within a block who could have eavesdropped on them. "Think I got an idea where he's put them carpet-baggers you been lookin' for."

Alarm bells started going off in Ryder's head. He kept his face deadpan and answered, "Oh?"

The sheriff nodded, just a bit too eagerly. "He's got a place downtown, on Walcott Street. Keeps some of his supplies there, for the Red Dog, if they won't fit into the saloon."

"So, something like a warehouse?"

"Not that big. There's a shop in front, dry goods. He owns that, too, and stores the other stuff in back, or else upstairs."

"Why would he take the Butlers there?"

"It's got a basement. Nice and private, if you get my drift."

"I get it," Ryder told him. And he wasn't buying any of it. "Will you show me where it is?"

"Be happy to. Can't promise they'll be there, but if they are, I'll help you get 'em out."

"No worries about disappointing Coker?"

"Comes a time, man has to do what's right or just give up."

"All right. Welcome aboard. You lead the way."

The hike from Camp Street north and west to Walcott was a winding journey, fourteen blocks by Ryder's count, watching for ambushes along the way. He didn't know if Travis had described an actual establishment or not, but he was reasonably certain that the sheriff's offer was a trick. He felt insulted in a way, that anyone would think him dumb enough to fall for it.

Ten minutes after starting out, the sheriff stopped and said, "We're almost there. Cut down this alley, here, and then another half block west'll take us to the back door."

"Anything you want to tell me now?" Ryder inquired. "Before we're in the middle of it?"

"I don't follow you."

"That's right. You've had *me* follow *you*. Knowing the

way you hate me, hate all Yankees, I'm not buying your repentant act."

"Reckon I'd try'n scoop you into trouble?"

"That's exactly what I think."

"Well, I can't help that. If you wanna help them others—"

Ryder raised his Henry, shoved its muzzle deep into the sheriff's gut, making him wince. "First thing, I'll have your pistol. Any fancy moves, I'll let the daylight through you."

Travis pulled his iron, a Colt Model 1861 Navy revolver, and handed it over. Ryder took it with his left hand, reached around, and tucked it underneath his belt in back. "That satisfy you?" he inquired.

"Not yet. You have a pocket pistol stashed away some- where? Maybe a derringer? Some kind of knife?"

"The Colt is all I carry. Never used it on a man."

"Just kids and women?"

Travis clenched his teeth. Said, "I know what you think a me an' every other southern man. The hell do you know about how we live or feel?"

"I know enough to tell you I don't give a damn. Next thing you want to do is tell me straight whether this place you're taking me is real or not."

"It's real, all right."

He didn't bother asking whether there would be a trap in place. That part was obvious. "Okay, then. Let's get to it. Anything goes wrong, you'll be the first to drop."

Does everybody understand the plan?"

Sly faces nodded at him.

"All right, repeat it for me," Coker said. He picked out one of them and pointed at him. "You."

Wayne Henley answered back, "The sheriff brings 'im

in. We're waitin' for 'em, but we don't do nothin' till you give the signal."

"Which is?" Coker prodded him.

"A whistle." Henley frowned. "I 'member it. Can't imitate it, though."

"You won't have to. Go on."

"We hear the whistle, ever'body draws down on the Yank."

"Remembering that . . . ?"

"You want him alive. If possible."

"That's right. If he starts shooting, which he may, try winging him. Arms, legs, something to slow him down and let us get the drop on him. I want to have a talk with him before he dies."

"An' what about the sheriff?" Orville Deen inquired.

"It would be helpful if he lived," Coker replied, "but it is not obligatory."

"Huh?"

"Means we can beef 'im if we have to," Ben Kyle clarified.

"If absolutely necessary," Coker said and realized the prospect did not faze him, either way. Travis was shaky, growing weaker by the day. If he could be disposed of, and his death attributed to Ryder, it would be a double benefit.

A silent moment passed before he said, "All clear, then?" and received another round of nods. "Go on and take your places. They should be here soon."

If Travis found the Yank, that was. Coker was never sure how much of any order Travis really understood or paid attention to. He'd been a fair choice as the county's sheriff, and the only competition for that job had been a unionist who cast his vote against secession, back in February '61. Between the two, there'd been no choice at all.

Coker took a moment to examine his LeMat revolver, even though he knew the gun was fully loaded. Better safe than sorry, when his life was riding on the line, along with everything he'd worked for up to now. The plan he had in mind wasn't ideal, by any means, but since his side had lost the war, it was the next best thing to victory in battle.

If his plan worked out, it meant more damage to his people at the outset. Some of them would likely die or lose their homes, but in the end, if he was resolute and led them well, the rest would benefit. Texans had beaten Mexico, not thirty years ago, when they had been outnumbered ten to one or more. Their problem in the last war had been putting too much trust in leaders from Virginia, Alabama, and the Carolinas, none of whom had kept his state's best interests in mind.

But this time, when his people rose in righteous outrage, Coker knew that it would be a marvel to behold.

They skipped the rear approach and passed the street side of the building, Ryder peering through the shop's display window to verify that is was closed, no customers still lingering who might be in the line of fire. From there, it was a short walk through an alley, two doors down, to reach the back door unobserved.

"No second thoughts?" he asked the sheriff. "Anything you want to say before we go in here?"

The bleak-faced lawman said, "I've told you all I know. You're gonna do whatever suits you, either way."

"Correction, Sheriff. You'll be doing it. The first man through that door, and first one down if somebody starts shooting. You can still fess up. If Coker doesn't have the Butlers here—"

"He does. At least, he *did*, last time I talked to him."

"And when was that?"

"'Bout half an hour 'fore I found you on the street."

"You saw them?"

"Nope. No reason why he'd lie to me about it, though, is there?"

"Maybe, if he thought it would improve your acting."

Travis frowned at that, considered it, then shook his head. "Uh-uh. He didn't like me poppin' in on him, like it was keepin' him from somethin' else. I figgered he was workin' on your friends."

"Nothing that bothered you about that?" Ryder challenged him. "I mean, since you pretend to be the law?"

"The only law we got in Texas now is what the Yanks tell us to do. Try livin' with your world turned upside down, see how you like it."

"Race is that important to you?"

"What else is there?" Travis countered.

"Did you ever own a slave, before the war?"

"Couldn't afford none. Didn't have no land, neither."

"But you're still working for the rich men. They still pull your strings."

"No poor man ever paid my salary."

"Which lets them tell you what to think."

"I *think*, okay? I know my place. If I ain't better'n a nigger, then what am I?"

Ryder dropped the hopeless line of argument. Some people were too stupid to be helped. Instead, he asked, "What's next? Are you supposed to knock? Give out some kind of signal?"

"Just walk in," said Travis. "After that . . ." He let it trail away and shrugged.

"They know you're coming with me?"

"How'n hell do I know? I can't even tell you who all's in there."

"You're about to find out," Ryder cautioned him.

"Still don't know what you need me for."

"Coker used you for bait, Sheriff. In fishing, bait gets eaten."

"You're supposed to be a lawman, too, ain'tcha?"

"I'm playing by your rules. They don't seem fair to you, you should've thought about it earlier."

Travis stood at the door, his shoulders slumping more than usual. He reached out for the doorknob, wrapped his hand around it, then turned back toward Ryder.

"Whatever we find in there, I had nothin' to do with hurtin' either one of 'em."

"You didn't stop it," Ryder said. "You swore an oath and broke it. You're as guilty as the rest of them."

Instead of arguing the point, Travis turned back to face the door. The knob, unlocked, turned in his hand. He pushed it open on to darkness and went in.

I t's been a long time since he left," said Anna. "Do you think he's gone?"

"I doubt it," Abel answered. "And it hasn't been that long."

"Are you having any luck?"

"Not yet."

Since Coker left, the two of them had worked on loosening the rawhide thongs that bound their wrists. Anna could feel the leather chafing at her skin, abrading it, and wondered whether she was bleeding yet. She didn't think so, but her hands were nearly numb, her wrists too sore to know for sure.

"You don't think . . . maybe . . . Gideon?" She was unable to articulate her hope, knowing it sounded desperate.

"Don't count on it," her brother said. "Don't count on him."

"He's helped us both. He's helped you *twice*."

"Because it fit in with the job he's doing. Don't set too much store by him."

"I'm not." And yet, her cheeks were flaming.

"I'm just saying—"

"Ssshhh! Somebody's coming!"

It was Coker, stepping through the door with a revolver in his hand. At first, Anna imagined he had come to kill them, contradicting what he'd said before about requiring information. But he kept the weapon's muzzle pointed toward the floor, regarding them with an expression close to curiosity.

"We are expecting visitors," he said. "A visitor at least. A friend of yours, I think."

Anna could feel her pulse quicken. *Ryder!* She tried to keep her face blank, give nothing away.

"No 'hallelujah'?" Coker asked. "Not even smiles?"

"We don't know who or what you mean," Abel replied.

"Don't you? Ah, well, perhaps not. You will have a chance to meet him, though. Or, at the very least, to view his corpse."

A sob caught in her throat on hearing that, but Anna tried to swallow it. She couldn't tell if Coker noticed, since he seemed distracted.

"As it turns out," he went on, "this should work perfectly. Killing the pair of you, no matter what the means, might not arouse our heroes at the garrison. A Secret Service agent, on the other hand . . . well, that should send a ripple all the way to Washington."

"You're not making sense," Abel told him.

"Oh, no? What do you think will happen when the blue-bellies are ordered to retaliate for Agent Ryder's death? Do you believe their captain will be able to control them? Think about the black troops, in particular. I personally think they will behave exactly like the savages they are."

"You have some gall!" Anna replied. "There's nothing in the world more savage than a lynch mob."

"That depends upon the cause, wouldn't you say? Threats

to a decent woman's honor, or her very life, bring out the rage in white men, I'll admit. They rise to the occasion in defense of hearth and home. In fact, I'm counting on it."

"So, you're what? Expecting a rebellion here, against the Union?" Abel asked him. "I'd have thought you would have learned your lesson from the war."

"Oh, yes, I learned a lesson," Coker said. "This time, I won't be trusting any outsiders, whether they come from North or South. A new Texas Republic's what we need, and we shall have it. Mark my words!"

With that, he turned and left, slamming the door behind him. Anna listened to his footsteps fading in the corridor outside, then said, "He's lost his mind."

"All the more reason to get out of here," her brother said, "if we can find a way."

Harlan Travis had started to tremble and hoped that the Yank with the gun at his back couldn't see it. Ashamed of himself for his fear, he still couldn't control it. Worse yet was the thought that Roy Coker had meant this to happen, had used him as bait, and would not miss him much if he died.

"You know—" he said, then swallowed it when Ryder poked him with the Henry's muzzle from behind.

"No talking!" Ryder hissed.

Against his better judgment, Travis stopped and turned to face his captor, stopping when he'd made three-quarters of the turn and found the rifle jammed beneath his flabby jawline, hurting him.

"You tired of living, Sheriff?"

Whispering, he told the Yankee, "Listen! Kill me if you wanna, but you need to know I wasn't in on Coker snatchin' them two what you're lookin' for."

"So what? You covered for him."

Travis nodded, best he could, the Henry gouging him. "Tha's true enough."

"I'm not your priest, and this is no time for confession."

"I can help you, though."

"You're helping now. Shut up and move."

"I likely know the boys he's got here, waitin' for you. I can try'n talk 'em out of it."

"Are you their boss, or Coker?"

"He is. But I'm still the law in Jefferson."

The smile that Ryder gave him back was harrowing. "All right," he said. "Go on, then."

"Gimme back my gun?"

"How stupid do you think I am?"

Travis managed a shrug without shuddering. "Okay, then. But if they start shootin'—"

"At *the law*?" said Ryder, mocking him.

"Awright, then. Have it your way."

Travis turned back to the hallway, doors shut tight on either side. Ahead of him, if he kept going straight, he'd wind up in the dry-goods store and visible to anybody passing on the street outside. The hostages weren't there, as he'd already seen. That left the basement or the second floor, both served by stairs located thirty feet or so in front of him. One flight, serving the upper story, was located to his left and quickly accessed from the shop. The other, going down, was hidden by the third door on his right.

"Hey, boys!" he called out in a shaky voice. "It's me, the sheriff! Listen up! There's been a change of plans."

No answer from the silent floor above him, though he thought he heard a floorboard creak up there. Somebody moving, or the building's normal settling noise?

"This thing has gone too far," he told the silence. "We're

just buyin' trouble that we can't afford. I'm takin' the two carpetbaggers outta here, and you'd be wise to stand aside."

He'd reached the point where it was time to make a choice. Stairs to his left, door to his right that opened on the basement. Even guessing where the captives were, he couldn't leave Roy's shooters at his back. He had to calm them first, persuade them to forget their orders and cooperate.

Travis turned left, to face the stairs, and peered up into murky shadows on the second floor. "I know you're up there," he advised. "You best come down now, with your hands where I can see 'em."

"Go to hell," a gruff voice answered from above. He saw a shadow shift up there, and then a blinding muzzle flash, before a storm of buckshot ripped into his chest.

The sheriff died with a surprised expression on his face. Instead of rushing to him, Ryder waited, standing well back from the staircase, Henry at his shoulder and his index finger on its trigger. Overhead, a muffled conversation reached his ears.

"You get him?"

"Hell, yeah."

"What about the Yank?"

"Don't see nobody else."

"Well, get down there and look!"

"Why me?"

"'Cause I said so!"

Chain of command, thought Ryder. It might work to his advantage, yet.

He stood and listened, heard footsteps slowly descending toward the ground floor. That would be the fellow with the shotgun, one barrel still primed and ready to release a spray of lead. Fair fighting didn't enter into it from this point on. His focus was survival and attempting to retrieve the Butlers from captivity.

A pair of boots came into view, their owner edging down the stairs until his legs and rump were visible, and then the rest of him. He held the sawed-off shotgun at his waist, still pointed toward the sheriff's ventilated corpse. When Ryder shot him in the back, his finger clenched around the weapon's second trigger and another blast of buckshot ripped into the lawman, who was long past feeling it.

The shooter toppled forward, plunging headfirst down the staircase. When he hit, his neck snapped. It would be a toss-up whether Ryder or the fall had killed him, and it didn't matter, either way.

One down. How many left to go?

A voice called down from overhead. "Orville? You hear me?"

"No more Orville," Ryder answered back.

"Goddamn you!"

"If you want what he got, come ahead."

"Don't think we won't," the angry voice replied, but no one started down the stairs.

"I haven't got all night," Ryder advised his unseen enemy. "I need to grab your boss before he slips away and leaves you with the short end of the stick. Time now for you to make a choice."

"What choice is that?"

"Whether you want to live or die."

"Big talk for one man on his own!"

A lamp hung from the wall beside him, giving Ryder an idea. "Throw down your guns right now, and come down showing empty hands, I'll let you walk away. You want to fight, I'll burn the place and leave you to it. See if you get roasted."

"I believe you're bluffing," came the answer, but the speaker didn't sound convinced.

"So, call me on it."

Raspy whispering upstairs, and then the same voice said, "Awright, we's comin' down."

"Guns first!"

"Yeah, yeah."

A pistol sailed through space and clattered near the bodies huddled at the bottom of the staircase. It was followed by two more, one striking Travis in his lifeless upturned face and gouging flesh.

"That's all of 'em," the mouthpiece said. "Don't shoot, now. We's unarmed."

Ryder stayed silent, rifle angled toward the stairs, and waited. Three men were descending, single file, hands down against their sides and hidden from him. When they'd nearly reached the bottom, they began to turn, half-hidden weapons rising, swinging in his general direction.

Ryder shot them each in turn, one round each from the Henry, rapid-firing with no need to aim at such close range. They fell together, dead or dying, in a heap beside their fallen friend and Harlan Travis, leaking blood and bile into the floorboards there.

He listened for a while, heard nothing more upstairs, and struck a match to light the hanging lamp before he took it down. Another moment, and he had the basement access door standing ajar, shouting downstairs.

"Anna? Abel?"

A muted sound came back to him, muffled by walls and doors.

Unhappy with his options, Ryder started down into the dark.

20

★ **H**e found the Butlers in a dirt-floored room, behind a padlocked door. The lock was cheap and shattered at the first shot from his Henry rifle, loud in Ryder's ears below ground, with the whole weight of the world on top of them.

They sat together, up against a wall, hands tied behind their backs with rawhide thongs. Ryder unsheathed his Bowie, cut them free, helped Anna to her feet while Abel got up on his own. He noticed Abel wince a little, pressing one hand to his ribs.

"Are you all right?"

"I will be," Abel answered, "once we're out of here and far away from Jefferson."

"Get moving, then," Ryder advised. "You think it's safe to stop at home and pack your things?"

"Should be," said Abel. "Coker's people won't expect us there."

"A few more minutes, and they won't expect you anywhere."

"What's that mean?" Anna asked him.

"Never mind. Go on, now. And at least consider going home. I mean your *real* home."

"Thank you," Abel said, shaking his hand, then starting for the stairs. "Anna?"

"A minute." She stepped close to Ryder, one hand on his arm. "Won't you come with us?"

"Sorry," he replied. "I still have work to do."

"Can't you just leave it?"

"That's not how it goes."

She rose on tiptoes, startled Ryder with a warm kiss on the lips, then turned and fled, trailing her brother up the stairs and out of sight. He gave them a head start, then followed, pausing on the ground floor near the heap of corpses. There, he pitched his lantern at the nearest wall and watched it shatter, streams of flaming kerosene igniting wallpaper, woodwork, the stairway's narrow strip of carpeting.

How long before the whole place was ablaze, flames threatening its neighbors? It was built of wood, dried out by Texas heat and a relentless sun. The walls and floors were little more than tinder, ripe for burning. If a breeze came up, he thought the fire might spread to take out half the street and make a nice distraction for him as he went about his business.

Hunting Coker.

Where to find him? On reflection, as he cleared the back door, trailing smoke, Ryder decided that his best bets were at home or at the Red Dog. Of the two, he figured the saloon would be his better choice. Coker would want a crowd around him when the killing happened, witnesses to prove he didn't have a hand in it, Knights to help him if the play went wrong. He might have money at the Red Dog, too, in case it seemed advisable to run.

The Butlers were long gone and out of sight when Ryder reached the street. He wished them well, the taste of Anna's kiss still lingering, and knew it was unlikely he'd see either one of them again. There'd been a moment, maybe more, when he'd connected with the woman, but it wasn't meant to last. She didn't fit his life, and Ryder knew he was a rotten fit for hers.

Too bad.

He put her sweet face and aroma out of mind and focused on the job at hand. The Red Dog, four blocks east and one block north, should have a decent early evening crowd of customers. He couldn't guess how many of them would be Coker's Knights, or simply innocents who didn't know they'd come to do their drinking on a battlefield.

Was *anybody* innocent in Jefferson, tonight?

Ryder reloaded as he walked, until the Henry's magazine was full once more, a cartridge in its chamber. With his pistol and the sheriff's, still tucked through his belt in back, he was as ready as he'd ever be to face a private army.

For the hell of it, he hummed "The Battle Hymn of the Republic" as he passed on through the dusk.

Roy Coker tossed a second shot of whiskey down and felt it sear his gullet on its way to calm his nervous stomach. It was disconcerting to be in the midst of friends, admirers, and to wonder if his plan might be unraveling beyond repair.

He trusted Henley and the others well enough to leave them on their own, let them dispose of Ryder for him, but he thought one of them should have come to fetch him back by this time. If they'd finished with the Secret Service agent, what was the delay? They didn't have to bury him straight off, just tuck him in a corner somewhere, then tell Coker it was safe for him to come back and interrogate the Yankee prisoners.

Simple.

Except they weren't here yet, and he was getting antsy, his imagination painting pictures that disturbed him. One more drink, and then he'd walk back to the dry-goods shop. Find out what the delay was and correct it.

"Another," Coker told the barkeep, smiling as three fingers of the amber fluid filled his glass. He lifted it, had almost pressed the rim against his lips, when someone barged in through the bat-wing doors and bellowed, *"Fire!"*

"Where at?" somebody asked the new arrival.

"Felcher's dry goods," came the answer. "Goin' up like Hell!"

The barroom emptied in a rush, civilians and Knights alike racing to catch the show, and maybe see if they could lend a hand in putting out the fire. His watchdog for this evening, Jeremiah Campbell, stayed at Coker's side and asked him, "Do you want to see it?"

"No. Those numbskulls couldn't do a simple job, we'll leave them to it. Flee or fry, I never want to see the four of them again."

"No problem. What about the Yankees?"

"Two of them are likely cooked by now. The other . . . let's just wait and see."

"What if he ain't, Boss?"

"Then we'll run him down and finish it. He's just one man, an outsider at that."

Coker drained his whiskey glass, then let his hand drop to the butt of his LeMat revolver with its metal lanyard ring. He hadn't shot a man since late November 1864 but felt the itch now, in his gun hand, agitated by a churning in his gut.

If Ryder had survived the trap, it meant he'd dealt with Henley's crew and Travis. Maybe he'd be wounded, even dying. Coker wouldn't know until he saw the Yank, and maybe had a chance to speak with him.

On second thought, forget that. There would be no talking, if and when they met again. Just gun smoke and a bloody end for one of them.

"You okay, Boss?" asked Campbell.

"Fine," Coker said. Thinking, *Come on. Let's get it over with.*

R yder watched from an alley as the crowd of Red Dog customers went streaming past him, toward the fire. Their voices jumbled all together, nothing he could make sense of in passing, even if he'd cared to try. He scanned the faces, didn't see Roy Coker's, and proceeded on toward the saloon as soon as they were gone.

Another problem when he reached it: how should he go in?

A quick peek through the street-side window showed him Coker and another fellow at the bar, glasses in front of them, both armed with six-guns. Add the bartender, who likely had a shotgun stashed away somewhere, and that made three. He didn't want to shoot an honest workingman, but that would be the barkeep's choice, if he sided with Coker in the fight.

It never crossed his mind that Coker would surrender voluntarily. It wasn't in him to admit that he was beaten, grant that he had failed. If Appomattox hadn't taken the starch out of him, he wouldn't back down now.

Given the atmosphere he'd found in Texas, and the odds against a jury of his Rebel peers convicting Coker, Ryder counted on a fight to settle things once and for all.

Whichever way it went.

He stood outside the Red Dog, breathing in the night, caught a tang of wood smoke on the breeze. More people shouting, back in the direction he had come from, and a bell was clamoring as someone tried to raise the fire brigade. He thought about the Butlers, wondered if they'd made it safely home or even tried, and knew their fate no longer rested in his hands. He'd done his bit and given them his best advice. Whatever choice they made, it would be their responsibility alone.

His job was here, a few yards distant, in the barroom.

Front or rear?

Without another thought, he shoved in through the swinging doors, rifle at his shoulder, with its barrel aimed midway between Roy Coker and his friend. They turned to face him, almost moving in slow motion, while the barkeep froze, a wiping rag in one hand and the other out of sight.

"I thought you might be joining us," said Coker. "Where's the sheriff?"

"One of your men killed him. Add it to your bill."

"What bill is that, if you don't mind me asking?"

"Murder and attempted murder, kidnapping, inciting riots."

"Quite a list. Even if true, however, those are state offenses. Where's your jurisdiction?"

"I was just about to say rebellion against these United States."

"Indeed? You make me sound ambitious."

"That, or crazy."

Coker's face grew dark at that. "If you're correct, it's never wise to prod a crazy man."

"I'll take my chances."

"Fair enough."

Both of them drew at once, Coker's companion being quicker, and the barkeep ducked to grab his twelve-gauge from a shelf behind the bar. Ryder triggered a shot and knew he'd missed all three, before he dived headlong below the nearest poker table, tipping it to cover him.

Which, as it turned out, didn't offer much in way of cover after all. The first shots from his enemies punched through the table, drilling tidy holes, but they were several inches high and only stung Ryder with splinters as they passed.

Too close for comfort, still.

Instead of giving Coker and his friends time to correct their aim, he rolled clear of the table, Henry rifle angled toward the bar, and triggered two quick rounds without much hope of hitting anyone. As luck would have it, though, his second round cut through the thigh of Coker's sidekick, spraying blood across the bar's wood paneling in front, above the brass foot rail. The man went down, howling, but still managed another pistol shot before his backside hit the floor.

Another miss.

Coker fired again, and now the bartender had found his shotgun, swinging it around toward Ryder with a pinched expression on his face, clearly unhappy to be there. His happiness went down another notch as Ryder shot him through the chest and slammed him back into the shelves of liquor bottles. Falling with a cry of pain, the barkeep fired both barrels of his weapon simultaneously, pointed toward the ceiling and the cribs upstairs. The buckshot blew a ragged hole some two feet square and loosed a rain of dust atop the dying shooter.

Coker's pistol gave a hollow boom, like something in its mechanism had exploded, maybe ripping off his fingers, but the sting of birdshot at his side explained the noise to Ryder as he gasped and staggered. A LeMat, damn it, and he'd be lining up another shot—a solid slug this time—while Ryder tried to get his balance back. The only answer to it he could manage was a quick shot on the fly, wasting the fifth round from his Henry, but at least it spoiled his adversary's aim as Ryder dropped into an awkward crouch.

Meanwhile, the leg-shot gunman had recovered well enough to try again. He had his Colt lined up on Ryder, more or less, when Ryder grazed him on the run, a headshot gone astray to clip the lobe from his left ear. More blood splashed on the bar, another cry of pain, and when the Colt fired, it was high and wide.

Pumping his rifle's lever action, Ryder fired again at Coker, missed, then swung back toward the other shooter, slumped against the bar, down on one elbow now, his six-gun wavering in front of him. They fired together, Ryder's .44 slug drilling home beneath the shooter's chin, while Ryder felt another razor line of fire lancing across his wounded side.

Instead of running now, Coker was moving toward him, shouting angry words that didn't register with Ryder's ringing ears. His chunky-looking pistol blazed and missed again, despite the narrowed range, its aim betrayed by Coker's rage.

One chance, thought Ryder, as he aimed his Henry through the gun smoke, squeezed the trigger, and saw Coker lurch backward, falling with arms outflung, a splash of scarlet on his white shirt, swiftly darkening. He hit the floor, heels drumming for a moment, then lay still.

Ryder rose slowly, painfully, and started for the exit, wanting to be gone before more Knights returned to tell their leader what was happening downtown. Outside, he left the smell of gun smoke and exchanged it for a pall of drifting wood smoke, wafted on the wind blowing in his direction from the dry-goods store.

The town was burning. Not a lot of it, so far, but he could see flames leaping over nearby rooftops, work enough to keep the fire brigade and any volunteers engaged for hours yet, he guessed. They'd likely save most of the downtown district, but with blackened scars to tell the tale.

Ryder considered what to do next. He was wounded, bleeding, though he sensed his injuries were not life threatening. He hadn't met a doctor yet, in Jefferson, and didn't fancy wandering the streets until he found one's shingle hanging from a doorpost. Even then, he might pick out a sawbones who was friendly with the KRS, if not a member in his own right.

He was angling toward the Bachmann House when someone spoke up from a darkened alley to his left, saying, "You're hurt."

It was a woman's voice, but Ryder swung his rifle that direction anyway. Tonight, unless he knew who he was dealing with, the rule was caution first, last, always.

"Who's there?" he challenged.

From the darkness stepped the Butlers, Anna letting go of Abel's arm to close on Ryder, while he let the Henry's muzzle drop.

"We couldn't just pack up," her brother said. "Well, Anna couldn't. We came looking for you. Heard the shooting."

She was pulling back the left side of his jacket now, saying, "Is this . . . ? My God, you're shot!"

"Birdshot," Ryder replied. "It shouldn't be too deep. The other is a pistol graze. It looks worse than it is."

And *felt* worse, too.

"Come back to our house," Anna said. "We'll clean this up and bandage you."

"It's best," Abel agreed. "In case the sheriff's looking for you, or the Knights."

"The sheriff's dead," Ryder informed them. "Back where Coker had you caged. You likely missed him in the body pile as you were leaving."

"Still, the Knights—"

"Don't know me, without Coker pointing them in my direction." With a glance back toward the Red Dog, Ryder added, "And he's long past pointing at anybody."

"Still, your wounds need tending. You can't go to the hotel looking like this. And you're still bleeding! I can fix this, if you'll just—"

She talked nonstop until they reached the house and ushered him inside. Abel was quick to lock the door and pull the blinds before he started lighting lamps. He had retrieved his old Colt Paterson, dropped in the living room when Coker's men kidnapped the two of them, and kept it ready, close at hand.

It was a slow and touchy business, cleaning Ryder's wounds, but Anna had skilled hands and minimized his grimacing. Abel stood guard, stepping outside from time to time and bringing back reports of progress with the fire. His final bulletin, as Anna finished taping Ryder's ribs, suggested that the blaze, if not extinguished, was at least under control.

Dressing, Ryder remarked, "I hope it didn't burn the Western Union office."

"Shouldn't have, from what I've seen," Abel replied. "But with the hour and all that's going on, I doubt you'll find an operator there."

Ryder assayed a shrug and instantly regretted it. "Won't matter. Long as I can get inside the office, I can handle it myself."

And would prefer it that way, if the truth be told.

"Wait!" Anna caught his sleeve as he was putting on his jacket. "Won't you stay here overnight, in case they're watching the hotel?"

"My guess would be the Knights have had enough excitement for one evening," Ryder said. "No one to give them orders now. They'll need time to recover."

And before that happened, Ryder hoped, someone in Washington could spur Captain Legere to start making arrests of KRS members.

"Will I . . . will *we* be seeing you again?" asked Anna.

"I wouldn't rule it out," said Ryder, edging toward the exit. "Washington's not too far from New York."

A fantasy, already turning into mist.

"I only wish—" she said, then caught herself and forced a smile. "Be careful, Gideon."

"I always am," he lied.

Ryder had Mexican for breakfast, something called *huevos in el purgatorio,* translated by his waitress to mean "eggs in Purgatory." What that meant, in practice, was two eggs simmered in spicy tomatillo sauce, with rice and hot chorizo on the side. He wolfed it down, relieved that no one interrupted him, then walked back to the Bachmann House, to finish packing up.

He'd gotten off a wire to Washington the night before, no problem getting into Western Union—which was locked up tight, as Abel had predicted. One of many things he'd learned while working for the U.S. Marshals Service had been picking locks, a skill Ryder believed that every lawman ought to have.

The clerk, same one who'd checked him in when he arrived, spied Ryder entering the lobby and called out to him. "Oh, sir! You have a telegram."

Ryder retrieved the flimsy Western Union envelope, checking for any signs it had been tampered with and finding none. He thanked the clerk and went upstairs to read the message in his room.

It was from Washington, of course. Chief Wood was spare with praise, but Ryder was becoming used to it. The message read:

CONCLUSION SATISFACTORY STOP LEAVE REMAINDER
TO UNITED STATES ATTORNEY AUSTIN STOP ATTEN-
TION NOW REQUIRED IN BONHAM TEXAS STOP
REGRET NO RAIL LINE ACCESS STOP DETAILS TO
FOLLOW STOP WOOD ENDS

Bonham? He'd never heard of it, would have to find a map somewhere and find out where it was, how far from Jefferson. "Details to follow" could mean anything, but Ryder guessed it would be trouble. Why else was he going there at all?

The part about no rail access was worrisome, until he thought about the local livery.

And wondered if that Appaloosa was for sale.